THE BALDWIN HOTEL

Lonnie Busch

UBiQ PRESS

THE BALDWIN HOTEL

A UBiQ PRESS BOOK
North Carolina, USA

https://lonniebusch.com/

Cover by Lonnie Busch

ISBN: 979-8-9871828-0-2

First Paperback Edition, 2022

AUTHOR'S NOTE

Out of observance of societal superstitions and fear of the unknown, many hotels omitted the numeral "13" when numbering their floors. In that same spirit, I have chosen to exclude *Chapter 13* from *The Baldwin Hotel,* but rest assured, no part of the story has been left out.

THE BALDWIN HOTEL

THEODORE

When I was fourteen, I set fire to the garage. I hadn't meant to, yet my mother almost died in the blaze. I blamed myself. My older brother, Linus, who helped put out the fire, never let me forget it. I took the flames to bed with me every night, wrestled with them in my head, never able to bring the event to a satisfying close.

A year before the incident, my father was killed in an automobile accident on his way home from work. I blamed myself for that as well.

Two years before my father's death, I underwent a series of shock treatments under the supervision of Dr. Winter at the Harris Gloams Mental Hospital. I had been twelve and inconsolable that spring. I never told my parents why. I couldn't. I had killed a boy, a neighborhood bully who was going to attack and brutalize my best friend, Woody.

The prior knowledge of that attack sprang from an event that took place a few months earlier during Easter Break. My family had been vacationing at The Baldwin Hotel in St. Louis when I glimpsed the future, or changed the past, I would never be sure. I had tried to explain what I'd seen and experienced in the stairwell of the hotel, but my parents had no reference for such a preposterous tale—my father became so angry he could hardly speak. My mother, I could tell, was worried sick. My brother just laughed. I never spoke of it again. What I had seen from the small window in the stairwell of The Baldwin Hotel altered the course of my life forever, a defining moment from which the rest of my life would spill like blood from a stab wound.

CHAPTER 1

———

Lightning crashed above Theodore as he limped toward the entrance of DreamCo, the black sky flashing green and white. He cupped his hands above his eyes to block the rain, then leaned in close to the glass, checking to see that everyone had left for the evening. The lobby was dark. He started digging in his pocket when a bright light snapped on behind him. He spun around to face it, his palm extended to shield his eyes from the glare.

"What are you doing there, fella?" a voice said.

"I work here," Theodore answered, blinking, jangling his key toward the spotlight. "I forgot something."

"It's awfully late. You got some I.D.?"

Approaching the police car, Theodore fumbled with the wallet in his back pocket and handed his license to the officer. The policeman studied the small card for a moment, before he handed it back.

When the officer nodded to his partner, the cruiser pulled away slowly, shining the spotlight along the building until they reached the end of the parking lot and exited onto Trenton Avenue.

Theodore unlocked the revolving doors and hurried across the marble floor to the reception desk, his sneakers squeaking out a trail of puddles. He shuffled through the newspapers on Otis's desk until he found what he was looking for. He pulled out his shirttail and with a black marker wrote several names on his stomach, along with an address and the current date.

After tucking his shirt in, he limped to the elevator. A curious feeling rose in his gut when he found himself giving the lobby of DreamCo one last curious look, a final farewell of sorts, he thought, then pressed the button.

When the doors of the elevator slid apart, the president of DreamCo stood in the opening. "I hoped tonight was the night, Edward," Cantwell said, erect as a soldier, his arms folded behind his gray suit.

When Theodore hesitated, Cantwell grabbed his shoulder and pulled him in. "Well, come on, Edward. Time is money!"

Theodore hated that Cantwell still called him Edward.

Cantwell's size seemed to warp the confined space of the elevator as the doors slid shut. With his features lit greenish-yellow from the fluorescent light, and his large hands clasped together as if in prayer, Cantwell looked like a glowering ringmaster in some furtive carnival. Theodore shuffled to the back corner of the enclosure.

"I'm sorry for what I said about your video game, Edward." Cantwell donned a sad smile, obviously as some mock proof of his regret. "But the good thing is… none of that matters anymore. We'll both have more money than we've ever dreamed of. Let's get started."

The elevator moved as Theodore pushed buttons in an arbitrary sequence, not only for Cantwell's hawkish eye, but to free his own mind of deadening thoughts. Cantwell fired questions at Theodore about the pattern, but there was no pattern, no rational reason or scientific hypothesis supporting the showy ritual other than to allow for possibilities. Theodore flipped open his spiral notepad scrawled with mathematical computations, hoping to distract Cantwell with important looking data, silence the inquiries. Unfortunately, the notepad served to intrigue Cantwell even more, prompting another salvo of questions.

"What are you doing now?" Cantwell asked, leaning forward, casting a shadow across the calculations. "What does this mean?" He poked a thick finger at the pad.

Theodore ignored him, focusing his thoughts on Sarah, picturing her still alive, remembering the smell of her hair, how her skin felt against his. He pushed buttons remembering how she'd looked the last night he'd seen her; that's where he wanted to go.

The elevator stopped suddenly. After a moment, the doors opened slowly revealing a dimly lit hall, then closed. The elevator moved. A minute later, the doors opened again, another empty corridor. Several more times the elevator moved, the doors opened and closed, nothing but the dark empty corridors of DreamCo. Cantwell pranced nervously.

"It's not working!" Cantwell said.

"Shut up!" Theodore shouted in frustration. "Here." He tossed the notepad toward Cantwell. Cantwell glared at Theodore, then bent over to pick it up.

"I can't concentrate if you're talking," Theodore said.

Cantwell flipped through the pages of the spiral bound pad, the tip of his thumb scuffing at each sheet, as though he knew what he was searching for. "This is gibberish!" he said. "I can't understand any of it! What the hell am I supposed to do with this?"

Theodore felt the weight of Cantwell's hand on his shoulder just as the floor began to vibrate, the small enclosure picking up speed. The thrumming inside the elevator seemed to have no source, surrounding them, everywhere and nowhere at the same time. Theodore gripped the railing of the elevator. Cantwell dropped the pad and looked up at the light, placing his palm against the wall to steady himself. After a few seconds, the elevator stopped. When the doors slid open, they found themselves staring into the empty space of another elevator.

"Now we're getting somewhere," Cantwell shouted, moving quickly into the alternate, yet identical, space. Theodore wasn't so eager. Even though he'd done this before, the sight of the matching elevator turned his knees to sand.

"Come on, boy! Now!" Cantwell said.

Reluctantly, Theodore followed Cantwell in, the doors sliding shut behind them. The elevator began to move again, but this time jerky, sporadic, jumping, then falling fast until Theodore couldn't tell which way they were moving. The lights flickered, the space accelerating, jerking from side to side, up, then down. Theodore wedged himself in the corner, while Cantwell spread his legs apart to brace against the gyrations. Without warning, the elevator came to an abrupt stop, tossing Cantwell off balance, throwing him to the far wall. He spun toward Theodore, his eyes wild, demonic, and started laughing. Just then, the light snapped off, the space suddenly and completely dark. For a moment, neither of them spoke.

"Are you there, Edward?" Cantwell whispered.

"Of course I'm here."

A loud groan bellowed in the elevator shaft above their heads.

"What the hell was that?" Cantwell said.

The elevator dropped again, but faster this time until Theodore could feel the pressure in his knees and chest. He huddled down in the corner, sliding along the wall until he was secure on the floor. Unable to see anything, Theodore was surprised to hear Cantwell whoop and holler like a kid on a roller coaster. There was nothing fun about this.

The elevator seemed to be free falling now, as if it had been dropped from an airplane. Theodore covered his head, preparing for an impact that would certainly crush them. But it never came. All sensation ended, and Theodore couldn't tell if they were stopped or floating. He was afraid to move, afraid he was not really there anymore, or anywhere. Uncoiling slowly, he felt his way along the floor toward the doors. Just as he touched the cold steel, the doors opened. Beyond the elevator, the lobby of DreamCo filled with glistening sunlight.

Cantwell was on all fours, staring at the ratty carpet on the elevator floor. "You did it, boy! You did it!" he shouted.

Theodore rubbed his eyes, trying to get to his feet, his mind on the carpet as well, but he had to focus, had to hurry or he'd be too late.

"You did it!" Cantwell yelled again, pulling himself up.

Theodore looked over at Cantwell. Brushing off his pants, Theodore bolted from the elevator toward the revolving doors of DreamCo.

"Wait, Theodore, tell me how you did it, boy!" Cantwell said, stumbling to catch up. "Come back. Tell me how you did it!"

Theodore glanced back over his shoulder, then pushed through the revolving doors and rushed into the bright parking lot, his mind on Sarah, then dashed across the pavement toward his white van at the back of the parking lot. Reaching the van nearly out of breath, Theodore hastily jerked the front door open and hopped in, then grabbed the keys from under the mat, and started the engine. It fired immediately.

Backing from the parking space, Theodore gave little attention to the world around him, focused instead on *time,* and how little of it there was to get to Sarah. He jammed the brakes to stop the reverse movement of the vehicle, then threw the shifter into drive and stabbed the gas pedal with his right foot, leaving a smoking blue trail of burnt rubber, never noticing the car pulling into the parking lot which floated dangerously concealed in his blind spot. The crash was a sickening cacophony of twisting metal and shattering glass, the impact slamming Theodore against the steering wheel, nearly crushing his chest, then hurling him against the driver's side door as the van tilted precariously on two wheels, as in defiance and observance of the laws of physics both at the same time. In that moment the axis of the world pitched, disrupting the balance of the universe, the movement of molecules and atoms, the blood cells pumping through Theodore's veins, the red sticky substance spreading along the old upholstery.

Even as the unfortunate event was approaching its climax, the flimsy compact car Theodore had smashed into was being dragged beneath his van, the occupant unconscious, bleeding from his head, unaware that any of this was happening. Moments later the hulking mass of metal and flesh and glass and rubber finally succumbed to the forces of friction and drag. The smoking conglomeration sat there gently rocking, an unrecognizable heap of scraped paint and shredded steel, leaking gasoline and antifreeze, the life blood of the vehicles spreading and mixing along the asphalt, alive with oily, diaphanous rainbows.

It took a good ten minutes before the sirens shattered the tranquil morning. They converged from numerous points in space, followed by red and white flashing lights that painted the buildings and sidewalks and signs with a deceptive carnival atmosphere. The jaws of life, metal slicing through metal, hoses washing away the residue of gas, fire fighters scurrying against time, EMTs desperately battling fate.

There was no pause in the urgency, the metal gurney rattling through the sliding hospital doors, the surgeons affixing their masks, the buzzing fluorescent tubes, the plastic oxygen cup pressed to Theodore's face, the brownish antiseptic applied to the wounds, the glint of the overhead light on the scalpel. Only time would tell.

On the sixth day of Theodore's hospital stay, his older brother, Linus, and his mother arrived to find his condition unchanged. Sunlight streamed through the opened curtains, illuminating the gazanias on Theodore's nightstand—the only color in the drab room. Theodore's mother, Madeline, bent to smell them, then lifted the card tethered to one of the stems, read it, flipped it over, then let it fall from her hand.

"Who they from, Ma," Linus asked, walking over to the bed, touching his brother's hand.

"Woody and Shelley," she said, sniffing the flowers once again. "Aren't they beautiful."

Linus nodded, throwing himself into the chair beneath the television.

Madeline sat in the chair next to the hospital bed examining the machine tracking Theodore's vital signs.

"You understand all that, Ma?" Linus asked.

"Yes, Mr. Wisenheimer," she said. "That's his blood pressure… and, well, the other number, I'm not sure." She took Theodore's hand into hers.

A man in a suit knocked on the doorframe of the hospital room, then entered, glancing briefly at the empty bed next to Theodore's. He introduced himself as Lieutenant Redmond and flashed an ID with a badge. He had curly red hair scattered across his head like cedar shavings, and slate gray eyes. His legs rocked lightly, as if he were balanced on stilts under his baggy brown slacks.

"Are you Mr. Trumball?" Redmond asked.

Linus nodded.

"Could I have a word with you in the hall?"

"What's this about?" Madeline asked, looking first at the officer, then at Linus.

"It's okay, Ma," Linus said, pushing out of the chair. "Just formalities, right?"

When Linus walked out in the hall, out of earshot of Madeline, he asked what the problem was.

"I'm sorry about your brother," Redmond said, pausing, staring at some notes jotted on a folded piece of paper. "I don't know how to say this… other than to say it. If your brother comes out of his coma, he'll be in a lot of trouble."

Linus's hands tightened at his side.

"You knew that Otis Williams died yesterday, didn't you?" Redmond said.

Linus eased his grip and shook his head.

"He was messed up pretty bad when your brother hit him with the van. His car looked like a ball of crumpled aluminum foil."

Linus averted his eyes toward the tile floor.

"Theodore could be charged with manslaughter," Redmond said. "I talked with Cantwell, the president of DreamCo, and he said that Theodore Trumball had an appointment with him later that morning. He said he didn't know why Theodore was two hours early for the job interview. Cantwell said he'd never met your brother before." Redmond seemed to be waiting for Linus to say something, but Linus was quiet, confused as anyone about the day of Theodore's accident, as well as the fire.

"Do you know where your brother might have been going in such a big hurry when he raced out of DreamCo's parking lot that morning?" Redmond asked. "Witnesses said he was driving like a madman when he hit Mr. William's Nova."

Linus shook his head. "I didn't even know he had an interview. I don't know anything." He was about to tell Redmond that his mom knew, but decided against it, not wanting Redmond pummeling her with a bunch of needless questions. Useless facts were not going to snap Theodore from a coma. All the questions made Linus realize how difficult it would be when Theodore finally woke up, having to learn about the accident, Otis William's death, the fire at Sarah's house.

"Do you think the accident had anything to do with the fire?" Redmond asked.

"How could it!" Linus shot back, frustrated with the inquiries.

"Of course," Redmond said. "Well, anyway, that's not why I'm here. Something else came up." Redmond dug in the pocket of his jacket and came out with a surgical mask. He handed it to Linus.

Written on the mask were the names, Theodore, Shelley, Woody, and another name, along with an address, Linus didn't recognize. "What is this?"

"Know those names?" Redmond asked.

"These three."

"What about the other one?" Redmond asked. "Do you know him?"

Linus shook his head.

"Kendall Blannert," Redmond said. "And Blannert's address."

Linus studied the detective's face. "Should this mean something to me?"

"The surgeon that stitched up your brother found that name and address written on Theodore's stomach, upside down, as if your brother had written it himself. The surgeon copied it on this mask before they prepped your brother for surgery."

"My brother does weird shit all the time," Linus said, wondering why Theodore had written 1979 on his stomach; was he afraid he'd forget what year it was?

"Well, your brother topped himself this time," Redmond said. "Blannert's very special, Mr. Trumball," Redmond said, fumbling with the mask. "Very special indeed."

CHAPTER 2

―――――

A perfect night for baseball. Early June, and Nolan Ryan, posting sixteen strikeouts, had just pitched the California Angels to a rousing nine-to-one victory over the Tigers. The crowd went wild, but then they had no way of knowing that Nolan Ryan, their Zeus-Buddha flame thrower, would become a free agent at the end of the season and point the *Ryan Express* eastward to sign with the Houston Astros for a crisp one mil.

The future was neatly tucked away.

Honking and shouting, thousands of crazed Angel fans jammed the freeways feeding out from Anaheim Stadium. By the time Theodore and Sarah made it back to Glen Valley after the ball game, it was just before midnight, the evening cool and sweet with the smell of rain.

Except for blotches of light from street lamps that lined the sidewalks, Rosemont Avenue was dark and quiet when Theodore and Sarah pulled into the driveway. Gravel crunched under the tires of the white Firebird as it slid slowly alongside the house. Sarah pushed the shifter to park. Theodore watched her from the dark passenger side of the car as she paused a moment to consider the junk piled in her open garage before turning off the headlights and springing from the car. The dome light startled Theodore, betraying his gaze, but Sarah apparently hadn't noticed.

"A glorious evening," she proclaimed, spreading her hands out toward the sky. Theodore followed her from the Firebird, bent his head back, and felt suddenly woozy from all the beer.

Sarah removed her sandals at the edge of the driveway and walked barefoot to the center of the backyard. The grass was moist with dew, wetting her feet and the bottom edge of her jeans. "What a beautiful night, but oh, how I miss the winter stars," she said, gazing skyward. "Orion's Belt. Sirius. Especially the Pleiades," she said, still looking up. "Seven Sisters, that's what the Pleiades are called. It's my favorite. Some people believe our ancestors came from there."

"They probably figured out how to predict and control the chaotic movement of electrons," Theodore said, measuring out his arm, reaching up as if to touch a star.

"What?" she asked, turning toward him.

"The Pleiades is about 400 light-years away. Even traveling at the speed of light it would take far too long. So if they came from the Pleiades, they came here instantly. It's the only way. In the quantum model, the Pleiades are no farther from earth than you are from me," he said, looking over at her standing a few feet away. "Distance is meaningless. Travel instantaneous."

She regarded him without words.

"My theory is that stars are really other dimensions, and that's why we can't physically travel to them, unless, of course, we learn to traverse dimensions. Like when we dream. Maybe we visit the stars when we dream. You know how freaky dreams can be."

Sarah shook her head. "Where do you come up with this stuff?"

"I don't know," he shrugged, "it's just what I think about."

She smiled, glanced up at the sky, then back over at him and touched his hand. "Happy Birthday! Did you enjoy the ball game?"

He nodded.

"So, how old are you today?" she asked.

"Twenty-nine," he answered, averting his eyes from the heavens for only a moment.

"Twenty-nine..." she shook her head and smiled, "...a long time ago for me, and yet, barely yesterday."

He looked at her, his eyes Budweiser-red, his lean frame, unsteady and wavering.

Sarah stared back, brushed some peanut shells from his plaid shirt, then started laughing.

"What?" he asked.

"You had too much beer tonight," she told him.

She turned toward the back of the house. "Oh, that porch light's burned out again," she said, searching for her keys. She opened her purse, tilting it slightly to steal light from a street lamp. "I think there's something wrong with the wiring. I love this house, but it's so old, and... damn, where are my keys? I just had them."

"I could repair that for you," Theodore said, looking up at the dark fixture.

"No you can't. You're my tenant. I'm supposed to take care of those things..." she said, then quickly succumbed to another laughing jag. "I may have had too much beer, too."

"Here, we can use my keys," Theodore said, jangling them behind her.

He followed her up the steps, then slid past her to open the screen, supporting it with his shoulder while he unlocked the back door. The back entrance led to a hall that led to the front door of Sarah's part of the house and a stairwell that led to the upstairs.

As soon as it opened, she pushed past him. "Wait here," she said. "Let me find the light."

She stepped carefully through the dark hallway cluttered with supplies for the renovation. Workmen had brought materials for the project several weeks earlier but had only worked a few days before they stopped coming, and hadn't called or been back in a week.

"Don't trip over the mess," she said, groping in the dark for the pull string. "I wish they'd get going on this place, but now I probably won't see them again for a month."

Theodore stepped in behind her, easing the screen door closed. Even though he was used to the mess, he waited for her to turn on the light.

When the naked bulb snapped on, Sarah's blond hair sparkled under the glow. Theodore studied her profile, traced her delicate eyebrow notched with a hairline scar, the gentle line of her nose, a dimple near the corner of her mouth that opened magically when she smiled. Her peach-colored sweater reflected a warm glow beneath her chin. They had spent many afternoons talking since he'd rented the upstairs apartment, and he'd always found her attractive, but tonight he couldn't stop looking at her. He watched her rummage in her purse, balancing it on her thigh, her knee up with the poise of a dancer, her bare foot dangling, glistening with dew, each toenail painted peach, matching her sweater.

She had been barefoot the day she came up to replace the curtains in his apartment. It was a few years ago and he'd just moved in, not yet unpacked. She'd been wearing a sleeveless blue shift cut an inch or so above the knee and had her hair pulled back in a ponytail. She climbed up on the bed, the curtains folded over her arm. He watched her painted toes sink into the mattress, her calves slide up into hard knots as she stretched to hook the curtains onto the bar. Her underarms were smooth dark shadows, her shoulders tan, and with the thin material snug against her body, it was obvious she hadn't been wearing a bra.

"Ah, ha," she said, pulling the keys from the pocket of her sweater. She unlocked her door and was about to go in when she sensed Theodore staring at her. "What's wrong?"

"Nothing," he said, wrenched from the recollection, embarrassed to be caught.

She pushed the door open and stepped in.

"Thanks for the baseball game," he said. "I enjoyed it."

She dropped her keys into her purse. "I was going to make some coffee. Interested?" She glanced at her watch. "It's a little past midnight. Do you have time before you pick up the newspapers?"

"I guess so," he said.

She let her purse fall to the carpet just inside the door, then carried her sandals toward the bedroom. "Make yourself at home," she called back, unzipping her jeans. "I'll put some coffee on in a minute. You can play the stereo if you find any of my records to your liking."

Theodore walked over to the shelf where she kept her albums and thumbed through them—Frank Sinatra, Louis Prima, Bette Midler, Roy Orbison, Charlie Parker, Billie Holiday. He pulled out the Holiday record, unsheathed it, and placed it on the turntable.

No sooner had the stereo started to play, than Sarah rushed in from the bedroom and turned it off. "Not that one, Theodore. Not tonight," she said, sleeving the record and shoving it back on the shelf.

"I'm sorry," he said.

"No, don't be, please. I'm the one that… it's me," she said. "How about Louis Prima?" She pushed the album into his hands. "I'm not in the mood for Billie tonight. Old memories." As she walked to the kitchen, Theodore noticed she had changed clothes and was now wearing baggy gray gym shorts and a pink T-shirt. Her hair was piled loosely on top of her head, held with a clip, exposing the slender shaft of her neck. He wondered how old Sarah was. With two kids of her own, both married, he figured she had to be close to his mom's age, 54 or 55, but that's where the similarity ended. Sarah didn't seem anything like his mom, and had somehow sidestepped the saga of aging. Theodore's mother, Madeline, would never wear gym shorts and a T-shirt. She'd be more inclined toward a long flannel gown, big fuzzy slippers, and hair stuffed with curlers under a stretchy net. Theodore couldn't imagine Sarah ever looking like that. Plus, Sarah had a library of interesting books, and record albums that she listened to regularly, not just collecting dust until company came. He knew she was crazy for baseball, jogged, loved the symphony, drove with the top down on her Firebird...

"Blueberry pie with your coffee?" she said from the kitchen.

"Sure," he said, perusing her bookshelves, something he felt drawn to do every time he was in her apartment.

"Theodore, I've been wanting to tell you how beautiful your violet asters look along the walk," she said. "And what are those bronze-looking flowers in your garden, the ones near the crimson gladiolus? They're amazing!"

"Hybrid gazanias. Named for Theodore of Gaza. He translated botanical works from Greek to Latin."

Sarah laughed. "A distant cousin, no doubt."

"It's called the *treasure flower*. I also have some hybrid *ruby* gazanias about to bloom," Theodore said. "I'd like to work with more hybrids. I've been wanting to talk to you about building a greenhouse if it's okay with you?"

"Theodore, it's more than okay. I'll fund it. How's that?" she said from the kitchen.

He nodded, forgetting she couldn't see him. "I have information upstairs on greenhouse kits. There's a company

17

that has one made out of redwood. You just put it together. It looks simple."

"That's exciting."

"I can show it to you tomorrow," he said toward the kitchen.

"That would be great."

Louis Prima sang *I've Got the World on a String.*

"How's the video game coming? You have another interview coming up soon, don't you?" Sarah said from the kitchen.

"Wednesday morning," Theodore told her, but it wasn't another interview, it was his last, and the finality of it filled him with a suffocating dread. He had exhausted his list of video game companies, none of which were interested in his game or in hiring him as a designer.

"You must be very excited," she said. "You've worked on that for over a year, haven't you?"

"Yes, about that," he said, knowing it was closer to twenty-one months with all the redesign. He didn't know what he would do next if DreamCo wasn't interested in the game, maybe go back to school and finish his PhD. He hadn't calculated his failure out that far yet, hadn't wanted to.

His attention drifted to a book he hadn't recalled from other visits. He read the back cover. "What's this book by Jung?—*Modern Man in Search of a Soul?* Have you read it?"

"I tried. Got lost about a third of the way through," she said, carrying the dessert in on a tray and setting it on the glass coffee table.

Theodore turned the book over and read the back cover to see what the book was about: Dream analysis, the primitive unconscious… The next subject caught Theodore's interest: The relationship between psychology and religion. Religion. Theodore hadn't thought about the church in well over a decade. What could this relationship between religion and psychology possibly look like? But there had to be one, Theodore reasoned. Not because Jung had evidently written about it in this book, but because everyone's life in some way is marshaled by religion: some belief in a higher intelligence, a powerful force that permeates the universe. Even atheists, in a rather ironic way, by taking the opposing side of the argument, to Theodore's thinking, gave credence to the subject, as if it were *something* that could have two sides, thus making the idea of God a *something*. In other words, if they acknowledged the *something*, how could they deny its existence? It seemed every aspect of our existence was up for debate. Jung's book itself was about examining the most contested areas of analytical psychology. Theodore couldn't help but wonder if the human race could truly agree on anything about our objective reality?

Sarah folded her legs under her as she nestled back into a corner of the sofa. "Oh, I completely forgot. Do you want whipped cream on your pie?"

Theodore shook his head, opening the front cover to read the colophon. "1933? That's when this book was published. You couldn't have even been born yet?" Theodore said, unable to face her, fearing she would sense his agenda.

She smiled. "Nice compliment, but a lame attempt. You're fishing, Theodore. Shame on you!" she said, sipping her coffee. "Come over and sit. I don't want to talk about Jung, my soul, or my age. I want to talk about the *Ryan Express* and the Angels. I don't know if you realize it, but tonight was extraordinary."

"How so?" he asked, lingering near the bookcases.

"Sixteen strikeouts by one pitcher in a single game!" she said, holding the coffee cup in her lap with both hands. "I know you're not into baseball, but let me tell you, sixteen strike-outs, that's incredible! Nolan Ryan is incredible. Do you know he throws over ninety-five miles per hour? He's been clocked at over a hundred."

"Radar guns?"

"Yeah. Behind home plate," she said, taking a bite of pie. "You really don't know anything about baseball, do you?"

Theodore shook his head. He didn't know anything about sports, hadn't ever been interested in them, unlike his father, Frank, and older brother, Linus. He felt that it was just one more thing that made it hard for his father to relate to him, and kept them on uneven turf.

"You know," said Sarah, "with Ryan throwing the way he is, the Angels could finish first this year. It's exciting. If they do, you have to go to the playoffs with me."

Theodore wasn't listening. His attention had drifted to a black and white photo on the bookshelf.

"I was a dancer… a long time ago," Sarah said in answer to a question he had yet to ask. "A different life. Before Mr. Bloom dragged me out to California and domesticated me."

Theodore's eyes roved over the miniature Sarah in the photo. She was gorgeous, a real showgirl, what his dad would've called a knockout—leggy, pinched waist, wearing a skimpy outfit designed for cleavage. Even at small scale, her smile was captivating, her eyes, infinite.

"You never told me you were a dancer," he said, still studying the picture.

"I was cleaning out the attic last week," she said, balancing her pie plate on her lap. "Found it in a box with other undeniable proof that I once lived a more exciting life."

He placed the picture back on the shelf, then glanced briefly at another framed photo. It was of an attractive young couple—a wedding picture. Mr. Bloom was extraordinarily handsome, a thick crop of wavy dark hair, block shoulders, a head taller than Sarah. Even in his twenties, Randall Bloom already had the appearance of wealth.

Theodore turned away from the bookcase and walked across the room, plopping down in the chair next to Sarah.

"Whoa," he said, grabbing his forehead.

"What?"

"The room is spinning."

"Drink your coffee. Here, the pie will help," she said, pushing it toward him. "You really put away some beer tonight."

"You think?" he said, leaning forward for his pie.

They ate dessert and Sarah talked about growing up in Philly and moving to New York to become a dancer. He told her that he'd never tried dancing because of his leg.

"Birth defect," he said, finishing his pie. "One leg's shorter than the other."

"Is there any way to correct it?"

"Not really. I can wear a lift. But it's no big deal. It doesn't hurt or anything."

When Sarah got up to carry the dishes back to the kitchen, Theodore tried to get up to help, but fell back, dizzy.

"Stay here," she said, smiling. "I'll get this. Want more coffee?"

"No thanks," he said. After they stacked the dishes on the tray, he insisted on taking it out to the kitchen. She refused, picked up the tray and was running water in the sink when Theodore walked into the kitchen and offered to do the dishes. She told him it wasn't necessary, so he ambled about the kitchen, reading the notes on her calendar, then the magnets on her refrigerator. While the dishes were soaking, Sarah went over to the table, poured herself more coffee and sat down.

"Sure you don't want a refill?" she said. "You need to sober up."

"Hey, remember tonight when the catcher and pitcher for the Tigers collided?" he said, ignoring her warning. He turned toward the table and began re-enacting the collision, a one-man vaudeville act, laughing and mugging, until he tripped over the trash can, crashing to the floor.

"Theodore, are you all right?" she said, unable to stop laughing. She got up and went over to him.

"I'm fine," he said, prone among the trash, holding up his hand as if he had caught a baseball. She knelt down next to him, trying to help him up.

"You're drunk, Mr. Trumball," she said, shaking her head, grinning.

"But I still caught the ball and prevented the triple play," he announced proudly, looking at her, the room swirling.

Obviously not interested in untangling his twisted baseball logic, Sarah slipped her hand under his neck to help him up. Theodore couldn't stop laughing, trying to untangle it himself. He tried to get to his feet, his arm around her shoulder, but fell halfway through the process, knocking them both to the floor. "Is that right? A triple play?" he asked, and now they were both laughing, stretched out on the kitchen tiles, Theodore on his back and Sarah draped across his chest. Theodore burped. "Excuse me," he said and they both started laughing again. Sarah raised up to look at him.

Her eyes were curious, her perfume sweet on his tongue. Gradually their laughter diminished. She studied his face for a moment, then pushed up off his chest. He was motionless. Arching her back, she grasped the bottom of her T-shirt and slowly pulled it up over her head, then unsnapped her bra. She slid his shirt up, then leaned forward until her breasts pressed against his bare skin. He started to turn her over onto her back, but she stopped him. She kissed him softly, her tongue exploring the soft crease at the corner of his mouth, then inside his lip.

After a few minutes, she stood and walked toward her bedroom. Theodore followed, clumsily trying to remove his shoes while watching her undress. She slid her gym shorts off, then her underwear, letting them fall in a pile near the bed. After getting under the sheet, she leaned over and switched off the lamp on the nightstand. The room fell dark except for the milky glow of a streetlight.

He felt uneasy as she watched him undress. When he got into bed, she scooted down, pulling him on top of her. She was wet and he entered her quickly. She raised her hips from the bed to meet his, her breasts swelling, rolling under him as he arched his back. He felt dizzy, the blood hammering at his temples. Everything was spinning in bursts of light, explosions in his head, flashes, the motion fluid at first, then savage, until he collapsed on top of her.

Rolling to her side, he glanced over in the dark. Her face appeared gauzy and vague in the dim light, almost ghostly. She smiled softly, then eased up until her face hovered above his chest. She looked like a teenager at first, then suddenly a hag. It threw Theodore, the sudden inexplicable transformation.

"You seemed to have sobered up," she said, nuzzling closer, her breath humid on his neck. Theodore let out a quiet groan, then glanced at her briefly, embarrassed, confused.

"Is something bothering you?" she asked.

He averted his eyes toward the sheets, unable to hide the awkwardness he felt.

She stared at him, trying to read his expression. "Are you sorry?" she asked. "Is it the age thing?"

"No... Sarah, it's not about that," he said. "I... I just..."

She kissed him softly before he could finish.

"I don't expect anything," she said. "It's one night. Let's leave it at that." She rested her head on his chest. They said nothing for a long while, lying in the dark, content with the closeness of each other's body. But Theodore couldn't help wondering about her, about Mr. Bloom.

"Do you miss your husband?" he asked, caressing her hair.

"Randall? Sometimes," she said. "But I think I miss the idea of him, the one I fell in love with. That Randall left years ago, long before he died."

"Did you ever wish you could have him back even for a minute, tell him something that you'd forgotten to say?" Theodore stared up at the ceiling.

"No… no regrets," she said. "Why?"

"Was he rich?"

"Randall? Yeah, he was born with it, but always thought he was a self-made man. I think that's why my dad always disliked him. My dad used to say, 'Randall was born on third base but thought he hit a triple,' " she said laughing. "My dad was pretty nutty for baseball, too!"

"Do you know I'm wearing a toupee?" Theodore said, moving his hand to her bare shoulder, wondering briefly why there was no light fixture on the bedroom ceiling.

"What?"

"I bet Mr. Bloom still had all his hair when he died, didn't he?" he said, picturing the wedding photo.

"What's all this stuff about hair?" she said, lifting up on one elbow. "What's going on?"

"I was nearly bald before I finished college. The hair on the sides and back is mine," he said, briefly combing it with his fingers. "But the top is gone. I started losing it around sixteen. Just started falling out."

"It's probably hereditary. Was your dad bald?" she asked, running her fingers across his chest.

"No. Neither is my older brother, Linus," he said. "You remember him, don't you? You met him last summer." Even if she didn't remember the meeting, Theodore did, the way Linus eyed Sarah, flirting with her—even Madeline noticed but didn't say anything. Later, when Sarah wasn't around, Linus made a crack about what a fox Sarah was. Madeline quickly informed him that Sarah was old enough to be his mother. Linus winked at Theodore and whispered, "So is Ava Gardner, but I wouldn't kick her out of bed, either!" Madeline overheard the comment, glared at Linus and said, "I hope you don't kiss your children with that mouth of yours!"

"Sure, I remember him," Sarah said. "You two are very different."

Theodore glanced over at her, wondering what she meant. It still bothered him that Linus's flirtations had not been lost on Sarah either, and that she seemed to have enjoyed the little game.

Sarah smiled and touched the side of his face. "What's wrong?" she asked.

He shook his head, ready to leave the subject of Linus. "I received shock treatments as a kid. I think that's what made my hair fall out," he said.

"You are *full* of surprises tonight." Sarah sat up, her knees resting against Theodore's side. "You had shock treatments? How old were you?"

"Twelve. My parents said I was eleven," he told her, distracted momentarily by her breasts. "That's why I got the shock treatments. We couldn't agree on what year it was."

"I don't understand."

"When I was twelve we went to St. Louis on vacation and stayed at this hotel near the riverfront. Have you ever been to St. Louis?"

She shook her head.

"Anyway, my dad was out somewhere, and my mom was getting her hair done in the lobby beauty parlor. I was playing in the stairwell of the hotel and got trapped in there," he told her, recalling the dismal space. "When I finally got out, something strange had happened, some kind of dimensional shift. I tried to explain it to my parents, but they looked at me like I had an axe sticking out of my head."

"They put you through shock treatments because of that?" she asked, unable to conceal her incredulity. "My God, you were twelve."

"I was inconsolable. But it wasn't just that. Something else happened…." he said, breaking off bluntly when the memory started unspooling in his head. He stared at the dark ceiling and saw Porky lying in the muddy grave, reaching up to him. Theodore shot upright in bed, his eyes wide.

"Theodore, you're shaking!"

He slumped over, wrapped his arms tightly across his chest, hugging his shoulders. She eased him toward her, resting his head on her chest. "It's okay."

They spent what was left of the evening holding each other in bed, saying little, until Theodore had to leave to pick up his newspapers. She walked him to the door.

"I enjoyed the evening," she said. Wearing just a robe, she stood in the doorway to the hall.

Theodore was quiet, studying the shaft of light stretching across the carpet.

"Are you okay to drive? You can take a quick shower if you'd like. It might wake you up a bit."

"I'm fine. Thanks."

"Listen, Theodore, if you want, you can come back here when you finish your route," she said, touching his arm. "I'll leave this door unlocked and you can let yourself in. When we wake up I'll make some breakfast… or lunch, whatever." She bit her bottom lip. "It's up to you."

He was listening to Sarah, weighing her offer when his thoughts drifted to Mr. Bloom, the successful investor, hunter, and bank president. Barely had he pushed Mr. Bloom from his head when he remembered Sid Carter, the tan middle-aged insurance underwriter from San Francisco who occasionally spent the night with Sarah when he was in town. *How can I compete with them? What role could I possibly play in Sarah's life, or her in mine?* Theodore wondered how he would explain Sarah to his mother, to Linus….

"It's probably not a good idea," he said, "you know, leaving your door unlocked."

Sarah touched him lightly on the cheek as he stepped into the hallway, then smiled, her expression fading as she guided the door closed.

THEODORE

What I recall most about my first shock treatment was that it took four nurses, two orderlies, and a doctor to slide me onto the table and hold me still until they could tighten the restraints around my wrists and ankles. I was twelve, weighed maybe 85 pounds, and my mother hadn't arrived yet that morning. The room was sterile, long, and filled with cold tables. Lashed to the tables were people, some that looked dead, some numbly awake, one even blue. A fleshy, black-haired nurse with thick glasses rolled a rattling metal cart along the end of each one. The cart carried a machine accentuated with knobs, switches, and lights, and fitted with two thick wires protruding from its side that reminded me of my dad's jumper cables. Lying on my back, I stared up at the bright fluorescent fixture above me, watching the grid of the acoustical ceiling slowly dissolve through my tears. Even when I closed my eyes, the harsh light seeped red through my eyelids, and with the pounding at my temples, I had the sensation of being bound inside a beating heart. The pungent smell of Pine-Sol hung in the air, concealing something acrid and sour. A nauseating sense of dread fell over me.

The leather restraints cut into my arms and legs. The rubber bit, held in my mouth by another doctor, tasted bitter and smelled of alcohol. It was rigid, cold. I gagged. I bit down, trying to snap it in two so I could breathe. I felt like I was suffocating.

Thoughts of The Baldwin Hotel, the stairwell, and everything that had happened in St. Louis raced through me, everything that had brought me to this moment. My skin sizzled at the thought of electric current.

Just then I wished I had said nothing about the stairwell, about what had happened. Why did I have to cry and argue, make such a fuss?—make my father angry, disgusted at the sight of me; my mother so frightened she could only regard me with sad, distant eyes, as she would a homeless stranger? I wanted to scream, to tell them I had made a mistake, or that I made it up, that nothing happened, that it was just another prank, that I was sorry. I wanted to go home, to my room, my books, the swing set in my backyard. But I couldn't scream, couldn't say anything, couldn't move, and all my objections melted into muffled grunts and useless gyrations.

The nurse's breath smelled of garlic. She applied cold gel to my temples that oozed down through my hair, into my ears, muffling the sound as if I were under water. She placed the cold metal discs on the chilly goo at my temples, then secured the leather strap around my forehead, pressing the metal firmly against my skin. I strained my head back to see her, plead with her. Dark bales of hair framed her bloated white face, her blank eyes bulging under thick glasses. I felt small, helpless, an insect under a magnifying glass.

CHAPTER 3

Theodore avoided Sarah for the next few days after the ball game. On Sunday afternoon, someone had knocked on his apartment door. He had been fairly certain it was Sarah, but pretended to be gone. He felt bad for the deception, more for himself than for Sarah, but he couldn't face her. No one knocked on his door after that. He thought it was strange that he could live upstairs from her and, if he chose to, could go for days without seeing her, or anyone else. He hardly ever saw Maria Lopez, Sarah's other tenant across the hall.

Theodore stared at his geranium, trickling water into the clay pot lettered with the name, Daisy. In less than two hours he would interview for a job he had anticipated for weeks, years, and now Sarah, not the interview or his computer game, was the governing force behind his thoughts. He studied the geranium as if at any moment it would speak and clarify his dilemma. Putting the pitcher down on the kitchen table, he rubbed his forehead, and peered out the window at the oak tree. A cool breeze rustled the leaves as the morning sun, minutes above the horizon, glared between the branches.

Theodore filled a small kettle with water, switched on the hot plate and set the kettle on the element. He searched the flimsy metal cabinet above the sink for a coffee cup, rummaging through the orphanage of dinnerware—Melmac, Waterford Crystal, colorful plastic cups, and empty jelly jars—before he found one behind a Flintstones glass. The blue coffee cup was imprinted with a white logo from Mr. Bloom's bank. After spooning instant coffee into it, then creamer, he waited for the water to boil.

His attention shifted to the white metal table sitting under his kitchen window, the tubular chrome legs, the slightest sign of corrosion near the feet. He rested his palm on the place mat where he ate his meals. The kettle squealed.

Snapped from his daydream, he jerked the kettle from the hot plate, filled his cup, then placed the hot kettle on a trivet. Stirring the coffee, he became aware of the Frigidaire humming behind him. It was old. The rest of the apartment was a halfway house for wayward furniture: a plaid couch that had traveled a great distance from Mr. Bloom's rustic hunting lodge, a cushioned lounger with rose-embellished upholstery, a worn black trunk that had found its true calling as a coffee table, and a knock-off dark mahogany antique dry sink that kept to itself in an isolated corner of the room. Above the dry sink was a shelf with Theodore's collection of antique glass flower vases.

The apartment, though sparsely furnished, provided everything Theodore needed: a bed, a place to eat, and a quiet space to think and work. Theodore brought few possessions with him when he moved to Glen Valley—an odd assortment of clothes, some books, and the hot plate and kettle.

After banking extra money from his paper route, he had purchased an Apple II computer with hi-resolution color graphics, 20k of RAM, and a fast cassette interface for saving work onto tapes. He created a workstation on a plain Shaker-style walnut desk that sat in the corner of his bedroom next to a lemon-colored bookcase.

Theodore stood before his opened closet, wrapped in a bath towel ready for his shower, holding his coffee cup, anguishing over clothing choices. Would the checkered polyester pants compliment the short-sleeve plaid button-down?—or maybe the rust-colored corduroys with the yellow-and blue-striped polo?—and how would the paisley tie work? After glancing at the alarm clock, he decided he was running out of time and settled on the checks and plaid, no tie.

Dressed, he surveyed himself in the bathroom mirror and noticed that his toupee didn't look right. He tugged and pulled at it, tried wetting it to make it behave. Baldness was not a trait of the Trumball clan, nor was it endemic to his mother Madeline's fork of the family tree either, but there it was. So, when Theodore was at Cal Tech, he decided on a toupee, the more permanent variety cemented to the scalp. But his existing hair, like a scorned spouse, was set on leaving and had receded below the toupee over the several years since he'd bought it, exposing a pale patch of scalp at the back of his head.

Theodore was about to switch off the hot plate and grab the cassette with his computer game when the phone rang.

"Hello, Edward speaking," he said.

"Hi, honey! I didn't wake you, did I? It's your mother. I wanted to call before you went to sleep. Did you hear about that dreadful murder in Glen Valley? I think it's the thirteenth one! How's Mrs. Bloom? Is she frightened? She must be beside herself! Well, at least she has you there, and that darling Maria. How is Maria? You should ask her out, she's so pretty. So, did you just get home from your paper route? I hope I didn't wake you?"

"No, Mom," Theodore said.

"And Teddy, why must you call yourself *Edward?*" she asked. "*Theodore* is such a lovely, proud name."

"I hate *it* as much as Linus hates his name!" Theodore answered. "Why did you have to name us after cartoon characters?"

"I picked your name myself!" she protested. "After the great president, Theodore Roosevelt! And Linus, well, that was your father's idea. He had an uncle or something named Linus who was in the merchant marines. But Theodore is a lovely name!"

"Yeah, if you're a chipmunk!" Theodore mumbled, remembering the abuse he had taken from the other kids at school. "Anyway, I need to get going."

"Oh really, aren't you going to bed now? I thought you just got home from your paper route?"

"I did Mom, but I have the job interview today, remember?"

"You *have* a job, Teddy! Your paper route! I thought you liked your paper route?"

"Mom, DreamCo creates video games."

"DreamCo? What's a DreamCo?"

"It's a company, Mom. A video game company."

"Oh!" was all Madeline could muster at first. "Will you be able to keep your paper route?"

"Keep my *paper* route? Mom...."

"What about that cute apartment at Mrs. Bloom's house? I thought you *liked* Mrs. Bloom. Where would you find another place as cute as that, and someone as nice as her? *Some* landlords are... well... let's just say I've heard stories..."

"Mom...."

"And your *garden,* Teddy! You've worked so hard, all your beautiful flowers. It's so nice of Mrs. Bloom to let you use her backyard. How are your gladiolus this year? Have they bloomed yet? I wish you would work on my garden when you're home next time."

"Mom...."

"And your paper route, how will you *pay your bills* if you quit your paper route? What about your school loans?"

"Mom...."

"Well, Teddy, you're still a young man," she said. "I suppose it's good to try wild things while you're young."

"There's nothing *wild* about it," he snapped back, frustrated with the direction of the conversation. "I'm sorry. It's just that I'll be late if I don't get going."

The phone fell silent. "Mom... are you there?" he asked, after a few moments.

"Of course I'm here. What about your PhD? Are you going to finish that? I thought that's why you moved to Glen Valley and took the paper route job to begin with?"

"I don't know. I'm more interested in designing computer games right now."

"But you're so smart," she said, then started stammering. "Not that *Linus* isn't smart too ... I just meant that...."

"Mom, please don't. You don't have to explain. Look, I've gotta go or I'll be late. I love you. I'll see you soon."

"Call me when you get back and tell me how it went."

"Sure, Mom, I've gotta go... I love you, bye!"

"I love you too, dear."

Theodore hung up the phone, quickly morose, thinking about his father, Frank. He often felt that his brother, Linus, was his dad's favorite and that he, Theodore, was the logical follow-up to the nuclear two-child family of the '50s. Not necessarily a mistake, but an aberration that sprung from the fact that Frank, maybe unhappy over having no brothers or sisters of his own, didn't want Linus to grow up an only child as he had.

Staring blankly past the idle phone, Theodore noticed the greenhouse booklet sitting on the end table. He picked it up and opened it to the page with the dog-eared corner. The redwood greenhouse was 8 by 12 feet, with two automatic roof vents, a full-length growing bench, and plant hanger assemblies. He would have to pour a concrete foundation, but he'd already found a book at the library on how to do that. He decided to show the brochure to Sarah that afternoon, after his interview, and wondered if she'd still be as interested. Checking his watch, he put the brochure down and headed for his workstation to get the tape with his game, OBO.

He decided to give OBO one last look before the interview. The graphics streamed across the screen and Theodore felt a sense of satisfaction over having finished the project. It even looked pretty much the way he had originally envisioned it. He popped the tape out and stuck it in its case, then put it in his pocket.

Leaving the apartment, Theodore thought to grab a vase from his collection and filled it with water. He locked the door and rushed down the stairs, the dull thud of his black oxfords echoing on the hollow wooden steps. He stepped carefully around the building materials in the hallway as he padded across a ragged remnant of carpet that Sarah had placed there to protect the floor from the contractors.

When he stepped out on the back porch, the sun was just tipping the chokecherries and alders lining the backyard. He hurried down the back steps and over to his garden on the side of the house. Kneeling on one knee, he bent over to inspect his ruby gazanias. They had bloomed beautifully, deep luscious red with bold, contrasting markings. He carefully clipped one from the profusion of vivid blossoms and placed it in the vase.

The morning was cool on his face. The scent of the soil still wet with dew mingled with the fragrant garden. He paused a moment, closed his eyes, and took a deep breath. After a moment of solitude, he hurried to the van, snatched a newspaper from the seat, and rushed back to the house. Sarah enjoyed the newspaper with her coffee. He always left one in the morning when he returned from his route.

Bending down in the hallway, he placed the vase with the gazania at the threshold of Sarah's door, then unfolded the newspaper and laid it out flat, headline up.

GLEN VALLEY WOMAN FOUND BRUTALLY SLAIN.

GLEN VALLEY KILLER BLAMED. STILL NO SUSPECTS!

Another woman was found raped and killed in her home on Monday!

13 women in last 5 months.

His stomach tightened as he read the boldface type. He decided to suggest extra locks to Sarah, and maybe one of those alarm systems that automatically calls the police, possibly even a guard dog. Did Sarah like dogs? He wasn't sure. But he worried about her, home alone at night when he was out throwing papers, even though Maria, a graduate student at UCLA, was usually upstairs in the evenings. And although Sarah never registered much fear over anything, at least outwardly, he knew that she sometimes had trouble sleeping when the house was empty and too quiet.

Mostly for company, Sarah had opened her house to renters after her husband died of a heart attack several years earlier. They had been married for over twenty-six years and Randall—an investment banker—had left her well off. Not needing to work, she filled her life with jogging, baseball games, the symphony, writing, reading, and a book discussion group that met a couple times a month. She had a boyfriend or two that she didn't talk much about, and her life was her own. Occasionally, on a lark, she would drag Theodore away from his computer to go bowling or play tavern shuffleboard at a nearby bar.

He stared at her door and wondered how their relationship had changed since the night of the baseball game. Would he still pause in the hallway when he came in from working in the garden, eavesdrop on her singing before he knocked, be invited in for fresh baked apple pie?—would they sit on the porch, drink iced tea in the afternoons and talk about TV evangelists, bungee jumpers, pro-choice, and Reagan? How would she look at him now?—would her sea-green eyes be too familiar?—or painfully complicated?—would her smile be restrained and self-conscious?

He liked how it had been before, even though he'd never trade his night with her for anything. He would always taste her breasts on his tongue, the way it felt to be inside her, the smell of her hair, her breath warm on his face, her skin, radiant, smooth. It all seemed so distant that for a moment he almost convinced himself that he'd imagined the entire evening, that none of it had happened, and that today when he got back from his interview everything would be as it was, the smell of freshly baked bread filling the house. But the memory of their night stirred an erection, only serving to confuse him further, causing him to revile his desire as amoral and distorted. Thinking of Sarah brought up thoughts of his mother; what would she say?—what would she think? His ruminations turned to sadness. He glanced at his watch. It was getting late. He hurried out the door and was almost to the van when he stopped and came back to the house, certain that something was wrong. He ran along the hallway, up the steps. Once upstairs, he checked the door to his apartment to make sure he had locked it. Temporarily satisfied, he went back out to the van, but returned, driven by obsession, to check the door several more times before finally leaving for his interview.

THEODORE

Annō Domini—in the year of our Lord. Agnostic, non-theist, or non-denominational, this is the defining moment in history, this is how time is book-marked in the world: before Christ, B.C., in the year of our Lord, A.D., annō Domini.

What I refer to as a defining moment—be it for the Western world or in one's own personal life—is the moment from which time is measured forward and backward. Everyone has one, probably many, but only the latest and most poignant moment has any real clout, has the ability to orchestrate your life, to arrange the events in your mind in some arbitrary manner; that which happened before the defining moment, and that which has happened since. For many, it's the death of a loved one, or a birth, a divorce, maybe a marriage....

A door that wouldn't open. That was my defining moment, sixteen years ago, in the stairwell of The Baldwin Hotel. The events in my life are arranged by that day, that moment: that which came before, that which came since.

What I remember most vividly was that when the door to the sixth floor wouldn't open—jammed, or locked, or held shut by some disenfranchised spirit, or fate—I knew my life was about to change, or already had.

It was 1963. I was twelve, my brother Linus was fifteen, and we had made our annual pilgrimage to St. Louis with our parents during Easter vacation. Every year we drove east from Bakersfield to visit my mom's sister, Trudy, her husband, Herb, and their four girls, my cousins. Because their duplex was small and their family large (they also were Catholic), we stayed at The Baldwin when we visited. It was downtown, in the heart of the city, not far from the riverfront, the Admiral, and the Jefferson National Expansion Memorial project, known simply as the St. Louis Arch.

    This particular day, Linus was in the lobby girl-watching. My dad had a job interview, and my mom, Madeline, was getting her hair done in the hotel beauty salon—I was playing in the stairwell. Bored, and lost in a peculiar daydream about a diagram of a DNA helix that I'd recently seen at the library, a disturbing image seized me; it was my friend Woody, battered and blind in one eye, beaten horribly by a gang of boys in Tathum Cemetery. It had happened the previous spring one day after school.

    The recollection had me sandwiched between rage and sorrow. I decided to go back up to the room, watch cartoons, flush it from my head. I started up the stairs, heading for the tenth floor. After climbing several flights, I decided to take the elevator. I came to a gray metal exit door with a red 6 painted on it, grabbed the handle and pulled, but it wouldn't open. I jerked harder and something curious happened, like a shadow cast from a cloudless sky. My skin prickled cold, followed by a sensation that I can only describe as the presence of nothingness, or no-time. It scared the hell out of me. I panicked and started yanking frantically at the door. It didn't budge. A chill sidled up my body as if I was being lowered into icy water. I screamed for someone to open the door. I pounded with my fists until they were red. My muscles felt weak, turning to mush.

    Frenzied, I ran from the landing, down the stairs, sometimes leaping five steps at once. My tennis shoes slapped on the cement, echoing up and down the concrete walls. But no matter how fast I ran, how many steps I jumped, the bottom of the stairwell was getting no closer.

    My chest was burning, felt like it would explode. I was sick to my stomach so I stopped to catch my breath. Bent over, holding my knees, I looked at the metal door, then looked up at the painted red 6, exactly like the one I had just fled from minutes earlier. I threw my body against the door, screaming and kicking, tugging at the handle, but nothing happened. I ran again, jumping, stumbling, falling, but no matter what direction I ran, up or down, or how fast, I found myself standing before a gray metal door with a red 6.

CHAPTER 4

Theodore was disappointed when he pulled into the parking lot of DreamCo. He had envisioned a contemporary structure, one of those chrome cubes, high-tech and ostentatious that tempered its austere visage by reflecting the surroundings. What he found was a nine-story brick building in need of tuckpointing.

He got out of the van and had taken only a few steps before he realized he'd forgotten to put his lift in and was limping like a three-legged dog. *Damn! I can't go in there like this!* He surveyed the parking lot as if providence might have dropped a size 9D lift for a left shoe, two centimeters in thickness at the heel and half a centimeter at the toe—no luck!—then pulled a small spiral-bound notepad from his briefcase, walked over to the curb, sat down under a flowering pin oak, and took off his shoe. He removed his gum and stuck it to the cardboard back of the notepad, placed the pad gum–side down inside the back of his shoe and secured it with a push. It wasn't his prescription lift, but it would do.

Walking toward DreamCo he was seized by an urgency, freezing him where he stood. Was it the interview? — he wondered—anxiety over the possibility that if he failed here, his dream of designing video games was essentially over, or was it self-doubt? Or was it something else, pulling from deeper within, a more encompassing sense of doom? His skin went cold. He turned toward his van following a pressing inclination to return home, then thought of the interview. Confusion coursed through him, undermining his ability to move until he stood like a post in the parking lot.

"Need some help there?" a uniformed guard called from across the lot, shattering his stupor. The tall man stopped momentarily, and smiled. Theodore quickly waved the man on, nodding a *thank you*, making it sincere by adding a smile. The guard turned away, shooting a glance over his shoulder before he reached the building.

Theodore exhaled, unaware that he'd been holding his breath. Agitation crammed his head, spinning his thoughts. He rubbed at the sides of his face, attempting to push away the dark premonition. After pumping several breaths through his lungs, percolating his blood with fresh oxygen, he decided to follow through with the interview, ignoring the barrier of discomfort creeping in.

When he reached the entrance to the building he stopped, ten feet from the façade, confronted by a peculiar anomaly— The Baldwin Hotel. Not the entire hotel, but the entrance, the revolving doors that had graced the hotel in St. Louis. At first he couldn't believe they were the same ones. He found them disturbing, yet familiar, then disturbingly familiar and out of place and a bit quirky for a building that was at one time clearly some sort of manufacturing company.

Above the revolving doors was a neon sign that read DreamCo. But below, demure by comparison, were the words,

The Baldwin Hotel, incised in bold elegant caps along the brass frame above the revolving doors.

Theodore's eyes fixed on the engraved words. A wall opened inside him and it was 1963, the Trumball family Easter vacation in St. Louis. His father, Frank, was excited about touring McDonnell Douglas, Anheuser Busch, and Grant's Farm, but more than that, he wanted to marvel at the engineering feat that was taking place on the riverfront: the Gateway Arch.

The Baldwin Hotel was located at the corner of Olive and Tenth, only a few blocks' walk from the Jefferson National Expansion Memorial, the future home of the Arch. Every morning after breakfast, the Trumballs walked down Olive to the Arch grounds to observe the project. Nothing changed much from day to day, but the walk was nice and the Arch project was impressive. Two massive stainless-steel legs rising from the ground 630 feet apart that would come together at a precise but intangible point 630 feet above the ground! It was astonishing for Theodore to think that two separate and distinct entities, which began from two separate and distinct points, could culminate in the exact same place, at the exact same time, six years later. The concept solidified his passion for numbers. The Arch to Theodore was living proof that mathematics was the key to determining the future and taming chaos.

Another noteworthy aspect of the vacation occurred one afternoon when the Trumball family visited the Mississippi riverfront and boarded the Admiral, a massive shiny steel boat that looked to Theodore like something out of Buck Rogers. Its sweeping lines, sleek curves, and long rectangular windows were more in keeping with a spaceship than a riverboat. The noise on board was deafening; the clamor of excited kids playing Skeeball, pinball machines, and a carnival collection of mechanical games. Flashing lights, bells, and buzzers combined with the din of a hundred screaming youngsters left Theodore with an indelible hunger to design games and orchestrate madness—wonderful, glorious madness.

But the most powerful moment of the trip occurred in The Baldwin Hotel. All at once, Theodore felt like he was seated in a dark theatre, observing a movie of himself, the thinly built boy of twelve, alone in the dimly lit stairwell. The image in his skull began to squirm; the steps in the stairwell like scales on the back of a huge serpent. Swelling, breathing, the stairwell slowly coiled up inside the enclosure of concrete and enamel paint, pressing against the walls, forcing out all light and air.

Theodore's eyes shot open. He shook his head, freeing himself from the recollection, then sucked in a deep draught of air. He glanced at his watch and was now five minutes late for his interview. Hurriedly, he pushed through the revolving doors and darted to the front desk.

A tall guard—the one from the parking lot—was directing a workman toward an elevator to the left of the desk. The workman was lugging a roll of carpet on his shoulder. Theodore glanced at the guard's nametag: Otis Williams. Otis turned and asked if he could help, but Theodore couldn't remember who it was he came to see. Just then it came to him, and without warning 'Cantwell' catapulted from Theodore's mouth like a dislodged hunk of food. Otis recoiled slightly from the outburst.

Otis asked his name, checked his list, then instructed him to use the elevator on the right and go to the ninth floor. A secretary would greet him there.

Theodore nodded.

Walking in the direction of the elevator, Theodore stopped when Otis called to him.

"Hey, hold on there, my man!" Otis said. Theodore turned around, startled by the command, and the disarming image of the imposing guard coming at him. The guard reached down toward Theodore's butt. Theodore jerked away.

"It's okay, I ain't gonna hurt you," Otis assured him, then plucked a leaf from the seat of Theodore's trousers. "Can't have you seeing the president of the company looking like a deciduous tree now, can we?" Otis laughed.

Theodore was temporarily distracted by Otis's comment, *a deciduous tree.* How many people ever used that term?

"Best not keep the big man waiting," he said, pointing Theodore once again to the elevator on the right. The workman with the carpet had laid the roll down and was measuring the floor inside the other elevator.

Theodore wasn't terrified of elevators, but they made him uneasy. Unsure if it was the confined space or the absence of control between stops, he disliked them. The doors opened, and he stepped in.

Averting his gaze from the numbers, he worked his eyes over the distorted visage reflected in the stainless-steel doors. His face appeared vague, widened, and spread out to the sides as if it were being stretched at the edges. It was a disquieting image because he could recognize his features even though they were blurred like he was moving at tremendous speed in opposite directions. But his eyes were the most unsettling aspect of the reflection; dark sockets hanging below a bright band of forehead. Within the nebulous dark blotches of his sockets were the faintest notions of eyeballs, smudges of dark gray surrounded by silvery almonds of light. Theodore looked down at the floor, too troubled by the distorted likeness.

The floor was linoleum in a pattern of faux parquet wood tile. *That's nice!* Theodore thought looking at the imposter under his feet. *I wonder why they're putting carpet over this?* His eyes traveled the roadmap of wood grain below his shoes. The elevator stopped and the doors opened. Theodore shot from the elevator as an attractive young woman stepped in.

"Excuse me," she said to Theodore, holding the door with her hand. "This is the sixth floor, don't you want the ninth?" she asked, looking at the lighted 9 button. Theodore looked first at her, then her red-painted fingernails holding the door, before his attention jumped to the numbers above the elevator. Sure enough, it was indeed the sixth floor. Theodore reentered the elevator just before the doors closed.

"Here for the interview?" she asked, glancing up from an armful of manila folders.

Theodore nodded, looking straight ahead.

"Macy," she said, freeing a hand from the stack. "You must be Edward. Kent's been looking forward to this interview all week!"

Already Theodore was sorry that he had lied about his name. He smiled, then looked away. He had spoken to Kent a couple of times on the phone and hadn't thought it would be a big deal to go by Edward, but now he felt bad about the stupid deception.

"No need to be nervous. Kent's great! You'll be fine," she said.

Theodore was upset that his emotional landscape was so easily betrayed. He was about to protest and tell the young woman that he wasn't nervous, just preoccupied, but decided against it. He knew he might start stammering and make it worse.

When the doors opened, Theodore checked the number above the elevator before he stepped off behind Macy. She smiled over her shoulder, nodding before she disappeared around the corner.

Walking from the elevator, he approached the amoeba-shaped reception desk. Behind it was a massive sculpture that upon closer scrutiny was an actual Piper Cub airplane that had been flattened like a pressed flower, wings and all. It spanned at least 35 to 40 feet across, was painted white with blue trim, and had *Sky King* lettered on the side. The wings had been re-welded to make the piece horizontal in orientation, but even with that, it still filled the 20-foot high tangerine wall that it was hanging on. It reminded Theodore of a balsa wood airplane his father had built and that Linus had accidentally flattened by falling on top of it.

"May I help you?" said the receptionist, a slender woman, fifty or so, seated behind the desk. Her hair was rusty-gold and cut like a smooth field of alfalfa, an inch long, even shorter on the sides. She was wearing a black sweater and large red hoop earrings.

Theodore was about to answer when a young Asian gentleman approached from his right.

"Hello, you must be Edward," he said with a broad smile, extending his hand toward Theodore. "My name is Kent Tanaki. I spoke with you on the phone." Kent, affable and stylish, in his twenties, had thick black hair that was medium length and uncombed. He wore black slacks, a loose-fitting gray silk shirt—quite a contrast to Theodore's attire.

For a brief moment, Kent's expression flashed queerly as he regarded Theodore's clothes, visibly trying not to stare.

"Am I dressed all right?" Theodore asked, looking down at his plaid shirt and checked trousers.

"Yes, of course… it's not you, it's… nothing. You're fine! C'mon, Cantwell's waiting," Kent said, motioning for Theodore to follow him. "Any trouble finding the place, Edward?"

"Kent," Theodore said, stopping abruptly. "I have to tell you something. My name isn't Edward… it's Theodore."

"Oh… I'm sorry, Theodore. How did I mess that up?"

"You didn't. I, uh…" Theodore stammered, regarding the confusion on Kent's face. "I… ah, it's a long story."

"That's cool," Kent said. He led Theodore down a hall to a double set of tall mahogany doors. Kent knocked, then pushed in.

"Come in, come in," bellowed the man behind the desk as he stood, unfolding like a hydraulic crane. Theodore thought Mr. Cantwell would never stop rising, he was so tall. The top of his head was covered with oatmeal-colored wavy hair, the kind Theodore figured never had to be combed and always looked great, even first thing in the morning. The gray pinstripe suit was impeccable on Cantwell's stout build.

"Edward Trumball," the large man said. "Frank Cantwell. I've been waiting for you, son!"

There was something in Cantwell's eyes that glinted mischievously as he shook Theodore's hand, as if they shared some private joke that Kent wasn't aware of. Cantwell winked knowingly, a clandestine acknowledgement of their private club. Theodore was confused.

"Actually, my name is Theodore," he timidly corrected.

"Oh, I'm sorry. How did I get that wrong?" Cantwell questioned himself, checking his planner. "I must've copied it incorrectly."

"No sir, it's my mistake," Theodore explained.

Cantwell laughed. "You got your own name wrong! I see. Well, I don't feel so bad then!" Cantwell's smile fell somewhere between a grin and a sneer, but it was the familiarity of his gaze that was unsettling.

"Have a seat, both of you," Cantwell said. "Theodore, it is still Theodore, isn't it?" Cantwell laughed again. "As you can see, I'm an adventurer," Cantwell said, spreading his arms, directing Theodore's attention to the proliferation of mounted animal heads scattered around the room. Some poses were fierce, some were grand, and all extremely dead.

"I love the excitement of the hunt," he told Theodore. "That's why I started this company! I was sick and tired of the pencil-necks and bean counters, and their tight-ass approach to life. I had to be free!" Cantwell said with a gesture of his arms that made him look like he might, at any moment, start ascending.

Theodore noticed that on both ends of Cantwell's vast gesture were hands the size of catcher's mitts.

"I wanted to try something that was alive, wild, adventurous!"

There was that word again: wild! Theodore's mother had used it earlier that morning. He wasn't sure what part of designing video games was *wild.*

"Video games! Theodore, that's where this world is headed," Cantwell howled. "Video games! We create illusions! That's what we manufacture in this great country of ours. Ideas! Concepts! Illusions! Entertainment! Fantasy! Leave the manufacturing of shoes and ties and toaster ovens to the Third World nations. We can't waste our time with that drivel!" Cantwell, wild-eyed like a beast in the jungle, rocked back in his thickly cushioned leather chair contemplating his patriotic dissertation, then suddenly bolted forward. "Are you afraid to fail, Theodore?" Cantwell blurted, a trace of spittle landing on some papers in front of him.

Theodore squirmed in his chair, not wanting to face the answer to that question. Wasn't everyone afraid to fail? After all, wasn't that the driving force behind human nature? Wasn't that the dark pit buried deep within everyone's miserable existence? Wasn't it in the Constitution, or at least the Ten Commandments? Thou Shalt Not Fail!

"I'm not afraid to fail!" Cantwell said, rescuing Theodore from the troubling question. "And you damn well better not be either if you want to accomplish anything in this goddamn world! People are waiting for you to fail. That's all some people live for, Theodore, to watch others fail!"

Theodore certainly could relate to Cantwell on this point. This was the grist for Theodore's inflated paranoia.

Kent listened quietly, obviously having heard this speech numerous times. Theodore felt like a piece of a Samsonite luggage being tossed about in a gorilla cage.

"I fix 'em, Theodore," Cantwell growled. "I shove my failures right up their ass!" he said, thrusting his huge fist toward the ceiling.

Kent looked over at Theodore, but said nothing. Theodore was mesmerized.

"Did you see the sculpture when you got off the elevator?" Cantwell asked.

Theodore nodded.

"That's no fucking sculpture!" Cantwell bellowed. "That's the first plane I ever crashed. I had just bought it for thirty grand, had less than ten hours of flight time on it when I crashed it on a beach near Malibu. Wind shear or some damn thing, who knows! While everyone was standing around whining and worrying, I climbed out of the wreckage, put the busted wretch on a flatbed and hauled it to the parking lot. I rented a steamroller and flattened the bastard myself. Hauled it over here and hung it on the wall. I've been offered up to $300,000 for that twisted piece of shit. See, Theodore, right up their ass!" Cantwell said, again thrusting his fist upward.

Theodore was sitting silent, stunned.

"Let's see what you got, young man," Cantwell said. "I'm very excited!"

For every ounce of Cantwell's enthusiasm, Theodore matched it with a pound of trepidation. Suddenly unsure of everything, Theodore was reluctant to pull out the cassette, fearing it could find a new home in his colon.

Kent took the cassette from Theodore and walked over to a computer near the back wall of Cantwell's office. After inserting the cassette, Kent waited a moment for it to start, but just as it did, the screen froze. Kent rebooted the computer and tried again. After several failed attempts, Kent, bewildered, glanced over at Theodore, while Mr. Cantwell impatiently loomed over them waiting for a show.

"Probably not enough memory," Theodore shrugged.

Kent ejected the cassette. "Let's take it to the viewing room. Better computers."

They hurried from the office with Mr. Cantwell following like a schoolmaster.

"Hold my calls, will you?" Cantwell said to the stylish secretary. She was busy reading the paper, seemingly bewitched by the headline:

GLEN VALLEY KILLER

"Is that my newspaper?" Cantwell said, wrenching her from her stupor. At first, she was embarrassed, then quickly surrendered the thick bolt of newsprint as if it were radioactive, thrusting it into Cantwell's meaty hands.

"Thanks," he sneered, grabbing the paper mid-stride without looking back.

The viewing room was a spacious rotunda with a glass-and-steel geodesic dome skylight above them. The conference room quickly brought to mind for Theodore the interior of a UFO, and although he'd never been in one, this seemed a fitting example. A large circular glass table, suspended from the ceiling by aviation cable, was the focal point of the room. A light source recessed in the floor directly beneath it beamed up through the glass and illuminated the table's edge, causing it to glow like neon.

Kent busied himself at the black-lacquered credenza filled with state-of-the-art computer equipment. He pressed a button on the remote in his hand and the canopy closed over the skylight dome above them, throwing the room into darkness. A rim of light sprung to life around the base of the walls, quickly washing the darkness from the space, leaving it pleasantly dim. In moments, Theodore's creation was up and running, but he hadn't noticed, obsessed with the feeling of having been abducted by aliens.

"OBO?" Cantwell commented as the graphics danced across the screen. "What's an OBO?"

"OB is a prefix meaning *toward* or *to* and the O is the Arabic cipher for *Zero,*" Theodore explained, a little nervous at first. "Oboe is also an electronics term for a navigation system. To me, OBO represents moving toward Zero point! Zero point is the beginning of all measurement, or the absence of everything we know. It marks the indefinite spot between the beginning and the end where nothing and everything exists!"

Cantwell didn't seem to grasp the arcane meaning behind Theodore's explanation. He mumbled something about the simplicity of the name being good for marketing purposes, but was quickly disappointed with the graphics, especially when a digitized image of a dog capered across the screen.

"What the hell is that?" Cantwell screamed. "A goddamn French poodle?"

"That's OBO!" Theodore said.

Cantwell grimaced, rapidly losing interest, and patience. He continued to watch the prototype, but his attention seemed to drift toward the newspaper rolled up under his arm. Cantwell fidgeted, seemingly about to excuse himself, when something new appeared on the screen.

"What's that?" he asked, his interest temporarily rekindled.

"It's a chimera," Theodore said. "There's also a three-headed alien...."

A grunt escaped from Cantwell's clamped lips.

"That's curious, Theodore. What is it?" Kent asked after a ghost-like flower appeared briefly, then disappeared.

"That's Daisy," Theodore said. "She's the Holy Grail of the game. If she likes how you're playing, she shows you entrances to the wormholes."

They watched another few minutes until the game went through several more screens, then ended. Kent hit the remote and the canopy opened above. Light rushed into the room.

Theodore was unnerved by the sour expression on Cantwell's face.

Kent also appeared disheartened by Cantwell's gnarled expression and stoic posture, as if he'd seen it before. Cantwell began an extravagant process of thinking; pained expressions, eye gyrations, highlighted by hand gestures, all coupled to the slow drumming of his rolled newspaper on the glass table.

"Why would anyone want to play this game?" he barked. "There're no guns! It's silly! Kids want aliens and space ships to blast. Nobody wants to play with a fucking Pomeranian lost in a maze chasing a flower down wormholes! And what is a fucking wormhole anyway!"

Theodore felt like he had just been punched in the face. Spots circled in front of him like flies swarming a severed head. Kent jumped in to defend him, but Cantwell waved his argument away.

"Let *him* speak," Cantwell said, his eyes searing into Theodore's.

Theodore felt the heat rise in his gut as Kent was silenced. Cantwell glowered at him, thumping the newspaper.

"The game is about patterns," Theodore said. "Every time one screen is completed, another one comes up that looks exactly the same but it's not. There are subtle differences and you have to treat them differently. Each pattern is altered slightly and the intensity builds because there are so many clues to concentrate on. If you make a wrong move, your OBO is trapped and disappears. And you only get five of them for a quarter. Each pattern is like a parallel universe—"

"Parallel universe? What the hell is that?" Cantwell screamed.

"One universe laid over another... uh, it doesn't matter, sir. The only thing that matters is the game, the patterns! The patterns are all that matter. With OBO, the score isn't even important—"

"Wait a minute!" Cantwell countered. "Nobody's going to play a damn game without a score. You're fucking mad!"

"The game *will* have a score though, won't it, Theodore?" Kent interjected, trying to appease Cantwell.

"The game will have a score, it's just not one that matters," Theodore defended. "The true gamers will know it's not about dogs or aliens or high scores; they'll know it's about the patterns! They won't care about the score. Keeping score is for losers!" Theodore's last statement had an abundance of fire in it, surprising everyone.

Kent's eyes were wide, his forehead taut and shiny. Cantwell glared, the skin of his face tight across his bony nose, his eyes narrowing to dark slits. Theodore stood firm until Cantwell began to stand, his large frame moving slowly upward toward the dome. Theodore instinctively stepped backward, unthinkingly resting his weight on his left leg. The metal wire of the notepad in his shoe dug into his heel. He grimaced slightly, but Cantwell hadn't noticed because he was almost to the door when Kent spoke up.

"Mr. Cantwell... sir!" Kent's words apparently came out more forceful than he had intended, so he tagged on the *sir*. "Before you leave, I would like to say something."

Theodore's eyes were riveted on Kent, his only ally and most likely his last chance of landing the job. Cantwell stopped at the door and glared at Kent.

"Mr. Cantwell, I know there are some problems with the game, but they're minor, they can be ironed out," Kent told him.

Cantwell stood unchanged as he waited at the door.

"But the true genius of Theodore's game is… that I think it will appeal to girls as well as boys. It will open up a market that hasn't really been tapped!"

Cantwell's eyes narrowed again, his expression softening.

Kent continued. "With the type of cartoon graphics that Theodore is proposing, OBO will appeal to a wider audience than the shoot-'em-up-testosterone-laden games that glut the market." Kent paused to allow the new insight to penetrate Cantwell's hardened defense. "I believe it's the wave of the future!" he added.

Cantwell paused a moment, then left the conference room without saying a word. Kent's head dropped. He glanced over at Theodore. "I'll talk to him."

Theodore felt empty. He couldn't speak. His chance had come and gone in less than forty-five minutes. Already, without a beginning, it was over.

"I thought it was fantastic," Kent said. "I really did."

Kent retrieved the cassette from the machine and was about to hand it to him, pulling it back at the last second. "Can I hold on to this for a while," Kent asked. "I'll protect it with my life."

Theodore nodded, lifting his briefcase from the glass table. Kent showed Theodore to the elevator doors and pressed the call button.

"Don't give up yet," Kent said. "I'll call you soon!"

The elevator doors closed slowly over Theodore.

When the elevator reached the first floor, it stopped but the doors didn't open. He waited, then after a moment pressed the OPEN button. Nothing happened. He pressed it again, then again until he started slapping at it with his palm.

"Hey," he yelled. "Is anyone there?" No answer. Putting his ear to the door, he held his breath, hoping to hear voices on the other side. All that returned was the thick metal silence of the door. "Hello, is anyone there?" he yelled again. "I'm stuck!

The doors won't open!" Panic wriggled up his spine and he suddenly felt short of breath. He pounded on all the buttons, yelling as loud as he could. Just then, the door opened, and with it, a rush of air swept in followed by the clamor of people in the lobby.

No one seemed to notice that the doors had been jammed. Theodore jumped from the elevator, throwing a wary glance over his shoulder when the doors slid shut behind him. He hurried past the reception desk, toward the revolving doors at the entrance.

"Hey, my man, how did it go up there?" Otis inquired, looking up from his newspaper.

Theodore shook his head.

Otis smiled with a shrug. "Have a good one!" he said and went back to his newspaper.

"Edward, how did it go?" a woman's voice asked.

Macy was standing behind him.

Theodore turned. "Okay, I guess," he said, then added. "Not really. Actually, it went pretty bad."

Macy frowned. "I'm sorry, Edward...."

"My name is really Theodore. Sometimes I go by Edward because... it doesn't matter...." he told her, too exasperated to care what she thought.

"Oh," Macy said. "Okay, Theodore. Well, are you sure the interview went as badly as you think?"

Theodore shrugged, picturing Cantwell behind the wheel of a steamroller flattening his newspaper van on the parking lot.

"What did he say?"

"Actually, he didn't say anything... he just walked out!"

"I'm sorry."

They regarded each other in silence for a few seconds.

"I better be going," he said.

She smiled. "It was nice to meet you."

Macy turned away, pausing at Otis's station. He watched Otis say something to Macy, making her laugh. He watched them from the other side of an illusory curtain in the same way he imagined the dead watched the living and felt excluded, removed from life like toxic waste. Much like when he was twelve, the several days he spent alone in the hospital, the shock treatments.

Because of Theodore's disconsolate ravings about The Baldwin Hotel, Frank and Madeline had taken him to a psychiatrist. But the psychiatrist had no luck consoling him either. Dr. Melvin, with his bushy eyebrows and shiny hair, listened, then showed Frank and Madeline into his office where he discussed the necessity of shock treatments in such extreme cases as Theodore's. "Shock treatments," he explained, "provide the greatest potentiality to wrest young Theodore from his delusions so that he can proceed to a fruitful existence." At first, Madeline refused, but after a few days of Theodore's continued rants, along with Frank's mounting displeasure, she felt no other recourse but to agree. The treatments were carried out over three successive days until Madeline halted them. Neither The Baldwin Hotel nor the shock treatments were ever spoken of again.

CHAPTER 5

———

Driving home from the interview, Theodore obsessed over the DreamCo debacle—the interview, the game, every agonizing detail. He analyzed the data, then analyzed it again. He had always felt he could defeat the vagaries of chance if only he had enough data to define the pattern. The pattern was the safe passage out of a chaotic world made even more chaotic by chance and happenstance. His theory eventually grew into the notion that he could actually change the past, as he had many years earlier, if only he had enough data to define the pattern in the present. But the only thing to emerge during the tedious drive home was the smell of newspapers wafting up from behind his seat.

Like Paul Revere with a paper route, Theodore would return to his life of spreading the news, entrenched in the dissemination of events already securely locked in the past. Old news, old scores, and old headlines. No matter how quickly a newspaper could relate an event, the event was clearly and irrevocably gone, the only proof of it lying in the aftermath left behind. And the aftermath would be the news of tomorrow! A newspaper couldn't even truly describe the present, Theodore felt, much less predict the future. The only items in the newspaper that foretold of future events were the ads that boasted of upcoming sales! It was clear to him that newspapers were tombs of the lifeless past.

When Theodore turned onto Rosemont Avenue, he saw the flashing lights of police cars dancing on nearby houses and trees. A police car at the end of Rosemont created a secure barricade, allowing no one within two hundred feet of the commotion. Theodore parked his van and walked down the block toward the throngs of onlookers, past the Channel 4 News van, toward the fire engines. Fire fighters in yellow jackets trudged sluggishly toward the red trucks dragging hoses thick as pythons. Pumper trucks sprayed water on nearby homes. At the center of all the turmoil was a charred stump of a house, smoldering, spewing dirty smoke.

The houses along Rosemont were a mix of older Victorians and Tudors, mostly two stories. At first Theodore couldn't tell which house had burned. He could see Mr. Miller's house with the green porch swing, and the Houston's with the faded burgundy trim; a second later he knew…

"Move, get out of my way! Please move!" he screamed as he pushed through the crowd. A small Chihuahua jumped from its owner's arms and began chasing after Theodore, yapping, biting at his trousers. He ignored the dog, shouldering people aside, shouting, "That's my house, that's where I live!" Theodore stopped a moment to make sure. He stared in disbelief at the jagged, smoldering timbers piercing the smoke-tarnished sky. "Sarah!" he screamed. There was no doubt now. Theodore bolted past startled neighbors who gasped, rocked their heads, covered their mouths.

A policeman spotted Theodore rushing through the crowd and hurried over to intercept him. News teams quickly trained their video cameras on Theodore being detained by the burly officer.

"Whoa, hold on there, son!" the policeman said, grabbing Theodore's shoulders briefly, then releasing him, but still blocking his advance. "You can't go in there!"

"I live there," Theodore cried, darting his head to the sides, trying to see around the large man. "In Mrs. Bloom's house. That's where I live. I've got to get in there!"

"What's your name again?"

"Theodore Trumball. I live there," he yelled, pointing. "I rent the upstairs apartment from Mrs. Bloom! Is she okay? Where is she?"

The officer turned gloomy in response to Theodore's question, not responding immediately. "Why don't you wait over there," the officer said, directing Theodore to a patrol car with the door open. "You can sit inside. Lieutenant Redmond will be over to speak with you."

Before Theodore could reach the police car, a reporter and her cameraman rushed through the crowd, pinning Theodore against the barricade that held the spectators back. Theodore winced when the cameraman switched on the bright flood lamp. The woman reporter, wearing a tan blazer with the Channel 4 emblem, began firing questions at Theodore. Disoriented, he stumbled backward against the yellow barricade. A man on the other side of the barrier pushed him back up and the crowd drew in tighter behind him to get themselves on the evening news.

"Did you live in that house?" the dark-haired reporter asked. "What's your name?"

Theodore was light-headed, unable to focus.

"Did you know the woman who died in the fire? Was her name Mrs. Bloom? Was she the owner of the house?"

"What?" Theodore asked, unsure of what he'd just heard.

"Mrs. Bloom? Was she the owner of the house?" the reporter demanded. "Were you her son?"

The crowd, the reporter, the cameraman, the smell of damp, charred wood, and the pulsing emergency lights congealed into a spinning blur. His legs tingled and he saw himself falling, drifting down through an infinite sea of blue sky and clouds. Serenity and warmth filled his body as he descended silently into a brilliant, bottomless chasm of light.

The sting of ammonia hit his nose, followed by the squeal of sirens and the deep rumble of diesel engines welcoming Theodore back to the world of the conscious. A man dressed in white was a vague shape, as was the metallic ceiling of the stationary ambulance. "Are you okay?" the EMT asked. Theodore nodded and tried to sit up, but the medical technician laid a gentle hand on his chest. "Just lie there a moment, catch your breath. You'll be safe from the reporters here," he told Theodore.

Theodore let his head fall back against the pillow, then stared at the pattern of metal supports and rivets that ran along the interior of the vehicle. It was shiny and clean, unlike Theodore's van, which had grown dirty, soiled from countless nights of nicotine before he'd quit smoking. Some nights, while running his paper routes, he would pull the van over to a curb when he got tired, crawl into the back, make a pillow of rolled newspapers, and stare at the ceiling just like he was now. Surrounded by the smell of newsprint and engravers' ink, he would lie with his head positioned under the slight angle of the back windows of his van and watch the stars as they made their pilgrimage across the night sky.

Someone shook his foot and muttered something. Theodore sat up slowly and focused on the middle-aged man wearing a brown rumpled suit.

The man asked his name again.

"Theodore Trumball," he answered.

The man introduced himself as Lieutenant Redmond of the Glen Valley Police Department. He inquired about the tenants of the house and asked if Theodore knew where they were. Theodore explained that besides him, it was only Mrs. Bloom and a young college student named Maria Lopez, who attended UCLA during the day and worked at Antonio's restaurant in the evenings as a waitress.

"Are you positive that no one besides you and Maria reside at Mrs. Bloom's house?" Redmond asked, his brow puzzled.

Theodore nodded weakly, searching Redmond's face for the source of bewilderment.

"Did she have a boyfriend or anything?" Redmond inquired.

"Yeah, maybe. What's all this about?" Theodore shot back, upset with the direction of the questioning, suddenly sickened by the thought.

"It's just that we pulled a man's body from the house, that's all," Redmond said. "I figured you might know who he was."

Sid Carter, Theodore thought. Sid was the freeloading insurance underwriter from San Francisco who took a cab from the airport as soon as he hit town and had a line for the women that was slicker than his hair. What Sarah didn't know about Sid was that when he wasn't gulping down her apple blintzes and sucking down her wine coolers, he was hitting on Maria while Sarah was at the grocery store. Maria, a repeat target for Sid's smarmy volleys, had told Theodore how she hated him and wanted to set Mrs. Bloom straight, but she never did.

"I didn't know her friends," Theodore told Redmond. "I try to mind my own business."

The detective seemed put off by Theodore's abruptness, but continued pushing for answers.

"You said there was a Maria Lopez living here also?" Redmond asked, checking his notes. "Do you know where Ms. Lopez is right now, Mr. Trumball?"

"Probably at school. Wednesdays she has classes from eight in the morning until six."

"Whose white Firebird?"

Theodore looked down, remembering Saturday, the baseball game. "Sarah's... Mrs. Bloom's," he told Redmond.

Redmond said nothing and scribbled in his notebook.

"Thanks. You can sit here a minute," Redmond said. "You have someplace to go tonight, friends you can stay with?"

"Mrs. Bloom? Is she okay?" Theodore asked.

Redmond's eyes tightened, his head drooped. "I'm sorry son, she... she didn't make it out either. Seems that the upstairs collapsed down on top of her bedroom. I'm sure she was killed instantly."

How could Redmond know if Sarah was killed instantly? Had he just told Theodore what he thought he needed to hear? Theodore sat motionless on the gurney in the back of the ambulance, tears welling stubbornly at the bottom of his eyes. A hard grief squeezed at his heart, then balled-up in his throat, until the turmoil around him melted away.

THEODORE

What I had told Sarah the night of the ball game was not completely true, the part about why I had received shock treatments when I was a kid. It wasn't that I had intentionally lied to her. My memory of things was vague at best for many years after the treatments and was only beginning to return in my early twenties. It was true that the incident at The Baldwin Hotel had caused me a great deal of distress, and that I had vehemently insisted to my parents what had happened. I knew they hadn't believed me, nor did they know how to respond. But it was after I killed Porky that I fell into a deep despair, followed by episodes of uncontrollable rage. I never told anyone about what happened with Porky, not even my best friend Woody, especially not him. So I chose rage. It was easier to cover my regret and guilt with anger, to hide from my parents inside a cocoon of madness, and it almost worked.

I regretted that I lied to Sarah the night of the ball game, but mostly for selfish reasons. It wasn't until it was too late that I realized I could've told her everything about The Baldwin Hotel, about Porky, about what I had done, and she would have listened with compassion and believed me, would've helped me to forgive myself, would've heard my confession. But I didn't take the chance, and the bus ride back to Bakersfield was one of the most tormented journeys of my life.

Gazing out the window of the Greyhound, I'd see her naked, lying in bed, feel my fingers trace the rise of her hip, the dip of her waist, her lips moist and warm against mine, and just as I would let myself taste her breath, smell her skin, the room inside my mind would burst into flames and all I could hear were her screams.

CHAPTER 6

———

"Come in, it's open!"
Kent walked in and closed the door behind him. Cantwell had his back to Kent, standing over his computer monitor, studying DreamCo's latest video game creation. Cantwell glanced over his shoulder at Kent, then back at the monitor.

"StarField is the ticket!" Cantwell said without turning around.

Kent didn't respond.

"When is it going to be ready to ship?" Cantwell asked. "I know it's going to be a killer!" He shot a glance back at Kent.

Kent was silent.

"Maybe we need more laser noises? Whaddya think?" Cantwell asked. "And can't we make the explosions louder, maybe add some screams! Yes, mix screams in with the explosions. Not the blood-curdling type, but subtle, almost subliminal, like sirens!" Cantwell was rolling. "What do you think, Kent? Are you just going to stand there like a lamppost? You worry me!" Cantwell slapped at the keyboard, turning brusquely from the console. The game on the screen withered and died as Cantwell marched back across his office and plopped down in his chair.

Kent glared at him.

"What?" Cantwell said, pulling a cigar from his pocket. "You look like a fucking zombie. What's with you?"

"How did you know what Theodore would be wearing today?" Kent asked. "Had you met him before? Do you know him?"

"Goddamn it, Kent, I hope to Hades you didn't come up here to bend my ear about that refugee from Tech school and his fucking canine-catastrophe of a game!"

The veins in Cantwell's neck strained against the starched white collar.

"I'm not gonna sit here and listen to a bunch of bullshit about parallel universes and wormholes," Cantwell continued, "whatever the fuck they are!—and flying potted plants?—for Chrissakes! Kids want spaceships... lasers!"

Kent reached in his pocket, pulled out a tangle of keys, and placed them on the desk.

"What's this?" Cantwell asked, leaning forward in his chair, picking up the keys and ringing them.

"The keys to DreamCo!" Kent said.

"You've got to be kidding! You're quitting because I won't hire the poster boy for Tartan wear?"

"I'm quitting because you hired me to make creative decisions, but when I try, you jerk me around," Kent argued. "We have a staff here that's struggling to keep up with an industry that's changing faster than Clark Kent in a phone booth. I need the kind of genius I saw in Theodore today. There's no room for copycat designs in this business and we're not going to lead the pack if we're swinging from somebody else's dick!"

"What the hell are you talking about? You're starting to sound like that vagabond chipmunk from Glen Valley," Cantwell shouted, snapping upright behind his desk. "Have you lost your mind?"

"We can't keep coasting on the back of other company's creations!" Kent said firmly. "We have to take a chance, break new ground!"

"Break new ground! What about StarField? That game is authentic, it's original, it's—"

"Space Invaders in a different box!" Kent yelled. "Everything we produce is a knock-off of somebody else's game! C'mon, Frank, you know it!"

Cantwell glared at Kent for several seconds before lowering himself back into his chair. He stroked his chin, his right hand hovering above the keys for only a moment before he snatched them up and dropped them in the open drawer.

"Pick up your check downstairs," Cantwell said coldly without looking up.

When Kent reached the door, Cantwell said, "Oh, by the way. You asked how I knew about our young Theodore's attire today. Well... the returning Messiah always wears checks and plaid! I think it's in the Bible somewhere."

Kent was clearly dumbfounded by the statement, but before he could say anything, Cantwell burst out laughing.

Several minutes later, Cantwell buzzed his secretary on the intercom.

"Yes, Mr. Cantwell?"

"Is Kent gone?"

"Yes, he just got on the elevator."

"Call down to Otis and have him stop Kent before he gets to the parking lot..."

"What should Otis do with him?"

"Send him back up here! Goddammit, do I have to spell everything out?"

"Of course, sir! Right away."

Cantwell rocked back in his chair, smiling, and lit a cigar. "God, this is fun!"

THEODORE

Magical thinking. That's what Dr. Melvin told my parents I was suffering from—along with paranoid delusions. Magical thinking, he explained to them, was a psychiatric symptom of a patient who believes that by merely willing an event to happen, or just thinking about it, could actually cause it to happen. Dr. Melvin went on to explain that it wasn't unusual for a child to experience wild imaginings, but, "in young Theodore's case, there is a predilection toward the morose, and an unhealthy, maudlin preoccupation with nefarious and phantasmagoric material."

He spoke to my parents as if I weren't in the room, probably figuring I couldn't understand what he was telling them.

He pushed the ECT (electroconvulsive treatment) consent forms across the desk.

Madeline sobbed. Frank signed the papers, then handed the pen to Madeline. Dr. Melvin grinned at me like I was a chimp in a cage.

CHAPTER 7

―――――

M ore milk, Teddy?"
"No, Mom," Theodore said, taking a bite of sandwich and staring out the window. The swing set in the backyard stood like a monument to his childhood, rusty and neglected. Only the top half was visible from the kitchen window, but Theodore could see that one of the chains was gone off the swing and one bar of the glider had corroded through. He imagined that the glider itself must now be lopsided, just like him with his short left leg.

Anytime he visited his mother he saw the swing set, but today it was different. Today it was in *his* backyard again, in *his* life and he would have to look at it every day. When he visited from Glen Valley it wasn't a big deal; he hardly ever noticed it. But since he'd moved back to Bakersfield, back into his mother's house, the dilapidated swing set was an annoying reminder that life, like the glider, never went anywhere.

"I'm gonna take down the swing set, Mom, before someone gets hurt."

"Who's gonna get hurt, Teddy? Nobody swings on it anymore. All the neighborhood children go to the park down the street. Besides, there aren't that many small children around here anymore. It's not like when you and Linus were growing up. Mostly older people now, and couples without kids."

But Theodore wasn't listening; his gaze fixed on the unsuspecting yard toy. He took another bite of his sandwich and said nothing while his mind entertained scenes of destruction. *A cutting torch would take that thing down in ten minutes, maybe five. Surely Linus would have a torch down at the garage.*

"Teddy, what are you going to do now?" Madeline asked, taking the seat across from her son at the kitchen table. A fresh breeze brought the smell of roses through the window. Madeline dried her hands with a floral dish towel, then laid it on the table, patting it down as if gravity alone couldn't be trusted.

"What about your paper route, Teddy?" she asked. "What did you do with that?"

"Sold it to Kurt Drescoll," Theodore told her. "That was easy, he always wanted it."

"What about your van?"

"I sold that too. What do I need with a panel van and a paper winder?"

"Won't you miss it, Teddy?"

Theodore grimaced and shook his head at the thought of driving his van until four in the morning through a maze of endless streets, mindlessly tossing newspapers onto manicured lawns. No he wouldn't miss it. He figured he could find meaningless work anywhere.

Every cloud has a silver lining. When one door closes another one opens. If you're handed lemons, make lemonade. Platitudes marched like soldiers across the trampled soil of Theodore's mind. He knew he had wanted nothing more to do with the paper route after his ledgers burned in the fire at Sarah's house. Too defeated to start over, he had called Drescoll on Wednesday afternoon, the day of the fire, and proposed the sale. Drescoll jumped on it and they arranged to drive the route together the next night so Drescoll could learn the customers and their addresses. Theodore stayed at a hotel for a couple of days until the details of the sale could be hammered out. While the settlement for the route was hardly munificent, Theodore was relieved to be free of it. When the deal was complete, Theodore took a bus back to Bakersfield.

"But you worked so hard, built it up from nothing," she reasoned, unable to understand Theodore's easy dismissal of it.

"I hated it, Mom," Theodore said bluntly. He hadn't built it up from *nothing,* as she was so quick to brag. Theodore worked for Mel Grossman, rolling and wrapping the newspapers in the back of Mel's van while Mel guided the vehicle down the sleepy dark streets of his dozing patrons. Theodore inherited the route after Mel was arrested for drunk driving for the third time and lost his license. Mel could have continued with the route, just having Theodore drive, but Mel, like a model of a clipper ship, was content to spend the last remaining weeks of his life crammed into a bottle. A month later, already drunk and sneaking a trip to the liquor store, he plowed his car into a tree and was killed.

"I'm glad to be done with it. I only did it to pay off my school loans and to buy the computer equipment."

"Oh, dear, and that all burned in the fire too!" Madeline's expression was an epitaph of despair. "I know how much you enjoyed your computer, Theodore."

Theodore, perturbed by the way she could make it sound like a hobby, was about to contest Madeline's last statement, but saw no point in trying to get her to understand. They regarded one another in silence while Theodore finished his lunch and Madeline brooded on the awful events of the fire.

"I'm so sorry, Teddy, about Mrs. Bloom," Madeline said, obviously reconstructing the terrible event in her mind.

Theodore rubbed at his eyes.

"Oh, Teddy!" Madeline said, going over to him when she saw he was crying. "Oh, sweetie, it's okay. Go ahead and cry, let it out."

Theodore convulsed under waves of grief, his body responding to each bitter swell as it crossed through his mind. After weeping for several minutes, Theodore, his voice soggy and garbled, mumbled something. Madeline, apparently unable to understand what he said, pulled back to face him.

"I think I killed her!" Theodore cried in a burst of spit and snot. "Mom, I think I killed her!" He began to shimmy like an old car, his eyes narrow and lost, his mouth parted, dripping drool. Madeline pulled him to her chest, squeezing him tight.

"No," she corrected. "Theodore, why would you think such a thing? That's just crazy!"

"No, Mom, the fire started in my apartment," he gurgled inside her grasp. Pushing his head from her chest his words became clearer. "It started in my apartment! My apartment collapsed on top of her; that's what killed her!"

One corner of her mouth pulled upward while she shook her head back and forth in general denial of his statement. "No, Theodore," she cautioned again. "You're wrong and I won't have you thinking like that. You had nothing to do with that fire. Do you hear me, Theodore? Nothing! You weren't even there!"

"Maybe he was flipping butts into a trash can?" Linus said, standing unnoticed in the hallway. Theodore and Madeline both turned to see Linus, his tall rangy frame looming in the doorway to the kitchen.

"Linus, that's enough!" She scolded, glaring coldly at the young man in grease stained overalls.

Linus, undaunted by Madeline's warning, proceeded to the table and grabbed an apple from the bowl. Theodore hung his head, embarrassed that Linus had seen him crying. Sniffing quietly, Theodore wiped discreetly at the tears with the ends of his fingers.

"C'mon, Ma, he burned down the garage and practically killed you doing it." Linus shot back.

Before Madeline could refute the statement, Theodore lunged from his chair, seizing Linus around the waist and driving him against the wall. Linus, his air knocked clear, was flailing his arms to free himself when he smashed the apple against Theodore's temple with an explosive thwack. Jagged chunks of fruit flew everywhere. For a second Theodore was dazed, stumbling backward when the bony knuckles of a right hook jolted him from his retreat. The sharp blow only succeeded in marshaling Theodore's anger into a raging rebuttal of wild punches to Linus's head and face.

Ceramic figurines crashed to the floor in shoddy explosions as the young men struggled along the back corner of the kitchen. Madeline's miniature spoon collection was ripped from the wall, then trampled under the brothers' dancing feet. Madeline rushed to the kitchen sink, turned the cold-water faucet on full and pointed the dish-rinsing nozzle and pulled the trigger. A cold spray of water shot across the room soaking both of them. "NOW, STOP IT!" Madeline screamed in concert with her attack.

They both turned to see Madeline standing in front of the sink, her arm rigid, holding the nozzle out in front of her body like a revolver, shooting a cascade of water in their direction.

"Mom, what are you doing?" Theodore shouted before he turned Linus loose. Saucer-eyed, Madeline glared at the dripping brawlers.

After releasing the trigger, Madeline held them at nozzle point. "I saw it on the news; police turned fire hoses on protesters! It seemed to work for them!"

Theodore, bleeding from his mouth, turned away from Linus, picking up his toupee from the floor. His scalp was bright red where the toupee had been ripped free. Madeline strained at the edge of tears. Theodore stepped away from Linus allowing Madeline to relax her defense. After returning the sprayer to its holder, Madeline righted a chair from the floor and sat down, slumping in exhaustion. Linus looked on pensively, half expecting a counter attack, but Theodore ignored him, too busy contemplating the mess strewn across the floor.

"Sorry about your *coonskin* there, Daniel Boone!" Linus chortled.

Madeline didn't hear the comment, but Theodore did. His jaw tightened. After a tenuous interlude, Theodore let the issue drop and turned back to face Madeline.

"Sorry, Mom," Theodore said, surveying the room.

"Is your toupee okay, Teddy?" Madeline asked. Theodore was holding it the way one would a kitten by the scruff of its neck. "Can you glue it back on?"

"Don't worry about it," he said, picking the chairs from the floor.

"I'll get the Elmer's, bro, we'll stick it back on!" Linus goaded. Theodore spun to face Linus with rekindled fury. Linus unflinchingly mirrored the gaze back, as if unsatisfied with the untimely end to the brawl.

"NO! THAT'S ENOUGH! I MEAN IT!" Madeline screamed, springing up from her seat.

She began shouting for mops, buckets, and brooms from the laundry room, dispensing orders like a drill sergeant, quelling any further uprisings.

After the mess was cleaned up, Theodore left for a walk while Linus was in the bathroom tending his eye. Madeline was at the sink finishing the dishes, watching Theodore from the kitchen window. She saw him lift the lid to the galvanized trash can, drop in the shabby toupee, then fix the lid back in place. He pulled a beret from his pocket and placed it on his head. After a few adjustments to the cap, he lumbered toward the street, his lanky frame tottering as if it were made from a jumble of spare parts.

Linus walked back into the kitchen.

"Why must you two always fight?" Madeline asked, keeping her eyes on Theodore as he walked across the yard.

"Ah, ma, it's nothing!" Linus grinned, pulling an ice cube from the freezer and placing it on his eye. "You make too big a deal out of it."

Madeline whirled around to face her eldest son, her hands dripping soapy water. "Too big a deal?" she shouted. "Look at my spoon collection..." Madeline pointed at the shattered shelf unit. "And my figurines!" She gestured toward the trash can. "Nothing, Linus? You ruined Theodore's toupee. He paid good money for that."

"He got robbed!" Linus laughed. "It looked like road-kill, for Chrissakes! I did him a favor."

Madeline shoved her hands back into the soapy water and rattled the dishes. She searched for Theodore out the window, but he was gone.

"Don't you have any compassion for what your brother just went through?" Madeline stated without taking her gaze from the window.

"What, ma?" Linus asked, checking the baseball scores in the newspaper while the dripping ice made soggy spots on the print.

Madeline swung from the sink, her eyes flaring. "Dammit! Linus," she shouted. "Your brother has just lost everything. He lost all his computer equipment, his business, his clothes, his pictures, everything! Don't you care about that, Linus? Have I raised a reptile?"

Linus hung his head. Madeline hardly ever cursed and when she did it usually consisted of an, "Oh, sugar!"—stated emphatically, of course.

"Look, I'm sorry," he said. "Theodore will be okay, he's brilliant. He'll figure out something."

"Will he figure out how to bring his friend, Mrs. Bloom, back from the dead, Linus? He loved her. She was a wonderful woman and a good friend. Are you so callous that you can't see that?"

"Sorry," Linus said standing up. "Look, I've got to go. Lisa and the kids are waiting for me to pick them up. We're going to the zoo. I just stopped by to see if Theodore wanted to go. He's hardly seen my kids since they were born."

Madeline's head dropped, her face somber as a blanket. She sniffled and wrung her hands into the towel. Linus came up behind her and hugged her. "I'll call you later, okay?"

Linus retreated; his work boots echoed along the hall, across the wood-planked front porch, then went quiet on the concrete steps out front.

From the kitchen, Madeline could no longer hear the boisterous departure of her son, only a silence that slowly surrendered to the electrical hum of the kitchen.

Several days later Theodore borrowed his mother's car and drove to Ballas Photo Lab on the other side of Bakersfield to meet his friend Woody for lunch. They went to the La Hacienda a few miles from the lab. After they ordered, Theodore excused himself to go to the bathroom and didn't return for over twenty minutes. Woody was getting up from the table to check on him when the waitress brought the food.

"Just set it down, I'll be right back," Woody told her, then headed past a line of booths in the direction of the restrooms. Theodore was standing at the sink washing his hands when Woody entered. Theodore hadn't noticed him.

"C'mon, Theo, they're clean," Woody said in a low, soft voice. Woody and his wife Shelley were the only ones who ever called him Theo. He didn't see himself as a Theo, but liked the sound of it coming from them.

Theodore looked up in the mirror and saw Woody standing near the door. Woody walked over, turned the faucet off and handed him a towel.

"Before our food gets cold," Woody said.

Theodore dried his hands with the brown paper towel and said nothing as he followed Woody from the bathroom.

"Has it started again?" Woody asked, after they sat down.

"A little, I guess," he said. Even though Woody was his dearest and most trusted friend, it was difficult to admit his recurring malady.

For a few minutes they didn't speak until Theodore asked about Shelley and the kids. Woody said that everyone was fine, that Rebecca was a handful, and Bryan would start school in the fall. They avoided talking about anything heavy, content to chat about Woody's time in the Air Force, and how he and Shelley were settling into their new home. When they finished eating, Woody brought up the fire, and Sarah.

"I'm sorry," Woody said. "She was a cool lady." Woody had met her on one of his business trips to Glen Valley.

Theodore was about to tell him about Sarah, how he felt about her, but then it all seemed so stupid, so unimportant now. What was he going to say?—that we had sex one night and now I miss her so terribly I can hardly breathe, and I feel empty inside every waking hour? How pathetic is that?

"You gonna stay in Bakersfield for now?" Woody asked.

"Yeah, I guess so," Theodore told him.

"Hey, what ever happened with that cool video game you were working on?"

"Nothing. DreamCo wasn't interested."

"Have you tried it anywhere else?"

"Everywhere else. DreamCo was the last shot."

"Are you working on anything new?"

"No, my computer got roasted in the fire."

"Ah shit! I'm sorry, Theo, I forgot… God, how stupid…."

"Forget it, Woody. It's no big deal."

Theodore changed the subject to the job at Ballas Photo Lab that Woody had told him about on the phone. Woody explained what Theodore would be doing at first, the training, and what he could expect down the road.

As Theodore listened, a disquieting thread unraveled in his stomach; his life was becoming everything he didn't want it to be—living back in Bakersfield, a nine to five job that didn't interest him….

"Why don't we go back and I'll give you the nickel tour," Woody said, palming the check from the table. "Lunch is my treat!"

Theodore thanked him as they walked to the car.

"Hey, Theo, you look good without Sylvester on your head," Woody said as he unlocked the door. "When did you lose it?"

"The other day. Linus and I got into it in the kitchen and he yanked it off."

"Ouch, that must have hurt? Did you thank him?"

Theodore nodded, "Yeah, I gave him a black eye!"

Woody laughed and unlocked the doors. "Oh, Theo, I almost forgot. Shelley told me to invite you for dinner tonight. Be there at seven, okay."

Theodore loved Shelley, but given the events of the past week, he wasn't sure he could handle the warmth of Woody's family, even though it might be the thing he needed most.

# # #

"Come in! You look great!" Shelley cooed, throwing her arms around Theodore's neck before he made it through the front door. Shelley's satiny-blond hair framed her almond face and conspired with her willowy figure to give her the look of an adolescent. Several inches shorter than Theodore, Shelley stood on tiptoes to hug him, then gave him a brief kiss on the lips.

"Right on time," said Woody, plodding across the living room with a young child clinging to his leg. She was almost two, shy, and playfully concealing herself from Theodore, peeking around her daddy's leg when she thought he wasn't looking, and giggling when he was. A young boy with a crew cut and fair skin, no more than five, sat mesmerized in front of the television. A quick glance in the direction of the front door was the only indication that the young boy had noticed Theodore's arrival.

Woody hoisted the young girl to eye level, holding her seated on his forearm. She bubbled coyly, then turned away.

"This is Rebecca, the flirt of Bakersfield," said Woody. "You haven't seen her since she was a baby, have you?"

Theodore agreed, even though he wasn't sure.

"Rebecca, can you say hi to Theo?"

Rebecca buried her face in Woody's shoulder and kicked her legs like a frantic bullfrog. Muffled giggles came from behind him as Rebecca continued her game of hide and seek with Theodore, her unwitting subject.

Shelley excused herself to the kitchen, coaxing Rebecca to help her finish dinner and lifted her from Woody's arms.

"Bryan, you remember Theo, don't you?" Woody asked, standing above the boy sitting cross-legged on the floor. The boy twisted toward Theodore, nodded with disinterest, then focused back on the screen.

"Yeah, well, okay then," Woody said, smiling at Theodore as they sat down.

After a few minutes, Woody brought up the subject of Ballas Photo Lab. "I know it's only been a couple of hours since we talked today, but have you had a chance to think about the job?"

"DreamCo called my mom's house today," said Theodore. "They offered me the job."

"That's awesome, Theo!" said Woody, stumbling over a toy truck as he jumped up from his lounger to shake his hand. "That is so cool! Did you hear that, Shelley?" he shouted toward the kitchen. "Theo got the job in LA!"

"Oh Theo, that is so wonderful," Shelley said, walking in from the kitchen, wiping her hands on her apron. "I can't wait to go to a bar and see your game there, that is, if Woody ever takes me out again!" Shelley gave Woody a jab in the ribs, then noticed Theodore's somber expression. "You're excited, aren't you?"

"Yeah... sure."

Woody looked over at Shelley, then back at Theodore.

"Do you need a ride into LA?" Woody asked.

"Linus is taking me on Friday."

"Well, I'm going to finish up dinner," Shelley said, stepping to the kitchen, glancing at Woody and shrugging. "It'll be on the table in five minutes!"

THEODORE

Thanatos is what Freud referred to as the "drive for death" in human beings. He postulated that all people, especially younger ones, secretly crave death. Some sources believe that cigarette companies have been exploiting this so-called "drive for death" through clever ad campaigns that entice smokers through subliminal death motifs. And because shock therapy creates the sensation of being killed, some proponents of ECT believe that a positive aspect of shock therapy is that it satiates the patient's desire for death, but in a safe and controlled way. I don't know if ECT satiated my secret desire for death, or if I even had one, but the treatments certainly created the sensation of being killed.

It's hard to pinpoint the exact moment the juice hits you because time-space reality bursts into a blue-white explosion of light, a loud crack inside your skull, but it's not your skull anymore, it's the entire world disintegrating in a flash, fierce, your guts ringing, your skin sizzling. Convulsions rip at your bound limbs, broil your organs, clamp your lungs; it's impossible to breathe. Searing pain shoots through your veins and you're hurtling down a brilliant vacuous cavity that echoes so loudly it feels as though it's melting your eardrums. A surge, a white-hot tremor blasts through you, and your thoughts, your fear, your sense of being, evaporate.

Your skin is hot, wet and tingling, leaving a metallic taste in your mouth. You're no longer sure if your eyes are open or closed, if your bowels have let loose, if you're alive or dead.

That was the first of three shock treatments I received during my six-day stay at Memorial Medical. After my third one, Madeline put an end to the procedures when I told her that the doctors were trying to burn me alive. The doctors informed her that my reaction was delusional, that there was nothing to worry about, that it was normal for patients to complain, and that patients experienced nothing but the slightest discomfort during ECT. I'm thankful she believed me instead of them.

CHAPTER 8

―――――――

When they left Bakersfield on Friday, a light mist hung in the warm morning air and the fresh smell of spring rose from the damp roads and wet verdure. Although they had ridden for thirty minutes without talking, the drive was not onerous with unspoken words, but instead, mellow with the absence of chatter. The radio played softly in the background of their silence.

It was curious to Theodore that barely two weeks had passed since the fire in Glen Valley had claimed all of his possessions, yet it seemed like a lifetime ago. So much had changed in such a brief period. And then there was Sarah. Theodore, oddly ambivalent over returning to Glen Valley, hadn't attended her funeral, a small memorial to honor her passing, even though her children, Thomas and Isabel, had invited him. They both lived in San Francisco and came to Glen Valley on numerous occasions to visit their mother, so Theodore had many opportunities to meet them, but never became close. Isabel had been the one to contact him in

Bakersfield to let him know of the service. "My mother loved you very much," she had told him on the phone. "Your garden made her happy!"

Theodore thought about his garden on the side of Sarah's house, how radiant it was in the soft sunlight that last morning, how the fragrance of moist soil filled his head when he bent down to snip the gazania for the vase. Theodore, like most unsuspecting beneficiaries of loss, regretted that he had not lingered a bit longer with the marigolds and gladiolus, had not paused to listen to the mourning doves cooing from the roof top, had not returned to Sarah's bedroom that morning after the ball game. Maybe things would've been different, or maybe he could've saved her, or maybe they could've died together like her and Sid. He saw her face, her eyes, he traced once again the rise of her hip, the dip of her waist, as he had done a thousand times. He tried to think of the last words they had spoken, the last thing she had said as she closed the door behind him...

"Linus, I'm sorry about the other day, attacking you and all," Theodore said, tearing himself from the memory.

Linus glanced over at Theodore, as if surprised by the sudden infusion of words into the silence, or maybe unsure what Theodore was talking about.

"That's where we're different, Teddy," Linus said, quickly glancing from the road to his brother. "I don't think about anything once it's over. I already forgot about it."

Once again, Theodore was reminded of how contrary he was to Linus and the rest of his family. Linus in a way was simple, not stupid or slow, just happily lacking complexity. His approach to life was much the same as his approach to shredded wheat; he ate it just the way it came out of the box. And afterwards he wasn't hounded by questions of degree, quality, or potential; he was merely satiated and left the table. And although he was not without his problems in life, Linus was basically, for the most part, happy.

"Linus, can I ask you something?"

"Yeah, sure. What is it?"

"Why did Dad dislike me so much?" Theodore asked, his eyes intense.

Linus appeared confused, his gaze drifting back and forth between Theodore and the road.

"You know, Theodore, for someone who's supposed to be so smart, you have no grasp of the obvious, do you?" Linus replied, with a chuckle.

It was true and Theodore knew it. Obvious conclusions were immediately buried under mounds of questions, while solutions attained too easily were quickly dismissed, presumed of little worth. Theodore believed that anything of real value, of real merit, must be hidden away like the Holy Grail, the Dead Sea Scrolls, the Ark of the Covenant. If a concept had its home in the mundane, then it was certainly endemic of the commonplace and no use to a thinking man. How else could it be? If the average man could lay claim to it, then it was nothing more than the embalmed folly of the masses. But for all his analytical posturing, he still couldn't understand Linus' seemingly arcane remark.

"What are you talking about?"

Linus's eyes drifted to Theodore, then back at traffic.

"You really don't get it, do you?" Linus said, grinning.

"No, Linus, enlighten me!" Theodore said, becoming impatient with his brother's gloating.

Linus savored the moment a while longer, stretching out the void before he spoke.

"Dad was a lot like me," he finally said. "I know he felt some of what I did, but I think he had it worse." Linus glanced across the seat. "The old man was crazy jealous of you, bro. That's why he treated you the way he did. You were smart, inventive, creative, like with the model building. While we were following the directions that came in the box, you were building crazy monstrosities from the trash we threw away. I saw the way he looked at the stuff you brought in to show Mom; he saw the genius in what you were doing."

"That's crazy, Linus!" Theodore objected. "Dad was brilliant, he was...."

"Dad knew how to follow directions," Linus interrupted. "He was good at what he did, following instructions, procedures. But he saw how you built from scratch, no guidelines. The problem was, if it didn't have guidelines or wasn't in a book, it was out of his reach... like it is for me. I don't see what isn't there, Teddy, I don't even try! I think Dad was haunted by it. But he loved you, Teddy, more than you'll ever know."

Theodore was quiet, unable to fit this information into the rotting photo album that he had buried away in his mind. It didn't seem possible that his father, this man who was always so sure of himself, so proud, could be the same man that Linus was speaking of. How could he be jealous of a gangly kid who walked with a limp and...? It made no sense.

"But Linus, I..." Theodore started speaking, but stopped when he lost the thread of his thought.

"Dad was out in the garage by himself one night working on something," Linus said, his eyes on the road. "I was doing my homework in the kitchen and Mom asked me to go out and get him for supper. It was dark and when I got to the garage door, I stood a minute, looking at him through the window to see what he was doing. I figured he would be building that new *Spitfire* he had gotten a few nights earlier, but he wasn't. He had one of your monstrosities on his workbench, studying it like it was the Mona Lisa. He was making sketches. I didn't knock. I sneaked back to the house, slammed the screen door and started singing down the back steps. By the time I got to the garage door, your creation was gone and the box to the *Spitfire* was opened on the workbench. I poked my head in and told him supper was ready and he said he'd be there in a minute. I waited by the door in the dark and watched him pull his sketch pad out from under the *Spitfire* box, rip out the page, and throw it in the trash."

Theodore was shaking his head, staring out the window.

"Don't be too hard on the old man, Teddy," Linus said. "He loved you the best he knew how."

Theodore burst into tears.

"What's wrong, bro?" Linus asked.

"I wanted him dead, Linus," Theodore screamed, pulling his knees up to his chest. "I wished him dead that day he left for work. I flipped him off behind his back and wished he'd never come back!"

Linus pulled the car to the shoulder and threw the shifter into park. The car stopped with a gentle jolt.

"Teddy," Linus said, turning toward him.

Theodore had pulled himself into a ball on the front seat.

"Do you know how many times I flipped off the old man when he wasn't looking? Or how many times I wished he would drive off a cliff? You didn't have anything to do with what happened the day he was killed; I guarantee it, no matter what you thought, *or* what you did."

Theodore pressed his face against his knees and wrapped his arms over his head. Not knowing how to believe Linus.

Linus placed a hand on Theodore's arm. "Hey Teddy, I'm sorry about what I said about Mrs. Bloom, and Mom, and the garage. I was just trying to get in your shit; I didn't mean it. I forget how seriously you take things."

Theodore raised his head slowly biting his lip. An eighteen-wheeler rumbled by, rocking the car.

"Come on, Teddy, you can't show up for your new job looking like Little Orphan Annie. Here wipe your eyes with this," Linus said handing him a McDonalds napkin from the glove box. "You okay?"

He nodded, wiping snot from his nose with the smallish paper towel. Linus put the car in gear and headed back onto the freeway. Theodore checked his puffy eyes in the visor mirror.

"Don't worry about it, Cinderella, you're beautiful!" Linus joked, smiling over at him.

Theodore pushed the visor back up against the headliner of the car, and fell into the rhythm of the tires on the pavement. After driving a while longer, Linus reached over and turned up the volume on the radio.

"... *residents of Glen Valley have had what police are calling 'a reprieve' from the recent brutal killings of middle-aged widows. The so-called 'Glen Valley Killer,' who had been striking with predictable regularity has not claimed a victim in almost two weeks. Police are speculating that the 'Killer' may have moved on from the area but urge residents to remain vigilant and to keep their doors locked, even during the day. Although officials have described the 'Killer's' approach as 'methodical,' the Glen Valley police report that they still have no solid leads in the case.*

Last week in an interview with Lt. Redmond of the Glen Valley police, the 'meticulous order' of the murders was blamed for the lack of any real leads in the case. 'Each murder is like the previous one, there is a definite pattern but no new evidence! He doesn't make mistakes!' Redmond was quoted as saying.

Yesterday, in other news...."

Linus turned the volume down until the announcer's voice was a murmur. "That's some freaky shit, ain't it?" Linus said, looking over at Theodore. Theodore's eyes were fixed on the blanched road stretching toward the city. The drizzle was gone, and the sun struggled to break through the haze.

Theodore remembered Redmond from the fire, and his certainty about Sarah's death. "Seems that the upstairs collapsed down on top of her bedroom. I'm sure she was killed instantly," he had told Theodore. But was Sarah asleep when the upstairs collapsed? Had she been drinking wine and reading late into the night, sleeping too soundly to feel the heat, hear the flames eating at the floor boards above her? No, of course not! Sid Carter was there. No, she wasn't reading....

"Teddy, where do we turn?" Linus asked, checking the exit signs. "Teddy?" he repeated. "Hey, bro!"

Theodore looked over, his heart pounding, then glanced toward the freeway. "Take the next exit."

They arrived at DreamCo shortly after one o'clock in the afternoon. When they got to the entrance, Theodore was about to push through the revolving door when Linus grabbed his arm.

"Whoa, little brother," Linus exclaimed. "Is that what I think it is?" he said looking at the revolving doors.

Theodore glanced up, then looked away.

"The Baldwin fucking Hotel! That's the hotel we used to stay at in St. Louis, isn't it?" Linus said. "I'm sure of it, Teddy. Remember how the manager came out and yelled at us for playing tag in the doorway. Shit yeah, what's that doing here?"

Theodore ignored the question, uneasy with the memory shifting through him. Linus followed behind.

"Hey, Teddy, I know you remember. No one could forget the stairwell incident," he said, laughing in the pie-shaped section of the revolving doors, looking at Theodore in the section ahead of him. Theodore heard the muffled laughter coming from behind.

Once in the lobby, Theodore padded briskly toward the front desk not waiting for Linus to bring the subject up again. Linus followed him, studying the bizarrely appointed lobby and probably thought his brother would fit right in. A fourteen-foot replica of Saturn floated above them, suspended by cables, with *DreamCo* in neon along the yellow ring.

"Hey, my man. I almost didn't recognize you without your... a... hair... thing!" Otis said, his wide grin as warm as sunshine. "You look good! Straight up!" Otis assured him.

Theodore smiled.

"Otis, this is my brother, Linus," Theodore said, moving aside to present his brother.

Otis extended a hand to Linus. "Nice to meet you, Linus," he said. "I have a cousin named Linus, plays football for UCLA. He's their big center, like a hippo in the middle of the field!" Otis laughed at his own joke, his eyes sparkling with genuine joy. "He hikes the ball and looks for someone to hit, but he's slower than shit. The defense is usually straddling the quarterback by the time ol' Linus finds someone to block! I don't know why they don't bench that boy," he said to himself, laughing.

"Is Kent here, Otis?" Theodore asked. "He told me to stop by when I got in town, he had a couple of leads on apartments."

"Yeah, I think he's waiting for you," Otis said, picking up the phone. "He told me to ring him as soon as you got here."

"Hello, Kent. Mr. Trumball's here," Otis said, listened a moment, then handed the phone to Theodore. "Kent wants to talk to you."

Theodore listened, said, "Okay," then passed it back.

"Kent wants to take us to lunch, do you have time?" he asked Linus.

After checking his watch, Linus said, "Sure, might as well eat before I go back! Hey, Otis, do you know where those revolving doors came from?" he asked, pointing to the entrance.

"I think they come from a hotel in St. Louis. Mr. Cantwell's daddy was the hotel manager there until it caught fire in '68. They had to tear it down. Cantwell bought the doors before they put the wrecking ball to it. Sure is strange, ain't it, walking through those doors? The Baldwin Hotel! I feel like a bellhop every time I come to work," Otis laughed.

"Our family used to stay at that hotel when we visited St. Louis. Last time was like '62 or '63," Linus told him. "They just started building the Arch around then. It was pretty cool!"

"Ain't never been to St. Louis. Understand it's a nice city," Otis said. "Love to see that Arch, but most of all I want to take a tour of that brewery, Anheuser Busch. I hear they give you as much beer as you want on the tour—*free!*" Otis wore a wide grin. Theodore avoided the conversation, hoping Linus would drop it as well.

"Maybe I'll take the wife and kids back out there for a vacation," Linus joked with Otis. "Drop them off at the zoo to feed the goats, while I visit with ol' Bud and Busch!" They laughed, as if each secretly entertaining the notion of free-flowing beer, while Theodore fidgeted, waiting impatiently for Kent.

"The hotel burned in '68, huh?" Linus asked, then turned to Theodore. "Hey Teddy, you think Cantwell's old man was the same guy that yelled at us for playing in the doors?"

Theodore, his mind jumping like a flea from one thought to the next, hadn't heard the question.

"Teddy? Earth to Teddy!" Linus said smiling.

"What?" Theodore blurted, jerking his head around.

"I said, do you think Cantwell's old man was the same guy who yelled at us for playing in the doors?"

Theodore pondered the possibility. The image of the square-shouldered gentleman with graying hair, fastidiously clad in a three-piece suit, crossed his mind, but before he could respond, Kent strolled up behind them and introduced himself.

"You must be Linus," Kent said, shaking his hand. "Nice to meet you. Do you design video games or was there only room in the family for one computer geek?" Kent asked smiling, glancing over at Theodore. Oddly, Theodore wasn't offended. Instead, he felt like he'd been included in an exclusive club with Kent as president.

"No, I fix cars and watch television," Linus announced proudly. "Theodore ended up with all the torment!" Linus laughed, hugging his brother around the shoulder, pulling him close. Embarrassed and surprised by the gesture, Theodore struggled gently to free himself. When Kent and Otis joined the laughter, Theodore forced a weak smile and straightened himself when Linus released him.

"Well, should we go to lunch?" Kent asked.

When they stepped out onto the parking lot, Kent offered to drive. Walking to his car, Kent asked about the fire in Glen Valley, said he saw it on the news, that's how he tracked down Theodore. Theodore described the afternoon, returning to the house, the police cars and fire engines, the total loss of everything, then became pensive over the recollection. He intentionally didn't mention Mrs. Bloom and hoped that Linus would keep his mouth shut as well. Kent changed the subject and asked Linus about his work and family. Linus boasted on his two girls, his beautiful wife, Lisa, and Trumball's Tire and Service Center, the business he'd started after high school.

"You seem real happy, Linus," Kent said as he turned onto Vandemont Avenue. "What's your philosophy on life, if I may ask?"

Linus, sitting in the front passenger seat, laughed. "I don't have a philosophy. I just don't worry about anything that I can't do anything about!" he told Kent and peered straight ahead.

Kent glanced over at him and nodded.

Theodore, sitting in back, was amazed that in less than five minutes Kent had succeeded in extracting the sole, defining logic that guided Linus through his life. He'd had no idea how

Linus felt about things and was a bit jealous of Kent's ability to bring people out.

"Hey, Theodore, I like the new look!" Kent said, regarding him in the rear-view mirror.

"Yeah?" Theodore replied, not sure what the comment pertained to.

"You look more *real* without it."

He finally realized Kent was referring to the absence of his toupee. It was still going to take some time acclimating to his bare head exposed to the world.

After they ordered lunch, Kent proposed a toast.

"To the newest member of DreamCo!"

They brought their glasses together with a brittle *'clink'* over the center of the table. Self-conscious over being the recipient of attention, Theodore excused himself to go to the bathroom.

As soon as he was in the lavatory, he locked the door and stood at the sink gazing into the mirror. The image that peered back was always a stranger, never quite matching the image he held himself to be inside. The reflection was a hideous being of immeasurable flaws, not at all the image of the rather bland fellow with soft eyes he kept expecting to see. As he washed his hands, Theodore pondered the dichotomy of form between the imagined and the real, and which was which. Which image did others see, or did they see something totally different from his impressions? The idea so confounded him that he began to wash his hands with increasing fervor until soap and water slopped about the sink and dripped from the bowl. So intent on trying to merge the inner image with the one in the mirror, he failed to notice the water splattering his trousers and shirt, painting an unattractive pattern at his crotch.

A knock at the door jolted him from his obsession. His heart pounded at his chest. "Just a second, I'm almost finished!"

"Theodore, it's Linus, are you okay in there? You've been in there for like a decade. I thought you fell in!"

Damn! Theodore whispered to himself. "I'm fine," he yelled through the door. "I'll be right there!" He heard Linus walk away, then searched frantically for the towels. Upon noticing the mess he'd created, Theodore realized that the hand blower was the best option. He twisted the nozzle in the direction of his trousers and hit the button; warm air streamed from the vent.

By the time he returned to the table, Linus and Kent were well into their lunch and laughing about something. Theodore took his seat, trying to act casual.

"I was telling Kent about our trip to St. Louis when we were kids and you're not gonna believe what he told me, Teddy," Linus said as Theodore was sitting down. "Kent said that Cantwell's old man paced for four days outside The Baldwin Hotel in a charred suit after the hotel burned down, talking to imaginary people and taking reservations on an old beer carton for the reopening!" Linus laughed as he related the story to Theodore.

Theodore looked at Kent questioning the validity of the story.

"Frank told me himself one—" Kent started to say.

"Cantwell's name is Frank?" Linus interrupted, his eyebrows raised.

"Yeah, Frank Cantwell. Why?" Kent said.

"That's our dad's name... and then The Baldwin Hotel and... I don't know, it's just *creepy!*" Linus said, twisting up his face. "Don't you think, bro?"

Theodore asked Kent how he knew about Cantwell's dad.

"Frank told me over cocktails a month or so after I went to work at DreamCo," Kent explained. "He was half in the bag and went on about how his old man lost his mind working at The Baldwin Hotel in St. Louis. Frank had to fly back to St. Louis and convince his mother to admit Monroe—that's his father—into St. Vincent's Hospital. Evidently, the police, after arresting Monroe, had called his mother and told her that Monroe was grabbing luggage and briefcases and shopping bags out of people's hands and placing them on imaginary carts in front of the burned-out hotel.

"So, when Cantwell found out about the demolition of the building, he purchased the doors and had them shipped out here—stored them until he bought the building. He said the doors of the hotel reminded him of his father's insanity. Frank said, 'It's important to keep your insanity close by, that way it can't sneak up on you one day like it did my old man!' "

"Hey, Theodore, tell Kent about the experience you had at The Baldwin Hotel." Linus said. Kent looked over, apparently concluding that something was bothering Theodore, and said nothing.

Theodore shook his head and stabbed at his lunch.

"All right, then I'll tell him," Linus announced with flair.

Kent fidgeted, as if sensing that Theodore was not in the mood for whatever Linus was about to share. Theodore was mortified but tried to hide it.

Linus took a drink and started the story.

"We were visiting our aunt and uncle in St. Louis, but because their house was small, we stayed at The Baldwin," Linus said as he chewed his food. "Since we were going to be out there anyway, my dad lined up a job interview with some big-deal firm. So while he's at his interview, my mom goes to the beauty parlor in the hotel. I stayed in the room and Teddy went with her.

"After a while, Teddy wanders off and goes into the stairwell. I guess you were like ten, maybe eleven at the time, hey, Teddy?" Linus said, but Theodore ignored the question.

"So, I got bored with TV," Linus said, "and walked down to the lobby. I was just about to the doors headed for the sidewalk to watch the bums and hookers, when our mom comes running out of the beauty parlor, screaming, 'My Teddy is gone!'" Linus started laughing. "You should have seen her, running with her arms above her head, her hair dripping that smelly-ass perm shit, her body tangled in this plastic floral cape. She looked like Wonder Woman on acid!

"I'm watching the whole thing as the manager, who we now know was Monroe Cantwell, comes running over to our mom, trying to calm her down. Meanwhile, people are gathering in the lobby of the hotel trying to see what all the commotion is. The manager tells my mother that if she will please calm down, he will send hotel security to search the premises, assuring her that everything will be fine. Of course, all the while he's phoning security and searching for Teddy, her hair is dripping that nasty perm crap on the two-thousand-dollar sofa and burning little white holes in the fabric!"

Linus started laughing, unable to continue with the story. Theodore glared at him, then considered getting up and leaving. Linus finally composed himself enough to proceed.

"Just then, little Teddy here comes running through the lobby like his ass is on fire screaming, 'The Arch is gone! The Arch is gone!' My eyes are as big as baseballs. My crazed brother here is knocking over plants and crashing into hotel guests, while our mom is destroying the hotel sofa. At that very moment, like it was choreographed, I shit you not, our old man comes through the hotel doors, sees my mother sitting on the couch like a fugitive from beauty camp and says, 'What the hell is going on here, Madeline?' Then, out of the corner of his eye, the old man spies Teddy making a beeline for the front door.

He's still screaming, 'The Arch is gone! It's gone!' Before the old man can get anything out of Madeline, Monroe runs over to her and asks, 'Is that your son, madam?'" Linus paused a second to take a drink.

"My mother sees me standing there—oblivious to the fact that Teddy just ran from the hotel—and cries out, 'No, it's the other one that's missing! The little one! My Teddy!' and starts wailing like a windstorm again. I'm in shock and can't move. The old man grumbles something and runs down Tenth Street chasing Teddy."

Linus started laughing. Kent grinned, then placed his hand over his mouth when he saw that Theodore wasn't amused. Theodore, head down, blankly eyed his half-eaten baked potato.

"So finally, I went over to my mom and told her that Teddy was okay and Dad went to get him. She quit crying and about then, Dad walks back into the lobby carrying Teddy kicking and screaming under his arm like a football. Teddy was still jabbering like a madman when we got him up to the room. Every morning until we left St. Louis, we had to take him down to the Arch grounds and show him that they hadn't even started building it yet. They were just clearing the land. It was hilarious, Kent!"

Theodore hadn't heard the story end; he was back in his garden on the side of Sarah's house. Kent looked over at him, then back at Linus.

"Come on, Teddy, it's a funny story!" Linus said, trying to coax him back to humor. "Don't be pissed. You were a little fart-head kid for Chrissakes; kids are supposed to do crazy shit! I think it has something to do with the onset of puberty, you know, all those dormant hormones springing to life!"

Theodore looked up at his brother, then at Kent, forcing a smile that to almost anyone would have seemed genuine.

Kent quickly suggested key lime pie for dessert. "It's the best in the city. Who wants to join me?"

By the time they returned to DreamCo, the day, which had started out misty and gray, was now warm and vibrant with sunlight. Kent offered to drive Theodore around to look at apartments, leaving Linus free to return to Bakersfield before dark.

"Nice to meet you," Linus said, extending his hand to Kent. "Thanks for lunch."

Linus turned toward Theodore and was about to shake his hand, but hugged him instead. "Take care, little brother. I'll talk to you soon," he said, releasing Theodore, leaving him moved and bewildered by the overture.

Theodore nodded, unable to construct a farewell of words.

Linus looked over his shoulder, smiled and waved goodbye.

Kent helped Theodore into the building with the bags and set them by Otis's desk. "Hey Theodore, if you're not too beat, why don't we go upstairs first and I'll show you some of our ideas on OBO and where we are with it."

Theodore followed Kent toward the elevators. Otis was busy with a repairman who had the word, OTIS, printed in large letters across his back. At first Theodore thought it odd to see Otis speaking with a man who had OTIS on his coveralls, until he realized that OTIS was a logo and the fellow with the coveralls was the elevator repairman.

Otis ushered the repairman over to the far elevator as Theodore and Kent entered the one on the right. As the doors slid shut, Theodore was struck by the smell of new carpet, something he hadn't remembered from his previous visit. When he looked down, he saw his shoes surrounded by wild swirls of color and exploding shapes as if the Big Bang had just taken place beneath his feet. Kent pressed the button for the seventh floor. Theodore was lost in the meandering design of the new carpet, straining to remember the floor from his first visit. He knew it wasn't carpet, not this carpet.

Theodore, nudged from his trance by the abrupt stop, looked up as the doors slid open.

"Thank God!" Kent said, stepping out, "Cantwell spends thousands on making this place look cool,"—then looked toward the carpet—"but hasn't sunk any cash into the guts of the building, in particular, these old elevators." Kent led Theodore down a hall to his office. "People are constantly getting stuck in them. They stop for no reason. They're just really old. They probably need to be replaced, even though they don't look too bad."

Theodore hadn't been in Kent's office on his first visit and was in awe of its understated elegance. Thin slatted aluminum blinds lined the huge windows behind his desk. The walls were painted dark gray, sparsely adorned with framed artwork and paintings. The dark ceiling was a relief map of pipes and vents. A video arcade game sat in one corner while a strange, almost prehistoric-looking, metal sculpture hung from the ceiling, rotating slowly under the spell of some inscrutable force.

Kent walked over to an elaborate computer console to the left of his desk and powered it up, then started to explain some of his ideas, but Theodore wasn't listening, suddenly preoccupied with the drive from Bakersfield, the fight with Linus, his father's funeral, the revolving doors....

"Theodore, are you okay?"

Theodore appeared sallow in the low light.

"I just need to sit down a second," he said, moving to the leather and chrome lounge chair near Kent's desk.

"I'll get you some water," Kent said and left the office.

Theodore fell into the chair and found it much more comfortable than it looked. He closed his eyes. Images of places and people raced across the inside of his eyelids until they eventually slowed to shadows, then shapes, dark purple, blues, bursts of orange, then red.

Kent placed a glass of water in his unsuspecting hand. He sat up, opened his eyes, looked at the water, then Kent. "Thanks."

"Why don't you take a rest, turn some music on if you like," Kent said pointing to the Harman Kardon stereo system on the glass shelves above the computer. "I have a couple things I need to do and then we can get going, find you a place to live." Kent smiled and pulled the door shut. Theodore slowly closed his eyes again, listening to the whir of the computer processor and was soon asleep.

A geranium in a clay pot floated down a muddy river. The geranium reminded him of Daisy from his game, but looked like a ruby gazania, but somehow Theodore knew it was a geranium. Unable to reach the flower from the riverbank, he grabbed a branch on the tree and broke it off, but as he did, the branch changed into a piece of electrical wire. Holding one end of it above the rushing water, he extended his arm to reach Daisy, but every time he touched the pot or the water, he got shocked. The flower and pot headed for a waterfall and were about to go over the edge when he dove in and swam toward the geranium. Just as he reached out to grab the edge of the pot, it went over. He fought hard against the current, but to no avail, and found himself tumbling over the edge as well. Soon he was falling, grabbing at the water, feeling heat rising from below. He looked down just as Daisy was engulfed in a tremendous blaze. Falling toward the fire, unable to stop, his heart pounding furiously, he opened his mouth to scream.

THEODORE

Squatting down next to my father's workbench, I lit my first cigarette, a Salem I had filched from my mom's purse. The Salem quickly threw me into a coughing jag, bringing Madeline, who had been hanging laundry in the backyard and singing along with Doris Day. When I heard the garage door open, I shot upright and flipped the cigarette into the nearby trash can. What's all this smoke in here? she cried, waving her hand as if battling a swarm of flies. I froze, gawking at her, watching flames shoot up from the other side of the workbench. The trash can had been filled with balsa wood scraps from model building. She screamed, told me to run to the house and get Linus, but I couldn't move, didn't want to, enchanted by the strange notion that everything would be all right. When I looked over, my mom was screaming, her dress on fire. She grabbed me by the shirt, dragging me stumbling from the garage. Linus rushed down the back steps when he saw the smoke and tackled her, then rolled her in the grass until the flames were out. He helped her to her feet and pushed her in the direction of the house. He told her to call the fire department, then ran to where I was standing, pale and cold, the front of my shorts soaked with piss. Linus pushed me aside, jerked the hose from the side of the garage and yelled at me to turn on the spigot. "Now, dammit! You little fucker, move!"

CHAPTER 9

―――――

"Want a beer?" Kent asked.

"Sure," said Theodore, admiring the sparse tasteful furnishings of Kent's apartment. Theodore could hear the tinkling of bottles as Kent rummaged through the fridge for the beer. Kent and Theodore had spent the afternoon looking for apartments for Theodore, finding one not far from Kent's, but not near as nice. Theodore wasn't even sure what his salary would be… or how long the job at DreamCo would last; Cantwell really seemed to hate his game.

A large photographic enlargement of The Baldwin Hotel's revolving doors hung above a purple futon. The image of the shiny brass doors with a street scene abstractly reflected in the glass filled the six- by six-foot glossy print. Recounting the episode over lunch and now looking at the odd reproduction was disquieting.

"I think you're going to like living around here," Kent called out from the kitchen. "This is a very cool area, old but quiet. A lot of interesting people, a lot of artists."

Kent came into the living room. "You probably never expected to see those in LA, huh?" he said, noticing Theodore's interest in the print.

Theodore shrugged, reaching for the beer that Kent offered. "Thanks."

"Do you want to talk about what happened at The Baldwin when you were a kid?" Kent asked, as if recalling how upset Theodore seemed to be at lunch. "It's certainly none of my business, Theodore, but I thought if you felt like talking… you know… I could listen—"

"Kent, would you just call me Theo?" he interrupted, the sound of his own name making him feel like a child.

"Of course," Kent said.

"I'd rather hear about DreamCo and the projects you're working on," Theodore said, knowing there was no way to tell Kent about what happened. The phlegmatic timbre of Kent's voice sent Theodore tumbling into the massive print of The Baldwin Hotel revolving doors, falling forward as Kent talked about Cantwell and DreamCo, Kent's voice trailing off into a long tunnel…

Construction on the Arch began in 1961, starting with the footings that would hold the structure in place. When Theodore's family came to St. Louis in '63, the two legs of the Arch were already seventy to eighty feet high; Theodore remembered that very clearly. Attached to the legs were huge creeper derricks that scaled the surface of each leg and would be used to assemble the rest of the Arch. Theodore had been especially taken by the engineering feat of the derricks.

After checking in at The Baldwin Hotel, the family had walked down to the Arch grounds and looked through the fence. It was amazing. Massive triangular columns of stainless-steel protruding from the ground. It was surreal at the time to think that three years later they would come together 630 feet above the ground to form a perfect Catenary curve along the St. Louis riverfront.

The day his mom went to the beauty parlor, Theodore grew tired of sitting in the room and fighting with Linus, so he went down with her, getting bored in a hurry and deciding to do some exploring. That was the day he'd gotten stuck in the stairwell. He'd finally stopped on one of the landings and tried to open the door. It was locked or stuck. Unable to get it open, he turned to the smallish landing window to break it out and yell for help, but there was nothing to break it with. He tried pushing it open but it was as stubborn as the door. It was then something outside the window caught Theodore's attention. Over toward the riverfront were tractors and bulldozers clearing the trees from the Arch grounds, but the two legs of the Arch, as well as the creeper derricks, were gone. As if they had never existed in the first place.

He stared at the barren red dirt, the huge empty holes that would eventually become the footings, and knew that something was very wrong. By the time he reached the main floor he was hysterical, just like Linus had said at lunch, except that Theodore had no idea where he was until his dad grabbed him running down the street.

"Do you want another beer, Theo?" Kent said in the shallow light of the quiet room.

"Sure," Theodore said numbly, one foot still in the past. He watched Kent head for the kitchen and wondered how Kent might have reacted to the story. Kent probably would have said, "So you went back in time or something?"

To which Theodore would have to respond with a resounding, "No! Time doesn't exist, and neither does time travel." Theodore believed Time was merely illusion, a construct of man with the help of clocks and calendars and schedules in some futile attempt to bring a new order to a world constructed on cycles. The universe was in a constant state of flux; seasons, orbits, ebb, flow. Not moving forward, or backward, but round and round, continuously. Even our bodies, Theodore knew, were in a constant state of dying and being reborn, that roughly every day millions of cells died, new cells springing to life, over and over, perpetual. Scientifically proven. And like the ceaseless cycling of cells, so was the case with parallel universes, infinite possibilities constructed from limitless choices, each universe some variation on a theme, a staggering, mind-boggling boundless number of outcomes, an inexhaustible plethora of fates. That's what happened to Theodore in the stairwell at the Baldwin Hotel. He found himself in an alternate fate, an outcome where Woody lived and Porky died. One possibility plucked from illimitable potential.

Theodore liked to think of it as a television with a hundred thousand million channels broadcasting simultaneously, all transmitting their own individual signal except that the programs beaming out might be nearly identical. The only difference between them very slight, possibly, like one where the eyes of a certain announcer were blue, while in another version they were brown, the difference so slight as to be nearly imperceptible.

In Theodore's mental experiment with television broadcasts, he wondered what someone would see when they started changing channels? A virtual seamless picture of the same thing with barely noticeable changes. Yet the origin of each image, even though it appeared to be identical, would be a different picture emanating from a unique signal, completely distinct from any other, just not very obvious to the viewer. Parallel universes. Physicists like Wheeler, and Everett, and others believe the universe is continually splitting into a multitude of parallel realities and possible outcomes. Theodore believed he somehow crossed into one in the stairwell of The Baldwin Hotel.

Kent set the beer down in front of Theodore, startling him. Theodore bristled.

"Sorry, Theo," Kent said. "You must have been lost in thought."

"Yeah, sorry." Theodore sipped the new beer and looked up at Kent. "Do you believe in parallel universes?"

"I've read a little about quantum physics. I don't know what I think about that theory. Why?"

Theodore shook his head. "Tell me more about that new game DreamCo is about to release. *StarField*, right?"

No sooner had Kent started talking, when a new query took hold behind Theodore's eyes: How would Kent react if he had told him his theory? Kent would probably say something like, "You and your family continued your lives at that point except now it was a year earlier. Didn't that freak them out?"

Theodore had wrestled with this question for years, until he realized that the shift only happened for him, lived and experienced from the perspective of his personal consciousness. He never understood why he had been privy to it, but believed that shifts happen all the time to everyone without their knowledge. Or maybe people get the slightest clue to the subtle change, something like déjà vu, that freaky notion that you've done this before, or been here before, or said that before. And that would be the end of it. But Theodore experienced the reality shift first hand, because the memory of Woody's terrible beating was still accessible to his mind as the alternate reality was unfolding, a disconcerting dichotomy that placed him at the helm of Woody's fate, as well as Porky's, a chance to live this different outcome, a different fate. To Theodore's parents (because they didn't have access to the prior knowledge of Woody's thrashing the way Theodore did), Woody had always been just fine from their perspective, and Porky, a classmate of Theodore's they had never met, died a tragic, meaningless death. And while the boy's demise was regrettable, that was all there was to be made of the unfortunate occurrence.

The fantasy conversation trundled on through Theodore's mind, like the train in his next example. "Think about this," Theodore imagines telling Kent. "An infinite number of trains traveling on tracks that are exactly parallel, right?"

Theodore pictures Kent nodding enthusiastically, as if he understands and accepts everything Theodore is saying.

"Then imagine that each train has a different fate, maybe something as insignificant as being a minute late to the next stop, or five minutes early, or conversely something as horrible as the train derailing, killing everyone on board. That's kind of what happened. I had been on the train where Woody was horribly beaten, and somehow, in the stairwell, I jumped to a different possibility, the train where I killed Porky before he could hurt Woody. But for some reason, I had awareness of both trains, both horrible outcomes. And still do. For me both things happened, yet I remained in the reality where Woody was saved and Porky died. That became my new reality."

"So, on your birthday when you thought you were supposed to be turning thirteen, you turned twelve again?" Imaginary Kent asks, obviously riveted by this uncanny conversation.

"Exactly, that's what my family believed, and that was their reality. So I had to accept it or go crazy. But there was never a shift in time, because time doesn't exist. The seeming *disparity* in time, or shift, was nothing more than an illusion caused by the overlap of both realities in my mind."

"This sounds like when you have to repeat the sixth grade because you flunked?"

"Sort of, except I was the only one who knew I was repeating the sixth grade, which in fact, I did."

Kent's face lights up with comprehension. "So, for that whole year," Kent says excitedly. "You knew everything that was going to happen because you had already lived it?"

"You would think so, but no!" Theodore tells his fictitious Kent. "This was a different train, the previous one inexplicably gone. Had I not made such a fuss about the Arch and the stairwell at The Baldwin Hotel, some things may have run along similar lines and that would've been pretty cool, but that didn't happen…." Theodore's thoughts suddenly drift to Porky, and Woody, then to Dr. Melvin and the shock treatments, and he realized for the first time that his fussing was part of his *new fate* in this alternate reality, as were the shock treatments, and everything that happened.

Illusory Kent looks over at Theodore, a new puzzle to his features. "I thought I understood everything, but now I'm confused again," he says, after much deliberation. "If you jump from one train to the other, then wouldn't you run into yourself, the *you* that's already on that train with your folks?"

"That's a good question," Theodore says, remembering how Woody had tried to grasp all of this, but had just accepted it because they were friends. "I told you the train illustration was a little lame to explain something as unknowable as this, but anyway, to answer your question—no."

"Why?"

"Because I'm the observer in my own life," Theodore tells him. "Until I observe the reality of the other train, it doesn't exist the way you think it does. Take for instance Channel 4 and Channel 5 on the TV. If I'm watching Channel 4, Channel 5 doesn't cease to exist because I no longer view it… or maybe it does. Some eastern thought would say neither channel exists at all. But that's another discussion altogether. But for our example, let's say Channel 5 continues to exist, running parallel to Channel 4, but waiting for me to observe it…"

"Theo?" Kent asked. "Theo? Are you all right?"

Theodore looked over at Kent who was leaning forward on his knees, his face wrinkled with concern. Looking around the room, Theodore was momentarily stumped by where he was, then looked back at Kent.

"Theo, you don't look so good," Kent said. "Are you feeling all right?"

The sound of Kent's voice echoed inside Theodore's skull, Theodore's attention warped as if awaking from an arduous dream, his mind pulled like taffy between disparate moments in time. The heat of embarrassment flushed up into his chest from the cauldron in his stomach.

"Kent!" Theodore said, as if surprised to find himself in Kent's apartment, like a thief who had broken in and got caught. "I'm sorry… I don't know what to—"

"No problem, Theo. I was just concerned. You seemed to glaze over and I thought maybe…"

"I'm not autistic or anything, if that's what you were thinking," Theodore said, with an edge of defensiveness. "I don't have Asperger's."

"No, nothing like that," Kent said. "I figured you were just exhausted from the stress of everything that's happened lately. That's all."

Theodore accepted Kent's explanation, even though he wasn't sure it was the truth. He picked up his beer and took a steady pull from the bottle, feeling a strange dysmorphic shape to the evening. For a moment, Theodore had experienced an ephemeral relief explaining everything to Kent, only to be plucked from his cerebral indulgence when he realized the exchange had only transpired in the vacuum of his skull.

"I wanted to ask you something," Kent finally said after a few moments. "Had you ever talked to Cantwell or met him before the interview?"

Theodore shook his head. "No, why?"

Kent shrugged. "Just curious."

THEODORE

I called them my father's "Dorothy" buttons. He was sitting in the corner of the hotel room, his index finger and thumb already wedged up under his glasses, the glasses hinged up against his forehead like the visor on a knight's helmet. His index finger and thumb worked gently across the balls of his closed lids and any second those two digits would search the thin bridge of his nose for his Dorothy buttons; the buttons he would squeeze while he wished he was back in Kansas or wherever it was that his life looked the way he had hoped. After squeezing the buttons, furrowing his brow with deep veneration, he removed the finger and thumb; the glasses fell back to his bridge and he glared over at me sitting on the hotel bed, explaining to my mother what had happened in the stairwell.

She assured me that nothing had happened, that the Arch grounds were just as they had been when we arrived in St. Louis, and that in a few days I would be back in Bakersfield playing with Woody. But that's not possible, I had told her, and tried to make her remember that Woody had been beaten unconscious, his broken ribs and missing teeth, and that he was blinded in one eye and that when he came out of the coma his parents moved back to Nebraska and that I hadn't seen him since. I reminded her of how disappointed I was at my twelfth birthday party when Woody couldn't come because he was still in a coma. She smiled, and shook her head and told me that that wasn't possible because I was only eleven, that I hadn't even had my twelfth birthday and I must have been daydreaming. I assured her I wasn't and explained to her in great detail about the Arch, the creeper derricks, my birthday party, Woody's horrible beating in Tathum Cemetery, her phone conversation with Edith, Woody's mother, the night of the tragedy, but I don't think she was listening. She had her eyes closed and a tear was running down her cheek.

I looked over at Linus, who was smirking and shaking his head, then glanced at my father, his thumb and index finger clamped to his Dorothy buttons.

CHAPTER 10

Kent helped Theodore move into his new apartment on Patterson Street. The apartment was a long narrow space above one side of a storefront with all three rooms lined up like a shotgun barrel, the long narrow space divided by two broad arched openings. The living room was in front, street side, kitchen in the middle, bedroom at the rear with a tiny bathroom off of it. In the hallway outside his living room was a staircase leading down to the front door. Across the hall was an identical space to Theodore's, only flopped. Another young man lived there, a musician, the landlord had said.

Although the apartment was furnished, the appointments were old and worn. The nine-foot walls were painted beige with dark stained crown molding along the ceilings of each room. A hideous crack extended up one wall of the living room, across the ceiling and down the other, slicing the room in half, as if, at any moment, the front half of the room could fall into the street and Theodore would be sitting in his underwear reading a book in full view of everyone who walked by below.

But the real disappointment for him was that there was no place for a garden.

Mr. Jafferty, Theodore's new landlord, didn't live in the building, but had informed Theodore that he would check in a couple times a month, and provided him with a pager number to call in case anything *blew up.* Jafferty made it very clear that he didn't want to be bothered unless it was an emergency.

The weekend went by slowly with Theodore acclimating to his new digs and stalking cockroaches with an empty Smuckers jar, only to set them free on the back landing. Jafferty assured Theodore that they weren't really roaches exactly, but *pimento* bugs, as Jafferty called them. Never really believing there was such a species, Theodore had always felt that palmetto bugs were nothing more than designer roaches, and every bit as wily and disgusting as *la cucaracha,* no matter what you called them. He was certain that Jafferty had been to Florida at some time in his life and had embraced the name for his infestation to ease the discomfort of his tenants. And discomfort was a mild term for the emotion aroused when one of these cigar-butt size insects crawled across your face in the middle of the night. Jafferty promised he would get someone out in the next week to spray, but Theodore wasn't at all convinced and picked up his own firepower from the store down the street.

Theodore figured he would set off the bug bombs the next morning before he left the apartment to catch the train for Glen Valley. He had decided to visit Sarah's grave.

Until this point, he had been able to avoid the full impact of her death, tucking it safely away as an abstract concept without real proof. After all, he had seen no spiritless corpse lying cramped in a narrow crevice of satin, no yawning hole cut from rich moist soil awaiting her casket, no sorrowful grieving beneath black veils or staunch dark suits filled with distraught men. Nothing was chiseled in stone.

When morning arrived, he wasted no time getting out of the apartment. After a quick shower, he threw on the same clothes he had arrived in, set off the roach bombs, then hurried into the hall locking the door behind him.

If Theodore walked at a normal pace, his limp was barely noticeable, a slight hitch at best. But when he was in a hurry, he rocked like a palm tree in a hurricane, appearing to be in jeopardy of dislocating an appendage.

He made the train just before they closed the doors, and since it was Sunday, and the crowd wasn't too large, he had no trouble finding a seat. Trying to catch his breath, he observed the station pulling away from the train. It was a strange sensation for Theodore, not knowing which was moving, the station or the train. Of course, his brain knew, or at least it thought it knew and presented a fairly convincing argument about the difference between kinetic and stationary objects. But Theodore's deeper logic told him that nothing is stationary, that every object is always in constant motion, even the largest, most seemingly immovable mountain, as long as the planet was spinning on its axis in the middle of a revolving solar system that was racing through space at tremendous speed. No, nothing was stationary, not even Sarah's body covered with six feet of worm-infested dirt.

Not long after the train had left the station, Theodore dozed, spinning in his own dreamy solar system hurtling toward Glen Valley. He had not slept well his first night in the new space due to the *pimento* bugs, and his saxophone-blowing neighbor trying to impress his young lady friend with his music and the intensity of his orgasm. Theodore was hoping that his new neighbor, whom he had yet to meet, wasn't one of those who was quiet all day, then suddenly came to life at midnight.

When the train stopped in Glen Valley, Theodore exited the subway station and hailed a cab.

"Where to?" the cabby asked as Theodore threw himself into the back seat.

"Whitemarsh Cemetery."

The cabby dropped the flag and started rambling about something as soon as the car started moving. Theodore, not in the mood for prattle, tried to ignore the driver's ranting without snubbing him. Whenever the cabby checked the mirror for validation, Theodore forced a smile and nodded agreeably. Even though the discourse proved a lively diversion from the glum morning, it grew tiresome.

The road through the cemetery was cradled on both sides by lush green lawns. Thick full maples, with a dark oval of shaded grass beneath each one, were scattered among the numerous headstones. In a few moments, the taxi slid up along the curb where the caretaker of the cemetery had instructed them to go and Theodore jumped out. He quickly slipped the driver a ten and told him to keep the change. Before he could get the back door securely shut, the car sped away, leaving him alone on the road, surrounded by the earthy fragrance of fresh-cut grass.

After scanning the area, Theodore spied a mounded scab of dirt on the ridge beyond the more manicured sites. He plowed arduously up the hill, deluged by memories of Tathum Cemetery and Porky Tucker. Although the nickname, Porky, might've indicated someone of portly stature, Porky wasn't really fat, just meaty. Almost five foot ten and weighing upwards of 175 pounds by the time he was fourteen, Porky was a tank without a war, so he created one any time he could. No one was really sure how Porky received the moniker, but rumor had it that he had bestowed it upon himself in reference to his male appendage. The one thing everyone could agree on though, was that Porky, even if he didn't have a fat prick, certainly was one. Only his little band of followers, which Theodore and Woody referred to as the Boneheads, were spared the brunt of Porky's debasement. And for whatever reason, Woody had become the prime target for Porky's aggression.

Theodore remembered the day he had walked to Tathum Cemetery. After telling his mother he was sick and couldn't go to school, he sneaked out of the house when Madeline went to the grocery. He had a pocketknife and a long stretch of black cord that his father used as a tether line for his gas-powered model airplanes. It was strong, thin, and hard to spot on a dead run. He had strung it between two wooden stakes about three feet in front of an open grave.

Theodore was eleven, or twelve at the time (depending on who was keeping track) and petrified over the stunt he was about to pull. He had concocted numerous pranks growing up, usually directed at Linus, but none of them could compare with this. Besides, all the other pranks involved a conspiracy with Woody, but this one he would have to execute alone, not even Woody could know.

Plodding up the hill toward Sarah's gravesite, his thoughts were still with Porky in the cemetery sixteen years earlier, the trembling in his legs, looking across the gaping maw of the open grave, practicing several times the leap he would have to make if the plan was to work. He saw himself moving the yellow sawhorse barriers to the left of the hole to block the path, careful not to make it conspicuous. From the safety of his head he watched himself moving the tarps and the wheelbarrow with shovels and picks to the right of the excavated earth to create a formidable obstacle, thwarting any attempt of a detour on the right flank. He had crept up within twenty feet of Porky who was busy listening to his Walkman. Even now, all these years later, he could still feel the cold stone in his hand, no more than an inch and a half in diameter.

The recollection pulled at him like a riptide. He took a deep breath, opened his eyes, and looked down at Sarah's grave, expecting to see Porky. But there was no hole, and no Porky, only several colorful floral arrangements that appeared very recent. The dirt was crumbly and rust-colored. All at once, Theodore was disappointed. He had intended to buy flowers for Sarah's grave but was so distracted by the taxi driver that he completely forgot.

He glanced around the cemetery and spied the ragged end of some woods buttressing the meticulously groomed hills. Not sure what he would find that was efflorescent, Theodore headed toward the rim of scrubby trees lining the verge. After a brief search in a tangle of saplings, Theodore found a single lavender iris. He knelt down next to it, plucking it from the earth by its base. To someone standing at Sarah's gravesite, it would have appeared that a balding young prince was kneeling in veneration to a thicket of small bushes and trees.

He ambled back down the hill to place the flower on the lightly packed dirt of her plot. As he knelt, the smell of freshly tilled soil spread up through his head—the smell of his garden. He closed his eyes and pictured Sarah.

THEODORE

The plan was simple physics: momentum and gravity. Get Porky to run toward the open grave, trip over the cord, and tumble into the hole. Simple.

Porky was seated on a large marble gravestone, occupied with his headphones. I stepped closer, careful not to rustle the leaves. I figured he couldn't hear me with the music playing in his head, but I didn't want to chance it. The stone felt insignificant in my hand. I reminded myself that it wasn't supposed to kill him just get his attention. I cocked my arm, inched a little closer, then hurled it at his head. The stone landed with a dull thud against his skull, not the loud crack I had expected with such a well-placed shot, but the effect was the same. Porky grabbed his scalp and spun around, his red eyes locked onto mine. I almost forgot to run, a crucial part of the plan.

It was all happening much faster than expected. In seconds, his bloody fingers were tearing at my collar. But it was the smell, like onions on his breath, that jolted me from my stupor, sent me twisting from my shirt to escape his grip. The plan was working wonderfully except that Porky was only three feet behind me and closing fast. I ran as swiftly as I could up the hill, but it wasn't fast enough. Just then, I felt his meaty hand land on my shoulder like a jackhammer. My legs collapsed under me. Tumbling along the ground, Porky stumbling over me, I was lucky he didn't fall on top of me, but his knee caught me on the nose. Everything went brilliant white, and my sinuses felt like they'd been filled with burning sand. Stunned, I struggled to my feet. Porky was still on the ground a few yards away.

He scrambled after me. We were both bleeding, closing rapidly on the open grave. Except for my heart pounding in my temples, the only other sound I could hear was Porky grunting behind me. At that moment, everything seemed to shift to slow motion. I could see the cord, knew I had to clear it with a natural stride so Porky wouldn't be suspicious, then time my final leap perfectly to carry me across the open grave. In mid-air, suspended in the middle of my jump, I heard Porky yell, 'C O M E ... B A C K ... H E R E ... Y O U ... S C R A W N Y ... M O T H E R F U C ...' then a thud, then silence. I stopped a few yards away and spun around, hoping to find a Porky-free landscape. Walking cautiously back toward the hole, holding my hand over my nose to slow the bleeding, I paused at the rim.

I don't know how long I stared down at him. It was sad, surreal, horrible. Suddenly detached, I seemed to float above the grizzly image, in a cloud, until I heard muffled laughter coming from the far side of the ridge. The Boneheads were coming.

Frozen on the image, I finally forced myself from the awful sight. I ran over to break the cord loose, but it was too tough. I pulled the pocketknife from my trousers and cut it, did a quick check for other evidence before I went back for my shirt, then bolted into the thick woods and didn't stop running until I was home, sobbing all the way.

CHAPTER 11

A thin veil of dusty light slipped through the window. Under the weight of a waking despair, Theodore lay motionless beneath the sheet, staring at the ceiling, thinking about the cemetery, about Sarah, then Porky. Was it a sin if an act of savagery was performed in an attempt to preclude another act of savagery? And how is one to atone for such a sin and move on? Certainly God would not be placated by the meager creation of even the most outstanding video game as compensation for a life. And how could He be cajoled if He couldn't be found? And, isn't the path to God paved with remorse? How, Theodore wondered, is one to make amends without remorse? To Theodore, remorse was the admission that you would do things differently if you had the chance to do them over, otherwise it was no more than empty sentiment, not unlike the pathetic soul who begs forgiveness on Sunday, only to start piling up the sins on Monday. Theodore wouldn't do things differently concerning Porky if it meant that Woody would suffer such an unacceptable fate.

Stretched out in the mausoleum of his bed, he forced the looping argument from his mind, switching his attention to roaches. Although none had crawled across his face in the night, he wasn't convinced they were gone. The bombs boasted in very clear terminology a guarantee of immediate triumph over the sinister arthropods, and that it should last for up to six weeks, but Theodore held grave reservations about the effectiveness of the little green cans. He imagined that the roaches were like children during a fire drill, walking very orderly in single file out of their classrooms to line up on the safe side of the playground until the firemen announced that it was okay to return. The roaches were probably seeking refuge in his neighbor's apartment, or in the hall, until the all-clear was issued and they could return *en masse* talking and giggling about the silly drill. He figured he was probably the only living creature remaining in the small apartment enduring the awful stench of the chemical attack, leaving him to wonder who was suffering most for his actions.

Still prone, inhaling the vile chemicals, his attention shifted to the overhead light fixture positioned in the center of the ceiling above his bed, a frosted square glass shade decorated with moose and deer against a backdrop of pine trees. He studied the design, concluding that the moose and pine tree motif accounted for the entire sum of artwork on display in his dank apartment. Believing it to be a peculiar furnishing, he wondered where Jafferty had purchased such a thing.

By now the light outside the window was yawning with more intensity. Theodore pulled himself from the flabby mattress and hauled himself to the shower. Hot water was stubborn in coming and stingy when it arrived, forcing him to finish the rinse part of his routine under a tepid sputtering from the rusty showerhead. After dressing quickly and foregoing breakfast, he grabbed his apartment key and headed out the door.

The stale odor of dead mice and mildewed wood hung in the hallway. He hadn't noticed the nasty smell when Jafferty had shown him the apartment a few days earlier, but then Jafferty had been smoking a cigar at the time. Theodore had thought it rude that his new landlord continued puffing his stogie during the walk-through, but now it was clear that the stinky cigar was essential in concealing the stench of the place.

The bus ride across town was short and dropped him within a block of DreamCo. The day was fresh, the sun vigilant, and the blue dome overhead was pristinely free of clouds. Unsure what time he was supposed to show up for work, Theodore had decided to arrive around seven thirty in the morning. Kent didn't seem overly concerned about hours; in fact, the whole pace of the organization had an ease that agreed with Theodore. As he walked through the revolving doors into the lobby, he was amazed to find little activity; even Otis was absent.

He walked to the elevator, pressed the call button, and waited. As he glanced around, he noticed the dramatic ceiling of the lobby, contending that it was over thirty feet high with a balcony and railing on the second floor that overlooked the reception desk. It was theatrical, especially the massive Saturn suspended above his head.

The elevator doors opened and Theodore turned to get on, then stopped, startled to find someone already standing there. Mr. Cantwell was not the first face he had hoped to see. As he stepped in, Cantwell peered straight ahead, perfectly still, ignoring Theodore. After pressing the button for the seventh floor, he thought it odd that Cantwell hadn't exited into the lobby. After all, there wasn't a basement as far as he knew, so Cantwell couldn't have been coming up. He concluded that Cantwell must have been coming down. So why did he stay on the elevator?

Finally, he decided to speak to the seemingly indifferent president. "Good morning."

Cantwell, in his shiny gray suit, glanced over briefly, then returned his eyes to his own silvery reflection in the doors. Theodore averted his eyes toward the colorful swirls on the new carpeting.

Cantwell glanced over at Theodore again. "Do I know you?" Cantwell inquired, mildly bewildered.

"Theodore Trumball. I interviewed with you a few weeks ago."

A glimmer of recognition eased across Cantwell's face.

"Oh yes, you were still Edward at the time, right?" Cantwell smiled, and laughed a little to himself. "Something about you looks different though," Cantwell said. "I didn't recognize you. Maybe it's the hair. Did you have it cut or something?"

"Well no... not exactly, but my name... it's really Theodore... or just Theo, sir." Theodore's words stumbled out.

"I'm glad you've finally settled on a name. Well, Theo, what do you think so far?" Cantwell said looking straight ahead, speaking to his own image in the shiny doors.

"Well actually, I just got here. It's my first day."

"First days, Theo," Cantwell gushed, a warm smile spreading across his face. "I remember my first day of school, the very first one. I was five. Notre Dame Grade School in St. Louis. It was on... let's see... Kienlen Avenue! Yes, that's it! Can you imagine that, Theo, I can still remember which street my school was on and it was nearly fifty years ago! My dear mother walked me to the bus stop that first morning. While all the other little kids were whining and crying and wiping their snotty little noses on their mother's housecoats, I stepped up to my mother, shook her hand and said, 'I think you can go home now, I'll be just fine!' Instead of smiling and being relieved, she gently patted me on the head, then reluctantly started walking down the street, crying. That's when I first realized that most of what she did was not out of protecting me, but out of her own fear. She was a wonderful woman, but terribly afraid."

Theodore said nothing.

"Are you afraid, Theo?"

Theodore stood perfectly still, unsure how to answer.

"Well, I think I've had enough for today," Cantwell announced when the doors opened on the seventh floor. "Let me show you to your office if Kent hasn't already." Theodore shook his head and followed.

Cantwell strolled down the hall past Kent's darkened office until he came to a doorway on the left and went in.

"This is it," Cantwell announced with outstretched arms. Cantwell's gesture evoked the image of Saint Francis of Assisi in Theodore's mind, except without the doves and stigmata.

"Will this do?" Cantwell asked, spinning toward Theodore. "Do you want to keep that print in here?" He pointed at an unframed poster of Les Misérables push-pinned to the wall. "I hope that's okay. I picked it out myself."

Theodore looked back and nodded, taking in the small, plain room. Except for the desk, the desk chair, and a cheap metal folding chair, the room was empty. Bare white walls, no windows, the ceiling a tangle of pipes suspended beneath a void of chipped and peeling paint. A lone fluorescent fixture flickered and hummed.

"We'll get that fixed," Cantwell announced, easing down into the chair behind the desk.

The desk was an ordinary metal and Formica issue that one would find in accounting offices all across America. The office chair was equally uninteresting. And no computer.

"My old desk from Amvest Securities!" Cantwell said proudly. "Do you have any idea how much money I made sitting right here at this desk, Theo? It's a thoroughbred!" He patted it lightly as if it had just won the Kentucky Derby.

The scent of Cantwell's after-shave made itself suddenly present—alcohol, limes, and some unknown but cloying ingredient.

"Sit down, Theo," Cantwell motioned toward the flimsy brown folding chair in front of the desk, which lent an unpleasant transitory quality to the meager space. "Don't worry about that… it's temporary. We've got some new chairs coming in a week or two. Did you like those black and chrome ones in Kent's office?"

Theodore didn't remember them.

"Well, they're not exactly like those. Kent's are original designs!" Cantwell stated. "But the ones coming are damn nice, orange, I think. The girls on the fifth floor have them in their offices. They love 'em! But I don't want to talk about chairs, Theo." Cantwell leaned forward, his elbows on the desk, hands steepled under his chin. "I want to talk about losers!"

The chair rattled when Theodore jerked unintentionally. Cantwell leaned toward the door, pushing it closed. The door clasped shut with a metallic snap that echoed in the hollow office.

"My old man was a loser, Theo," Cantwell said, leaning back from the desk. "Don't get me wrong, I loved him, I always will, but he would tell you himself if he had the balls, and, of course, if he were still alive. He knew he was a loser, but the problem was, he couldn't admit it. If he could've, he wouldn't have gone crazy like he did!

"I don't judge losers. It's just that some people are winners and some are losers. It's not important that you're one or the other, only that you know which one you are."

Cantwell's eyebrows met near the middle of his forehead and flared up at the outer ends like steer horns. His eyes were sapphires, rimmed with iridescent gray, aimed at Theodore.

"See, the problem with my old man was that he denied he was a loser, always striving to prove he wasn't. Ruined his life! And my mother's.

"Are you a poker player, Theo?" Cantwell asked, leaning back in his chair until his nostrils were revealed in an unnatural, unattractive way.

Theodore shrugged. "I've read about game theory."

"Um, I see. Well, Theo, there's an old saying in poker that probably didn't show up in your books," Cantwell said. He rotated forty-five degrees so that he faced the closed door, then cocked his head back toward Theodore. "The old adage goes like this: If you can't figure out who the sucker is when you sit down at the poker table, then the sucker is you!"

Theodore didn't know what to make of this strange poker axiom.

"Mind if I smoke?" Cantwell said, pulling a cigar from the inside of his jacket.

Theodore thought a moment, then said, "I'd rather you didn't."

Cantwell laughed and put the cigar back in his pocket. "See, now that's what I'm talking about," Cantwell bellowed. "Any other little turd who was trying to suck up might have agreed, gone along, even though he didn't want to sit here in this crappy little office choking on the boss's smoke. But you stood your ground, Theo. I admire that. But Theo, while I admire it, it's the sign of a loser! You either know how to get by or you're a loser, it's just that simple."

A shiver went up Theodore's spine.

"See, my old man worked for Crown Industries, a corporation that bought up successful independent hotels across the country. He'd been with them thirty-five years, started as a bellboy when he was fourteen. They moved him here and there, all over the country until he ended up working some flophouse in St. Louis as hotel manager, The Baldwin

Hotel, where the revolving doors came from. Monroe Percival Cantwell, that was his name. He didn't know when to go with the flow, how to change, and always thought his way was better than the folks running the show. But see, Monroe forgot the most basic tenet of his existence—he was a loser. If he could've accepted that, God only knows where he might've gone! Maybe somewhere besides crazy!" Cantwell lit his cigar and puffed.

"There's no shame in being a loser, just hardship for everyone you love when you don't recognize it," Cantwell said, getting up from behind the desk. He checked his watch. "Take your time getting settled in." He walked out, leaving the door open.

Theodore slumped in the metal chair, listening to Cantwell's Gucci shoes click a trail down the hall toward the elevator. The light fixture hummed monotonously. After a few moments, Theodore folded his arms on the desk and buried his head. He wasn't sure how long he'd been resting there when he heard Kent's voice.

"Theo, what are you doing?" Kent asked, standing in the doorway.

Theodore looked up. "Uh… sitting in my office… waiting…."

"Christ!" Kent said. "This isn't your office. It's a storeroom! Goddamn Cantwell! I should've known he was up to something when he had the janitor clear the stuff out of here."

Kent looked around the room, his eyes snagging on the old Broadway poster. "That's from the goddamn lunch room!" He shook his head. "Cantwell can be the biggest asshole." Kent ripped the poster from the wall and rolled it loosely. "C'mon, I'll show you your office."

Theodore followed him out.

"Where did you run into Cantwell?" Kent asked as they walked down the hall.

"On the elevator," said Theodore.

Kent smirked. "Frank is weird. He usually gets here before anyone else and rides up and down on that damn thing like he's meditating or something," Kent explained. "Cantwell says there's strong energy in there, that's where his ideas come from." Kent started laughing.

"What's so funny?" asked Theodore.

"Cantwell doesn't have ideas," Kent said. "He's rich. He buys them."

When they got on the elevator, Kent began describing the problems they were encountering with the OBO prototype, but Theodore's thoughts were still with Cantwell, intrigued by something entirely alien to Kent's discussion: the extent of Cantwell's prank. Why would the president of a successful company, or any company, expend time and energy just to humiliate a new employee that he didn't even know? Or any employee? Weren't there more important things to tend to? And why ride up and down in the elevator? Cantwell was obviously a very strange man.

"I'm sorry I wasn't here when you arrived this morning," Kent said. "Otis was supposed to show you to your office when you came in, but I think he had some kind of an emergency." Kent unlocked the door.

Light from two expansive windows washed across the polished oak floor. The walls were pale gray with dark gray baseboards. Along the ceiling hung rows of track lights illuminating the sleek aluminum desk, the black lacquer credenza, and a gallery wall hung with framed prints.

"You can hang whatever you want over there. I just had those put up so the place wouldn't be so empty. I hope this is okay?"

Theodore nodded, sliding his hand along the aluminum surface of the desk. He tapped on the keyboard, then sat down in the cushy swivel chair facing the computer. Leaning forward, he pushed the switch and the computer hummed to life.

"Oh yeah, Theo. There's a meeting this afternoon at three," Kent said. "It's about *StarField*. It'll give you a chance to meet everyone. I'll talk to you later."

THEODORE

Everything belonged to Porky; the blue sky, the summer afternoons, my mom's homemade pizza, her cherry cobbler, my books, my showers, my sleep, my thoughts. It was all his, every day, every moment. After that day in Tathum Cemetery, hardly a minute went by that Porky was not with me, flashing in my head, writhing in that hole, churning my stomach. I became life support to his memory, a silent shrine in his honor. His squirming torso, his grim, frightened expression, his blood; it all seeped deep into my tissue, into my bones, and I ceased to exist.

I don't know how much longer I could've lasted with the guilt and fear. When I planned Porky's death, it felt justified, necessary, like I had no other choice. I had witnessed the unacceptable, the impossible. It had to be overturned. But lying there, in the bottom of that hole bleeding to death, Porky no longer seemed like the embodiment of evil I had imagined him to be, no longer an ominous threat, just a big clumsy kid who wanted attention, whose body grew too big too fast, who felt odd and alone, who was so much like me I started to cry.

I was already unraveling when they took me for the shock treatments. And although I felt like I was being burned alive during those three days, being killed in bursts, the current jolted the horror of Porky from my head, flushed the guilt, the shame, the remorse, until the events in Tathum Cemetery seemed like nothing more than vague reruns on television. Every aspect of my conscience was erased, every memory extinguished, leaving me numb, my life tolerable, at least for a while, until my memory started to return.

CHAPTER 12

"*T*hat's what these kids want!" Cantwell shouted with the fire of a Bible-belt preacher. All eyes around the conference table were trained on him.

"They've had all the *goddamn flower power* and touchy-feely *crap* they can swallow," Cantwell continued. "These kids have *troubles* they need to work out and they can't do it by picking *daisies* and wearing *peace* signs. They want *adventure*, they want to release *hostility*, and they *need* a safety valve! *That's* what we're all about, that's what DreamCo is all about... providing an outlet for their aggression... and their *money!* And I'm not afraid to say *money!* If you are, if you have forgotten what we're doing here... well... maybe it's time to hit the dusty trail, *amigo...* "

Cantwell searched each face. "...only *losers* lose sight of what it's all about. That's why they're losers!" Cantwell turned and started walking from the room. "Have a nice evening everyone, see you all tomorrow!"

When the meeting ended, it felt as if Cantwell had taken all the joy and most of the oxygen with him when he left the room. For several minutes, people shuffled papers, thumped pencils, attempting to fill the void that Cantwell left in the wake of his departure. Everyone was dumbfounded by the speech, unaware of the hidden battle Cantwell was waging against Theodore, everyone except Kent; he was well aware of Cantwell's purposeful warheads and for whom they were intended.

"*Hey*, congrats to everyone on *StarField!*" Kent said, shattering the solemnity. "The '80s belong to DreamCo!" Kent raised his Coke can in a toast. "Also, I would like to introduce the newest member of our team, Theo Trumball."

Theodore nodded and smiled. People walked up and welcomed him, shaking his hand, introducing themselves. Macy came over.

"Remember me?"

"Uh… Macy, right?"

She extended her hand and smiled.

Theodore shook it gently, noticing her nails were painted a pale blue today.

"Some meeting, huh?" she said. "Like a recital! Frank gets pretty fired up sometimes." She pushed her hair behind her ear. "So, have you found an apartment yet?"

"Yes, not far from here," he said, thinking what a dump it was, the roaches, and his saxophone-playing sex-crazed neighbor.

"Well, good. So… well, I guess I'll be seeing you around then."

Contemplating his future at DreamCo with much trepidation, Theodore tried for a smile. "Yeah, sure."

After she left, Kent and Theodore were the last ones in the meeting room. Kent was busy putting evaluation forms into a folder, scrawling notes before he slid them in.

"Theo, you ready to go?" Kent said, closing his briefcase.

As they walked down the hall in the direction of the elevator, Kent was the first to speak. "I know that some of Cantwell's rant was aimed at you? Are you okay?"

Theodore didn't like the innuendos Cantwell had slung his way, but Theodore was the new guy. He'd take his lumps… as long as Kent was on his side.

After a moment Kent said, "Forget all that crap Cantwell said this afternoon. That's just Frank!"

Theodore didn't respond.

"What are you doing for dinner tonight?" Kent asked while they waited for the elevator.

"I don't know, I'm not really hungry."

"Have you eaten today?"

"Uh, yeah. I had some peanut butter crackers from the machine earlier. Some days I don't eat much."

The doors slid open and Kent stepped in. "C'mon, Theo, let me buy you dinner tonight. We'll *celebrate!*"

Theodore was about to step in but reconsidered. "How about another night? I've got some things I want to do here before I go home."

"Okay, but don't work too late. It's your first day, don't kill yourself!" Kent smiled, pulling his hand from the elevator doors. "I'll see you in the morning!"

Feeling strangely alone in the empty hall, Theodore went back to his office and sat at his new desk. He fiddled with some pens, then looked in his drawer to see what was there: paper clips, rubber bands, a few pencils, and stamps. Outside it was dark. DreamCo was quiet. Occasionally, he'd run his hand along the smooth surface of the desk, then survey the room once again, taking it all in, as if at any moment it could disappear. He thought about his game, all the afternoons he spent designing it in the upstairs apartment at Sarah's house.

Sarah. What would she think about his new office, his new job? What would it be like going home to Glen Valley after work? He pictured her in the Broadway chorus line, her pert smile, her satiny hair, and wished he would've asked to keep the photograph. He could put it on his desk. Look at her every day. He felt his fingers trace the dip of her waist, the soft flesh of her tummy. He tasted her lips, her breath. The memory brought him to the edge of tears. He cupped his hands over his head, letting his forehead fall forward and bang on the desk.

"You all right?"

The smooth, mellow voice poured across Theodore's mind. At first, he imagined it was God. He'd read stories about people who had heard the audible voice of God; unfortunately, most of them were madmen, psychopomps, or Nazis. Out of the corner of his eye, he detected the silhouette of a figure filling his doorway. He turned to see a plump, but fit, elderly man with glistening ringlets of gray hair. The old man, wearing tan coveralls, was guiding a yellow bucket on casters by the long handle of a mop, the mop head concealed beneath scummy brown water. He regarded Theodore with eyes that were warm and clear.

"You all right?" he repeated, this time raising his brow, stretching his face, almost comically, as if it were made of elastic.

"Yeah… hi, I'm Theo," he said to the elderly gentleman.

"Pleased to meet you, Theo," the old man said with a bright smile. "I'm Adam."

Releasing the handle of the mop, he extended a thick callused hand. The rough hardness of his palm surprised Theodore, like cowhide wrapped over steel.

"Why you here all alone this late at night, Theo?"

"I'm not alone, Adam, you're here!"

Adam laughed and shook his head, concealing his wondrous eyes for a moment behind eyelids of smooth skin. "I guess you're right," Adam conceded, laughing and scratching his head. "I heard an awful *bang* when I was coming down the hall. And by the big shiny red spot on your forehead...." Adam chuckled, pointing a crooked finger at Theodore.

"Oh," Theodore said, chagrined there was a mark, and that Adam had seen it. He rubbed at his forehead to make light of it. "Little accident, that's all. It's nothing."

"Problem with the game?" Adam said, with unsettling resonance.

The game? Theodore thought. *What game is he referring to?*

"A man bang his *head* on a desk, I figure he's having problems with the game." Adam laughed again. "God *loves* a good game, Theo. He *loves* to see how we play, and He don't give a *snort* who wins and loses." Adam laughed again, then paused for a moment. "The way I figure it, you don't take your victories and defeats with you to the Promised Land, just your soul," Adam said, meeting Theodore's eyes briefly before he turned to leave.

"Nice to meet you, Theo," Adam said, then pushed his mop bucket down the hall, humming.

THEODORE

The seed of Porky's death grew slowly inside me, burgeoning into a compelling, almighty force. I could kill. And not in the clumsy, mechanical fashion, like with Porky, but with the smoothness of thought, intent, like I had killed my father a year later, a simple gesture, my middle finger, extended.

Not long after that I almost killed my mother when I set fire to the garage. It wasn't intentional, but the fire didn't know that and gave her third-degree burns on the backs of both legs. But she didn't die.

Maybe the curse was gone? But then there was the fire at Sarah's. Stupidity? Negligence? Bad karma? I don't know but the blaze had started in my apartment. Maybe it was the hot plate, or the rug over the extension cords, but whatever it was, it felt like a killing force had taken up residence in my soul.

I felt omnipotence, to be sure, wielding power with the gods, the stuff of Olympus, and I didn't want it.

Eventually, I would come to believe that this strange force had led to the death of my best friend, Woody. Indeed, the power, and my delusions about it, had grown too magnificent, too horrendous.

CHAPTER 14

―――――――

At first, Theodore wasn't sure where he was when he woke. The pale light outside his office indicated morning, while the yellowish cast further defined it as early. He checked his watch, pushed himself up from his desk and walked down the hall to the restroom.

Standing at the stall, he recalled the previous evening. He had worked on OBO well into the morning hours, making moderate progress with the more stubborn elements of the original design. So much of the infrastructure of the prototype had to be reconfigured, with much of the source code requiring a complete overhaul from scratch to fit the arcade paradigm, as well as changes Kent had written down for him. He wasn't sure when he had fallen asleep, but knew it was after 4 a.m.—that was the last time he'd checked the clock on his computer.

As he washed his hands at the sink, he glared at the ruffled fellow in the mirror. *They're clean, Theo, you can stop washing them now,* he heard a voice imploring him from inside his head. But he couldn't stop, and his gaze fell toward the sink. His eyes, like the sudsy water, were instantly drawn to the dark hole that spoiled the perfection of the white porcelain. Immediately he felt himself being pulled down, swept deeper into the dark throat of the drain, surrounded by the deafening *whoosh* of gushing water in the cramped pipe. He struggled to free himself, but couldn't—unable to move his arms, unable to breathe...

"Theo?" a soft voice spoke.

Theodore jumped, like someone awakened from a nightmare, unintentionally throwing water across the floor and onto Kent. "I'm sorry...I...."

"No, Theo, it's fine, really. Are you okay?"

"Yeah, I was just thinking... about the game... you know and...."

"Did you stay here all night?"

"Yeah, there were some things I wanted to work on."

"Theo, why don't you go home, take a nap... come back later this afternoon."

"Okay... thanks."

"I'll talk to you later, okay?" Kent said, patting him on the back.

Theodore hurried down the hall to the elevator and was about to push the button when he remembered Cantwell's curious meditation practices. He felt too fragile to deal with him this morning.

There was a red exit sign at the end of the hall for the stairwell. He studied the sign until the letters etched on the back of his brain. *What are you waiting for? Open the door, go down the stairs.* Under a rush of adrenaline, Theodore flung the door open and attacked the stairwell. In seconds, he was bounding down the steps, the loud clap of his shoes on the metal stairs reporting like gunshots off the concrete walls.

In his haste, Theodore hadn't noticed the gray interior of the stairwell, or the 40-watt bulbs burning sour yellow. He raced toward the bottom, confronted by the disquieting sense that the landing below seemed to be pulling away. He knew he wasn't alone, that he was being tracked by some inscrutable entity, a white-cold fear that nipped at his neck, that caressed his spine, that had followed him all the way from St. Louis across hundreds of miles, across sixteen years and was now barely a breath behind him. He jumped two and three steps at a time, stumbling, catching himself at the last moment, clutching the cold metal railing, then attempted to jump an entire flight in one leap, crashing to a heap, jumping back up... *Don't run on the steps, you'll break your neck! Don't leap without looking... Don't ever look back....*

Gulping air, he jumped to the bottom landing and smashed the palms of his hands against the long door handle but it didn't budge. His mouth was parched with the coppery taste of blood. His stomach went sour. He pushed hard at the door, banging it, butting the long bar with his hip. Suddenly the door burst open, throwing him into the lobby.

Stumbling from the unexpected release, he crashed to the floor. Otis was seated behind the reception desk reading a newspaper and looked up.

"Theodore, my man, are you okay?"

Theodore nodded, catching his breath, scrambling to his feet. He heard the metal door clamp shut behind him.

"That door gets stuck sometimes. Something wrong with the latch," Otis said, shaking his head, studying Theodore as he walked toward the reception desk.

"Whew, your eyes look like minestrone soup!" Otis said. "You didn't work all night your very first day, did you?"

Theodore nodded without looking up as he tucked in his shirt.

"You have to pace yourself, son, or you'll end up like my poor brother-in-law!" Otis laughed. "He's working three jobs to pay off his gambling debts and passed out at the breakfast table from pneumonia yesterday morning. His face fell flat in the cereal, *splat!*" Otis slapped his hands together laughing. "I had to drive him to the hospital. If that boy don't work himself to death, he'll probably end up drowning in his own breakfast!" Otis said, grinning.

Theodore was quiet, smiling nervously. He bit his lip as he turned from the reception desk and hobbled toward the entrance.

"Take it slow, Theodore!"

Harsh shafts of sunlight squeezed into Theodore's bedroom, burning narrow trapezoids onto the bare wood floor. He was aroused from his sleep by a roach crawling across his cheek.

"Damn!" he screamed, sitting up, swiping his hand across his face, bouncing the bug off the far wall. It landed with a solid *tick,* on its back, its legs racing nowhere in mid-air. Theodore leveled his gaze on the insect and couldn't help but think of poor Gregor Samsa lying in his bed that fateful morning, his little legs motoring in the air just like the poor creature across the room.

Watching the insect, Theodore tried to figure how the bug had crawled up on the bed. After a few minutes, he slid down under the covers and was almost back to sleep when something crawled on his leg.

"Damn!" Jumping up, he threw off the blanket and jerked the sheet from the mattress. "Where are you fuckers coming from?" he shouted, standing in the middle of the room in his boxer shorts, wearing a horrible grimace, like Edvard Munch's frozen scream. He ripped the sheet from the mattress and shook it out like a demented Ahab trying to exorcise a spirit from the main sail. He did manage to wrench loose another roach, which flew up in the air as if it had been shot from a pistol, hit the ceiling, then plinked to the floor. Grabbing his shoe, he smacked the escaping pest as it wearily tried to reach the wall.

Disgusted and sweating and knowing it would be impossible to get back to sleep, Theodore slung the big wad of bedclothes into the center of the mattress and glanced at the clock on the dresser. One-thirty in the afternoon. The room was thick with humidity and stale air, and the breeze outside the window lacked the gusto to stir the yellow-stained curtains.

He sat on the edge of the bed, studying the smashed guts of the tiny infestation in the corner of the room. And although the smell of chemical warfare from the roach bombs still hung thick in the room, it was a black oxford, size 9D, that delivered this fellow's final curtain call.

Sitting on the edge of the bed with his elbows on his knees, he plowed his fingertips along his burnished scalp. Thoughts drifted to Glen Valley, Sarah, his garden, the fire. Rubbing with more fervor, he cleared the inside of his skull until all that was left was the visage of Macy, and his mind stopped bucking.

He tried to hold it, but another image bled through with the wicked obstinacy of an ink stain. Charlotte Miller! Macy didn't really remind him of Charlotte. On the contrary, Charlotte was an unwelcome intruder in Theodore's mind since high school. She was the first girl he had sex with. That was one evening that would never go away.

It was senior year at Sisters of Mercy High School and a bunch of kids were meeting at Mike Lerner's house because his folks were out of town. Woody had heard about the party and talked Theodore into going. There was the usual drinking, dancing, and pot smoking that eventually led to a game they called Carnal Concentration, a variation on an old TV game show that wasn't the least bit carnal. In this homemade version, a regular deck of cards was used and enough pairs were pulled from the deck so that everyone would receive one card. The pairs were split up into two sets, one set for the girls and one for the boys. Then the cards were shuffled, dealt out face down in front of everyone. One by one each boy turned the cards face up, then the girls. Matching cards determined who was paired up. Charlotte got Theodore.

Charlotte lived at St. Theresa's home for girls. A couple of years older than the other kids in the senior class, she was eons ahead in experience. Having moved from foster home to foster home when she was younger, she finally ended up at St. Theresa's when she became too wild for anyone to handle. She had been held back a year in the eighth grade and another in the ninth after getting caught stealing a car with a couple of male friends. And while she was hardly the most popular girl in school, practically every boy at Sisters of Mercy High School was intimately familiar with the rose tattoo on her pelvis.

Charlotte stood up slowly from the circle, flung her hair back like a cape, and puckered her moist red lips. "You're mine, little man!" she said looking down at him. Her eyes glistened, not soft and beautiful, but dark like a dying animal. She stood over him, holding out her hand amid the whooping and hollering of the other boys in the room, Woody leading the cheers. Even as a memory, he could still see her glistening red nails, her long naked legs protruding from beneath her dark skirt, could smell her perfume hanging like a fog in his head.

The twenty minutes he spent with Charlotte would be the most memorable sexual experience of his life, and the most humiliating. Not only did Theodore get a case of crabs, but at the graduation ceremony when he went up to get his diploma, half the students in the graduating class began braying like donkeys, the sound he supposedly made during his orgasm, according to Charlotte.

Still sitting on the edge of his bed, Theodore could not restore order to his jumbled thoughts, Charlotte's naked ghostly form rising like a dead body floating up from the bottom of a lake.

He jerked to his feet and walked over to the window. Blanched by the blazing sun, the sidewalk and buildings were bleached of all but the faintest pastel hue. After a few minutes of staring at nothing in particular, he stepped back from the window, allowing the yellowed curtains to fall back across the opening.

He washed his face, dressed, and headed to the bus stop, stopping at a bakery for coffee and a doughnut. Maybe he would just sleep at his desk again tonight; at least there were no roaches.

When Theodore arrived at DreamCo, the lobby was bustling with people. Otis was busy on the phone. Theodore looked forward to Otis's greetings, his pleasant smile and familiar way. But this afternoon, Otis didn't even notice him. Theodore spotted Macy by the elevator with an armful of folders and books.

"Need some help?" he asked.

She spun around to face him.

"You bet," she said, handing him the stack of books. She juggled the folders, rearranging them so she could hold her coffee cup in her right hand and took a sip. "Thanks."

He smiled, but then averted his eyes toward the books that Macy had placed in his charge. When the elevator doors opened, they stepped in. A young man rushed through the doors just as they were about to close. He stood between them, to Theodore's dismay, but only went as far as the third floor.

When they reached her office, she went in first to clear a spot on her desk.

"Just set those here," she said.

He set the books down and stepped back as she scooted the folders onto an edge of the desk, pushing some other papers out of the way.

"I've got to clean this up soon!" she said. "Let me buy you a coffee. I could use a refill."

Macy led the way toward the lounge, Theodore following, unaccustomed to her brisk gait. "Kent told me you worked all night. How's the game coming?" she asked, as they turned into the drably appointed room.

She laughed before he could answer, "I'm sorry, you've only been here one day, how could it be coming!" The smell of fresh coffee, cinnamon and vanilla hung in the air. A stout woman, wearing a long flowing black skirt decorated with gold and blue swirls, and a turquoise blouse, stood with her back to them in front of the coffee maker.

"Hi, Macy," the woman said, glancing over her shoulder. "I just made a fresh pot!"

"Great," Macy said. "Annie, I'd like you to meet one of our newest designers." Macy put her hand around his arm and tugged him forward, the way a wife might cajole a bashful husband. "Annie, this is Theo."

Theodore smiled, mostly because of Macy's hand on his arm; a touch so delicate it sent a slight tremor down his back.

"Nice to meet you, Theo," Annie said, taking his hand firmly. Annie was probably in her fifties. Her round face and satin smooth skin brought to mind an opera singer, while her jewelry—the hand-made turquoise necklace, silver enameled bracelets, and numerous rings—created the illusion of a gypsy belly dancer. Her teeth sparkled, stained slightly with a smudge of red lipstick.

"I figured I would hide out down here for a while so Frank couldn't find me. He's got me collecting newspapers from all over the country, lugging them up to his office every day," Annie said, rolling her eyes. "You'd think I was delivering Christmas presents, the way he practically drools when I put them on his desk. Then he can't get rid of me fast enough."

"Really?" Macy said, surprised. "I thought he was more focused on the release of *StarField* than his stupid sports results?"

"It's not just sports. He had me research every state that has a lottery, then get every local newspaper that carries the drawing results. I feel like a research librarian," Annie said. "Well, I've got to get back. I'll leave you two kids alone." Annie turned with a swish of her long skirt and drifted toward the doorway. "Nice to meet you, Theo." She waved with a glance over her shoulder.

He smiled and gave a slight wave.

"Cream and sugar?" Macy asked, standing at the coffee machine.

"Yes, please," he answered, confused by the new edge to Macy's tone.

She handed him a styrofoam cup with coffee, then pulled out a chair at the table.

"Thanks," he said, then asked, "is anything wrong?" He sat down opposite her and sipped his coffee.

Macy sighed. "Nothing, I guess." Her demeanor had turned sullen. "This is the first time I've had a chance to sit all day. Cantwell's had me going up and down the elevator like a yo-yo, schlepping production costs, market analysis, licensing info…" She paused. "Now I find out that all he's interested in is his stupid scores!"

Theodore said nothing.

"I just can't believe him sometimes," she said, her eyes dark, her mind busy.

Theodore noticed the cream swirling in a spiral in the top of his coffee. Soon it melted to a consistent tawny shade.

"So enough about that," Macy said, her eyes twinkling, catching the overhead light when she tilted her head back slightly. "Kent said you had lived in Glen Valley. My mom lives in Glen Valley. That's where I grew up."

Theodore nodded. "I moved to Glen Valley to go to grad school, but I'm originally from Bakersfield. That's where I grew up." He looked down at his coffee then glanced up at the wall clock.

"Do you need to go?" she asked.

"I don't know," he said. "I was just coming back when I saw you at the elevator. I haven't seen Kent yet."

"Oh, don't worry about Kent. He's a real sweetheart!" Macy assured him. But it wasn't Kent he was worried about.

"Kent said something about the house you were living in burned down or something? That must've been horrible," Macy said with a concerned frown.

Theodore fidgeted in his chair, thinking about Sarah.

With her hands around her coffee cup, her elbows resting on the table, Macy regarded him in silence, steam from her coffee rising slowly past her lips. "Did you lose everything?" she asked.

"Yeah, pretty much."

Macy shook her head. Theodore was about to tell her about Sarah, not about the night of the ball game, but what a cool lady she was, and how she'd died in the fire....

"Macy! Pretty hectic today, huh?" someone said from behind him.

Theodore instantly recognized the voice.

"Not too bad, Mr. Cantwell," she said, her tone casual, hiding her frustration with him. "How are you? Have everything you need for now?"

Cantwell walked over to the coffee maker and filled the ceramic cup he'd brought with him. "Um, smells fresh!"

Theodore could hear Cantwell tinkling the spoon against his cup, stirring in the cream and sugar. Macy glanced at Theodore—his back to Cantwell—and smiled.

"Oh, Macy, I need to talk with you about something when you get a chance," Cantwell said, turning from the counter and walking in the direction of the doorway. "There's no hurry, though."

"Sure, I'll come up in a little bit," she said.

Cantwell stopped at the door, then pivoted slightly. "Oh, Theo, if you get a chance, you may want to check in with Kent," Cantwell said, stirring his coffee again. "He's been looking for you all day. Talk to you later, Macy."

Macy glanced over at Theodore as Cantwell walked out.

"Are you okay?" she asked.

Steam swirled from the styrofoam cup. She reached over to touch his hand. It was trembling. "Theo, are you all right? Theo?"

Like a rocket, he shot up from his seat, upsetting the flimsy table, sending coffee across Macy's blouse. She jumped back. After checking her blouse, she then looked back at him. "Theo?"

"Oh, God… I'm real sorry!" he finally said when he saw what he had caused. "Here, let me get a towel." He ran across the room and grabbed a roll of paper towels from the counter, ripping a wad of them from the bolt and thrusting them at Macy, then grabbed more and wadded them, plopping them on the muddy river of coffee running across the table, dripping from the edge. Macy blotted her blouse and skirt, smiling up at him. "Don't worry about it," she said. Bent over, looking through a space in the hair draped down over her face. "I'll send you the cleaning bill!"

"Please do," Theodore said gravely. "I'm so sorry!"

"I'm kidding," she said, laughing. "I spill stuff on my clothes at least three times a day; I thought about having them Scotchgarded!"

She finished dabbing the coffee from her skirt. Picking up the soggy towels from the table, she carried them to the trash can. "I'll put some water on it later." She looked over at

Theodore; his face was dark and grim. She touched his arm. "Hey, don't worry about it," she said softly.

"I better get going," he said, pulling away from her. "I'm sorry!" He looked back at her stained blouse, then at the floor before turning away.

"Theo, I'll stop by your office later, okay?" she said, pushing her hair from her face.

He looked back at her, his expression blank.

In moments he was standing in front of the elevator, waiting alone, thinking about Cantwell. The doors rumbled open and Theodore stepped in, then pressed the button for the seventh floor. The metal doors squeezed the last bit of hallway into a tall vertical sliver, then shut completely with a final suck and the elevator jolted to life. Theodore was still picturing Macy's stained blouse when the elevator doors opened.

"Hey, Theo," Kent said, standing in the hall.

"Sorry, Kent, I thought you knew I went home."

"I did," Kent said. "Actually, I didn't think you'd come back this afternoon after working all night."

Theodore was stepping from the elevator when the steel doors closed against his shoulders. He pushed at them impatiently. They reopened. Glaring back at the doors as if they had purposely conspired to crush him, he stepped clear.

"I couldn't sleep," Theodore said, smoothing his rumpled clothes.

"Theo. You don't eat. You don't sleep," said Kent. "You're like the Bionic Man, or something."

He glanced at Kent. "You were looking for me?" he asked, his expression dull. Kent seemed puzzled.

"No, I wasn't looking for you," Kent said. "Why?"

Theodore shook his head and said nothing.

"Theo, relax... don't try so hard." Kent touched his arm. "I'll talk to you later, okay?" Kent smiled and walked away.

Theodore went to his office, pulled the door closed, and collapsed in his chair. He poked the button on his computer with his index finger and leaned back while the computer gathered its senses.

With the afternoon outside his window fading to dusk, Theodore worked on OBO. The bustle of people in the halls gradually diminished to silence. Kent had made a visit or two, but other than those few interruptions, he worked in solitude all afternoon.

Immersed in the only world that made sense to him—the world of code, the universe of numbers, symbols, and patterns—he had all but forgotten about Cantwell and the calamity in the coffee room earlier that afternoon. For a moment, he thought he heard a knock at the door. Maybe it was just Adam cleaning the hall, slopping the mop against the baseboards. The knock came again.

Theodore pushed back from his computer screen. "Come in."

"Hi, Theo, I hope I'm not disturbing you," Macy said, her soft lips arched in an uneasy smile. For a moment, she brought to mind a Girl Scout selling shortbread cookies, nervous and unsure. "I was just getting ready to leave and was wondering if you wanted to get some dinner?"

Theodore looked at her, noticed the amoebae-shaped stain on her blouse. Something condensed inside him. "I can't tonight," he blurted, his chest pounding monstrously in protest to his self-pitying response.

"Maybe some other night then," she said. "I'll see you tomorrow. Don't work too hard." She turned away and he listened as she made her way down the hall.

He wanted to tell her to wait, accept her invitation, but the words sank haplessly toward the bottom of a dusky void. Bolting to the door, he spotted her just as she entered the elevator. In seconds the doors closed and she was gone. He stared after her until the rumble of the departing machinery faded into the empty hallway.

CHAPTER 15

Theodore glanced at the time on the computer screen—3:27 a.m.—massaged his eye sockets, ran his fingers across his scalp, then glared back at the screen. "Enough!" he said, shutting down the computer. By the time the screen went dark, his thoughts—released from the protective track of concentration —ran wild like children after the final bell, swiftly becoming unmanageable. He shot up from his desk and walked to the window.

Neon snakes reflected in the darkened wet streets. Cars rushed past, sizzling along the damp pavement. Were the buses still running? How long would he have to wait for a cab? Then there was his roach-infested apartment; he dreaded going back. Another night sleeping in front of his computer monitor? No, not again—not tonight.

After calling Yellow Cab, he shut down the office, then stepped into the hall and pulled the door shut, locking it. At first he didn't know why he bothered, nothing in the office was his anyway. But there was Cantwell to think about. An unlocked door was invitation to chaos—crazy pranks, far more insidious than a whoopee cushion, rubber doggie poop, or a converted storeroom masquerading as an office. He double-checked the door.

The hall was deserted except for billions of buzzing electrons in the fluorescent light fixtures. Theodore's head was pounding dully at the center of his forehead. He rubbed at the offending pain as he padded down the carpeted hall.

Pausing at the elevator, he thought he heard a noise, someone singing, or moaning, he wasn't sure. He looked around, saw no one, and pressed the call button. He heard the noise again and figured it was Adam, cleaning offices. But the noise wasn't in the building—maybe outside, in the street. He ignored it, waited for the elevator, his mind drifting back to Macy's dinner invitation. Why hadn't he gone with her? He pictured himself seated across from her in a booth, talking, laughing, finishing dessert and sipping coffee. He watched her fork slice into the coconut cream pie. A roach ran out from the custard filling, followed by another, then another, but she didn't notice and raised the bite to her lips. By now, roaches were exiting the pie like clowns from a trick car, scampering across the tablecloth, over the napkins and utensils. Macy smiled and laughed and took another bite of pie. He couldn't figure out where all the roaches were coming from, or why she hadn't noticed them. He looked around the restaurant, then under the tablecloth. Cantwell was under the table with a canister of bugs, releasing them into tubes that went up into the pie. Theodore jumped up, tipping the table, dumping the pie and coffee, dousing Macy's blouse. She screamed, surprised at first, then angry.

"How can you be so stupid!" she shouted, looking at her ruined blouse, her breast showing through the thin, soaked material.

"Is that why you did that, so you could see my breast?" she cried, then slapped him and spun away from the booth, storming from the restaurant. Cantwell began laughing under the table, joined by Charlotte, and the entire graduating class, who were also in the restaurant, laughing and cheering. Annie, from the coffee room, started singing an opera (it was in German so Theodore couldn't understand it), while everyone applauded—standing ovation.

When he tried to exit the booth, everyone crowded around, singing songs, and clapping. He climbed up on the table to see over the throng. Outside the window, there was a face at the glass, a burned disfigured woman shaking her head slowly back and forth. He didn't recognize her at first, until her identity became painfully clear—Sarah. Her scalp was singed bare, covered with melted blotches of skin and black oozing sores. Theodore clambered across the top of the crowd, clawing his way toward the window. He tried to glimpse the woman again, but by then she was gone.

"No!" he screamed, jolting himself from the disquieting fabrication. The elevator doors opened. "Shit!" he screamed, his heart racing, staring at the open elevator. When the doors started to close, he shoved his hand between them. They slid open again. He stepped in, letting the doors shut behind him, then pushed the button for the lobby.

For several minutes he stood motionless, his mind rewinding the bizarre daydream with Macy and the coconut cream pie and Cantwell, before he realized that the elevator wasn't moving. He pressed the button again, even though it was still lit. Nothing. He slammed the button, then hammered at all the buttons until they all glowed. The elevator didn't budge.

"Come on, goddammit, go!" he shouted, pressed the Open button, nothing. "Is anyone out there?" he yelled, pounding his fists on the stainless steel. Was this another of Cantwell's twisted pranks? How far would Cantwell go to get rid of him? Or was it just to make him miserable? Theodore tried to wedge his fingertips into the slit between the doors and pry them open. No luck. Suddenly, the elevator jolted to life, moving downward. Relieved, he slid back against the rear wall. He closed his eyes, tried to calm himself, his lungs sucking roughly at the air. Cantwell's comment slid up behind him, *"Kent's been looking for you all day!"* He saw the table tip, coffee exploding across Macy's blouse—her breast, a ghost of her dark nipple rising through the soaked clothing. He'd hoped she hadn't noticed him looking.

Theodore straightened suddenly, threw open his eyes, flooding his head with light. He was angry, then anxious, then an unnatural mix of the two which gradually gave way to claustrophobia in the tiny space of the elevator. He rocked from foot to foot, tilted his head back, dropped his jaw to take in more air. The numbers over the elevator doors were a blur.

He pressed the button again as if repeated instruction would make the elevator travel faster toward the lobby. All at once it came to a rest. The doors opened.

About to step out, he stopped, arrested by the anomaly before him. He shook his head, trying to clear what most certainly must be a mirage caused by exhaustion. Moving slowly forward, he stuck his hand into the space as the doors began to close, then jerked it back to let them shut, hoping to extinguish the mirage. Even Cantwell couldn't pull this off. With the doors shut, the elevator was perfectly still, obedient, patient. Theodore hit the Open button. The doors slid open effortlessly, but the anomaly remained. He felt the slow prickling of panic gnawing at his legs. He shuffled toward the opening, his skin suddenly cold, tingly.

Before him was not the lobby of DreamCo that he expected to see, or Otis's desk, or the revolving doors of The Baldwin

Hotel, but instead, the interior of another elevator identical to the one he was standing in, like a mirror image.

He fell against the back of the elevator. The doors slid shut but the elevator didn't move.

Instantly, the space seemed stingy with its air. He cried for help as he darted forward, pounding the doors, then the panel of buttons. The doors slid open. He paused a moment, studying the empty elevator before him, then scanned the one he was standing in. He straddled the space between the two.

After a few moments, the doors slid shut against his body, then opened after sensing the obstruction, closing again after a few seconds. The doors continued their incessant closing and opening against him as if they were determined to slowly pulverize his skeleton.

From the space between the elevators, a leg in each one, he inspected the acoustical ceilings, the carpeted floors, the panel of lighted buttons along the right side of each interior. They were identical, down to the scratches and imperfections. The doors continued slicing back and forth. He wasn't sure which elevator he had started in, and didn't really think it mattered anyway. He finally committed to one, stepping in, or out, who could tell, and allowed the doors to shut. He pressed buttons, all the buttons, with no concern for which ones he pushed. The elevator started moving, slowly at first, then picked up speed until the movement made him dizzy.

An impression sluiced over him, a feeling of timelessness, a disquieting sensation—no-time, like he'd felt sixteen years earlier. As a Time denier, Theodore couldn't quite parse this feeling of *timelessness*. What was it exactly? Just then, the elevator jolted to a stop, throwing him to the floor. The doors opened.

He sprang from the floor, hurled himself into the other elevator and began slapping buttons. The doors closed, the elevator jumped to life, moving swiftly, direction indiscernible, then halted, knocking him to the floor once again. The doors remained shut.

He stared up at the buttons, recalling The Baldwin Hotel, the feeling of being trapped in the stairwell. Pulling himself to his feet, he poked the buttons this time, then hammered his fists against the stainless steel.

"Open up, goddammit!" he screamed, pounded, retreated, attacked again. Just then the doors opened, throwing him into the lobby.

Stumbling from the unexpected release, he tried to keep his feet but couldn't and ended up sprawled on the carpeting. He noticed that the lobby was bright, like morning. He checked his watch. Eight-thirty? He knew that couldn't be possible; he hadn't been trapped in the elevator for over four hours.

"Theodore, my man, are you okay?"

Surprised that someone was there, Theodore scrambled to his feet. The elevator doors slid shut behind him.

Otis was seated behind his desk, looking up from his newspaper.

"That damn elevator gets funny sometimes. Mr. Cantwell should get that fixed," Otis said, shaking his head.

Everything seemed familiar, Theodore thought, brushing himself off.

"Whew, your eyes look like minestrone soup!" Otis said. "You didn't work all night your very first day, did you?"

Theodore was confused. "What? What did you say, Otis?"

Otis repeated himself. "Your eyes look like minestrone soup!"

"No, the other thing."

"You didn't work all night your very first day...?"

Theodore tucked in his shirt, pondered Otis's statement. "What day is it?" he asked.

"Tuesday." Otis smiled. "Yesterday was Monday. I know 'cause I took the day off."

Theodore looked down at the floor, almost certain now what had happened. If he was right, Otis would tell him about his brother-in-law with pneumonia who passed out at the kitchen table, and how he had to take him to the hospital.

"You have to pace yourself, son, or you'll end up like my poor brother-in-law!" Otis laughed. "He's working three jobs to pay off his gambling debts and passed out at the breakfast table from pneumonia yesterday morning. His face fell flat in the cereal, *splat!*" Otis said, slapping his hands together and laughing. "I had to drive him to the hospital. If that boy don't work himself to death, he'll probably end up drowning in his own breakfast!" Otis said, grinning.

Theodore was quiet, smiling nervously. "If you see Kent, will you tell him that I went home for a while? I'll be back this afternoon?"

"Sure thing, Theodore. You take it slow, now!"

The morning was fresh. A cool breeze carried the faintest scent of sea air. Theodore walked to the bus stop, obsessed with the elevator, the lost day, the lost evening. And where did it go? He knew he couldn't have been trapped in the elevator for more than twenty minutes, if that, but the entire night had evanesced in less than a third of an hour, melting seamlessly back into the previous day, or so it seemed.

Taking a seat near the back of the bus, he watched out the window as the storefronts, pale and indifferent, rushed silently by, slowly becoming The Baldwin Hotel, the stairwell, the rip in the fabric of reality from years ago.

If only he hadn't been so scared, he thought, he could've paid closer attention to what was happening in the elevator. Maybe there was a pattern? There had to be a pattern, some logical formula that opened a portal to an alternate reality. Did he want to know?

But it was crazy, like something from television, or movies. Glancing out the window, he saw the Sud-Z-Duds Laundry slip by and realized he had already passed his apartment. He jumped up and yelled to the driver. The bus pulled to the curb in front of the convenience store.

Theodore stood in the exhaust of the departing bus as it rumbled down past parked cars. An ad for "Raid Roach Bombs" displayed under the rear window. He turned up the street and started home, his shadow tilting out in front of him, leading the way. As tired as he was, he was certain he wouldn't be able to sleep. Distressing thoughts crowded his mind: Cantwell, Macy, DreamCo, the elevator, and roaches, cunning palmetto bugs, and parallel realities.

After napping for only a short while, Theodore got up, showered, and headed for the bus stop. The afternoon, though still early, had turned surprisingly humid. Riding back to DreamCo, he wondered about the consistency of this phenomenon. Would the lobby be filled with people as it had been before? Would Macy be juggling a pile of folders and books, waiting for the elevator? Would he help her to the fifth floor, go with her for coffee, relive the scene with Cantwell in the lunchroom?

When he arrived at DreamCo all his questions were answered. The lobby was filled with people just as it had been before, but Macy wasn't waiting at the elevator, so there would be no coffee, no Cantwell, no embarrassing scene. Theodore strolled unnoticed to the elevator, rode upstairs to his office, and closed the door.

Sitting at his desk, he wondered if maybe he had imagined the whole thing, the incident with Cantwell, the spilled coffee, Macy's soaked blouse. Had it just been a mind skit? —synaptic theatrics?

Theodore grabbed the phone from the cradle and rang the front desk.

"Otis, it's Theodore. Can you tell me if someone named Annie works here? I don't know her last name."

"Yeah, there's only one Annie, Annie Johnson."

"Where's her office?"

"The fifth floor. Want me to ring her for you?"

"No, that's fine. Thanks."

In minutes, he was searching offices looking for Annie's. The door was open. He knocked on the jamb and went in.

"Hi, I'm Theo. We haven't met," he said, extending a hand. "You weren't at the meeting on Monday."

Standing, she reached across the desk, and smiled. "Nice to meet you," she said. "I'm Annie. Macy mentioned that we had a new designer. I'm guessing that's you."

When she stood, he saw that she was wearing the exact same skirt he remembered from before, the same blouse, the same assortment of jewelry and rings, even had the smudge of lipstick on her teeth. He was certain now that it hadn't been a daydream or hallucination; something had warped inside the elevator, allowing for this disturbing shift. But was that necessarily true? Couldn't this just have been a common case of déjà vu? Otis's comments, Annie's attire? Nothing more than a mental hiccup?

"I need to be going," he said, deflated, and walked out, leaving behind a bewildered Annie standing at her desk.

"Theo, hi!" someone said from behind him as he threaded his way down the hall. He glanced back.

"What are you doing down here?" Macy asked.

"Uh, just… looking for you. I was pretty sure your office was on the fifth floor."

"That's a nice surprise. Is there something I can help you with?"

He hoped Annie wouldn't walk into the hall. "Um, well… no, yeah, but I forgot. I forget sometimes," he said, turning away. "If I remember, I'll call you."

"Hey, Theo," she yelled after him. "Have time for coffee?"

He paused, pondering the invitation, thinking about Cantwell, but now he was forearmed. "Sure."

Theodore and Macy had a pleasant visit in the lunchroom. Annie wasn't there, Cantwell didn't show up, and there was no coffee mishap. Afterward, with new vigor for his game, he went back up to his office and buried himself in OBO.

With the light fading outside the window, he caught himself checking the clock on his computer, trying to remember when Macy had come up in the alternate timeline to ask him to dinner. At once, he heard his thoughts, and was struck by how strange it seemed to be thinking in terms of "alternate worlds." There was only one reality, the one he was in, but what other explanation could define what was happening? The whole phenomenon left him with a dreamy residue, a vacuous feeling in his stomach.

Maybe he was psychic and what he thought was an alternate reality was nothing more than a premonition? Even dreams seem real while you're dreaming. So, what was a premonition? How did Edgar Cayce see the future? How did psychics perceive events that had yet to take place? He thought about the Hopi Indians, and their ability to predict future events. Did the Hopi predict events, or had they already lived through them in some parallel existence?

His head was reeling with conundrums, the most frustrating part being that he knew he couldn't tell anyone what was happening. And why should anyone believe such strangeness? After all, he could barely parse the events for himself.

He got up, opened his door and scanned the hall. It was empty. The building seemed deserted. He listened. Nothing. He went back and sat at his terminal.

"Shit," he said, then checked the time. It was twenty past eight and he knew that something further had changed. Macy wasn't going to come to his office to invite him out for dinner. Most likely she'd already gone home for the day.

He started to wonder if the only reason she had asked him was out of pity, wanting to ameliorate any embarrassment he might have endured over the spilled coffee. His gloom was returning.

Unable to focus, he decided to test the elevator again. Maybe he could discover a pattern. He grabbed a notepad and a pencil from his desk, locked the door, and padded down the hall. The building was like a tomb.

When he pressed the call button, an enervating anxiety swept over him. The elevator doors opened, and for a moment he contemplated the stairwell, then entered. The doors slid closed behind him. He pressed first the button for the lobby and before he could make a note on his pad, the elevator began to move. He waited, watched the lights above the doors as they lit up and went out in descending order. The elevator stopped and the doors slid open. Theodore looked out into the lobby. It was dully lit, the night outside the revolving doors, black. He pressed the Close button, the doors responded, then he hit the one for the ninth floor. He made a note as the elevator jerked to life, stopping him on the ninth floor. Theodore continued, frustrated, trying every sequence of numbers he could, finally pressing all of them at once, pounding on them like he had before. The elevator started, stopped, bucking spasmodically. Theodore braced himself against the wall. Now we're getting somewhere, he thought. The elevator speeded up, then jerked to a stop, then started moving again, then stopped abruptly. He waited, his eyes fixed on the stainless-steel doors, his reflection stretched and distorted, staring back. The doors slid open.

"Everything okay, Theo," Adam asked, standing in the opening with his mop and bucket. Theodore shot a glance past

Adam, toward the revolving doors. It was still night, the building still deserted.

"I heard the elevator go up and down, up and down," Adam said. "I thought maybe it was Mr. Cantwell. Then I thought, maybe it's just on the fritz again. That old elevator looks new, but its innards need an overhaul. One time it actually caught fire, up in the motor house," Adam said, pointing up, his eyes following his finger.

"Theo, are you okay, boy?" Adam asked, observing the pained expression on Theodore's face, his eyes drifting to the note pad in Theodore's hand. It was filled with numbers, mathematical equations, algebra.

"Yeah, Adam, I'm fine," he said, stuffing the notebook in his trouser pocket. "Just code stuff, you know." He hurried past Adam toward the revolving doors.

"Good night," Theodore called over his shoulder.

"Good night, Theo. Take care now." Adam shook his head, then boarded the elevator with his bucket and mop.

THEODORE

I have memory of things that others don't. For instance, Woody had no knowledge of the brutal beating he took at the hands of Porky and the Boneheads, but I can still remember it, his battered face, his torso bandaged from chest to waist. But for Woody it never happened.

Macy had no knowledge of the incident in the lunchroom, when I spilled the coffee across her blouse, but I remember the fiasco clearly.

And in St. Louis. I can still see the creeper derricks on each leg of the Arch, and how the stainless-steel legs, some eighty feet above the ground, glistened in the sunlight. But my family denied it. It wasn't until my dad saw photos depicting the various stages of the Arch project in an engineering magazine that he was forced to speculate on how I knew about the creeper derricks, the same creeper derricks that I had described in great detail. He was baffled but there they were, illustrated in the photographs, exactly as I had described them nearly a year earlier.

Often I wondered if what I had experienced were merely vivid perceptions, so vivid, in fact, that I believed they had really happened. But had they? It would be hard to know and impossible to prove.

One could argue that because I had prior knowledge of certain events, that that was proof of my theory and I've used that argument on myself many times. But prior knowledge denotes nothing more than a vision, a precognition of events to come, second sight, not proof of having experienced alternate realities or multiple universes, or that one could shift between them. There's just no way to know for sure.

Quantum physics has observed an electron in two separate locations at the exact same time, raising the issue of the existence of parallel universes. But even this knowledge does little to alleviate the confusion and ambiguity that I've felt over the years. And while quantum physics has underpinned the possibility for my experiences, it certainly doesn't substantiate them.

CHAPTER 16

After the incident in the elevator, the remainder of the week and weekend had passed quickly. When Theodore arrived at DreamCo the following Monday morning he felt refreshed for the first time since coming back to LA. He had spent the weekend cleaning the apartment, stocking the fridge, battling roaches, and reading. The weather had been pleasant so he took several walks around the area and had found a nice coffee shop where he could hang out.

Otis greeted Theodore with a smile when he approached the reception desk.

"Good weekend, Theodore?" Otis inquired, his newspaper lying in front of him.

"Very good," he answered.

Otis started talking about baseball, but a small headline, partially hidden by the sports page, caught Theodore's attention.

Glen Valley breathes easier! Glen Valley Killer...

But the headline was cut off by another page.

"The Angels are going all the way this year," Otis said, smiling. "I know it's a little early to predict, but, they sure look good."

"Oh, uh, really?" Theodore said.

Otis began quoting stats, talking about other teams in the division, bragging on Nolan Ryan, but Theodore was already thinking of Sarah, and Anaheim Stadium, the smell of her hair when he came back with refreshments, her shoulder against his in the narrow seats, her delicate painted toes peeking out from her sandals. Everything was crisp and clear that night, the stadium lights glistening off Sarah's hair, the green grass of the outfield and infield contrasted the orange dirt, the bases, white and square like Chiclets, the white chalk lines, the bright splashes of cheering fans, the sticky concrete beneath his shoes, the faint promise of rain in the night air.

"Theodore?"

His attention snapped back to Otis.

"You want the sports page?" Otis asked.

"Yeah, sure… if you don't need it."

Otis passed it across the desk.

Theodore smiled and walked to the elevator, thinking about Sarah and the sports page he was holding in his hand. He studied it as he rode up to the seventh floor, not sure what he was supposed to be looking for. There was a picture of Nolan Ryan on the mound. Under the picture were the words, *The Ryan Express*. He recalled Sarah making that same reference.

When he stepped off on the seventh floor, he was still with Sarah, what she was wearing the night of the game, how her teeth sparked under the stadium lights when she laughed. His reverie was broken by an argument coming from the direction of Kent's office. He slowed down to listen, almost certain it was Cantwell bellowing threats. Just then, Kent's door flew open.

When Theodore turned toward the commotion, Cantwell was glaring at him from the other end of the hall. He made a pointing gesture with his finger, slowly mouthing the word, *You*. Cantwell snarled, his indicting thick finger pointing like a gun. The scene fired a familiar image inside Theodore's head: The Uncle Sam poster in the window of the recruiting office in Bakersfield: "I Want You."

Cantwell dropped his arm and leaned forward, seemingly straddling a decision to march down the hall toward Theodore, or leave. He straightened slowly, as if filling with air, his sinister Uncle Sam sneer morphing to a Scrooge grin. He strolled away toward the elevator.

Kent appeared in the doorway, grim and frazzled, glanced in the direction of Cantwell's departure, then at Theodore. He wavered a moment, considering something, then slipped back into his office and slammed the door. Theodore started for Kent's office but decided against it.

Sitting at his computer, Theodore's thoughts congealed, the scowl on Cantwell's face, the long Uncle Sam sausage of a finger poking at him. YOU—the word flashed in his mind, stark as a newspaper headline. Malaise slipped through him until he could no longer envision the code for OBO, could no longer follow the thread of his own game.

Kent appeared at his door. "I need to talk to you a minute, Theo. Can I come in?"

Theodore looked up and nodded, pushing out from his desk. He felt compelled to stand, like a private in boot camp. Kent had a magazine rolled in his hand and waved it toward him, directing him to sit down.

"Look, I'm sorry, Theo, but we have to talk," Kent said, pulling up a chair, his expression gloomy.

Theodore sat.

The magazine unfurled when Kent placed it on the desk. "Are you familiar with this magazine, *Modern Gaming?*" Kent asked.

Theodore nodded.

Kent flipped to the Post-it note stuck in the pages.

Theodore looked at the small blurb of copy circled with a highlighter pen, then looked at Kent.

"Someone leaked *StarField* to *Modern Gaming!*" Kent said. "*MG* blasted it! The review was terrible and we're barely in production. They called it a, 'knock-off of *Space Invaders*, but not nearly as interesting,'" Kent told him. "Cantwell is freaking out."

Theodore glanced back at the article, then at Kent, unable to grasp Kent's point.

"This is bad, Theo. Cantwell didn't want any press on this game before it came out. It's important to hit the market fresh..." Kent said, sitting back roughly. "He thinks you leaked it, Theo."

Theodore had to think on Kent's statement. Leaked it. What did that even mean? "I don't understand, Kent."

"He thinks you told *Modern Gaming* about *StarField!*"

"I didn't!" Theodore protested. "Why would I? I would have no reason to... I mean, what...." Theodore paused to ponder the antagonism that had grown between himself and Cantwell since their first meeting. "I didn't, Kent. Please believe me. I wouldn't do that."

Kent looked down at the floor, then at Theodore. "Cantwell's convinced you did. I don't know what it is between you two, but..." Kent shook his head. "Cantwell wants somebody's ass. I think it's yours!" Kent said, grimacing. "He's not going to get it but I need some help here, Theo."

Theodore looked down at the review.

"Don't give Cantwell any more ammunition, all right?" Kent said. "Do you know what I mean? Steer clear of him until I can find out who did this, and...."

"What?" Theodore asked.

"Nothing, just... steer clear, okay?"

Theodore nodded, still regarding the magazine on his desk.

"I'm sorry for all of this shit," Kent said. "It shouldn't be like this."

Theodore shrugged. "Yeah, I'm sorry, too."

Kent got up to leave. "I'll talk to you later," he said, closing the door behind him.

The remainder of the afternoon trudged by. Theodore took numerous breaks from OBO, went to the restroom several times, the lunch room, the snack machine on the second floor, careful to avoid everyone, then back to his office for more street gazing and people watching. He had heard there was a good view from the roof but hadn't been up there yet. Between his breaks he had managed to move the game along, writing new code, creating directories and sub-directories, but was quickly becoming fatigued. It was a little past seven when he locked his door and headed for the stairwell, avoiding the elevator all together.

After a quick and uneventful trip down the steps, he pushed effortlessly into the lobby, letting the door close quietly behind him, turning to see someone sitting at Otis's desk.

"Hey, Theo," Macy called. She was reading Otis's newspaper, closing it when Theodore approached.

"Why do you use the stairwell?" she asked. "Exercise?"

Theodore accepted the easy excuse with a nod.

"Are you headed home?" she asked.

"Yeah," Theodore responded flatly, fatigued by the tedious afternoon. He found himself dwelling on Cantwell's accusation.

"Want to grab a sandwich?" she asked, her eyes bright under Otis's desk lamp. "I know a place not far from here, casual, kind of funky, but the food is great."

"Sure... okay," he said.

They were almost to the revolving doors when Otis's phone rang. Macy paused with the thought of answering it, then reconsidered. "Cantwell's still here. Let him answer it," she said, and pushed through the doors.

"Does he always stay late?" Theodore asked.

"I don't know. He's usually still hanging around when I leave."

She unlocked the passenger side of her blue Mustang, walked to the driver's side, unlocked it, and slid her legs under the steering wheel, smoothing her skirt before she started the engine.

It was about a fifteen-minute drive to Pastori's Deli. Most of it Theodore blanked out, engrossed in Kent's visit and Cantwell's disturbing antics. Macy was talking, but he wasn't in the conversation, merely nodding at appropriate intervals.

It wasn't long before they parked the car and were standing at the deli counter.

"Do you know what you want?" Macy asked.

That was the question that always confounded Theodore more than any other. He often thought he knew, but now wasn't sure. Sometimes what he wanted seemed like the right thing until he got it. Was DreamCo one of those things? He certainly hadn't expected so much animosity, or to provoke so much ire. One thing he loved about the paper route (the only thing, really) was the ability to perform his job in anonymity, in solitude, in the night while everyone slept. That was the attraction to designing video games as well, the excitement of the challenge without the conflict of human interaction. If only he could be left alone to do what he did best, design video games, interact with the computer, exist in a world of numbers and code...

"Theo, do you know what you want?" she asked again.

"What?" he said, startled. He looked around at the people waiting in line behind him, then at the chalkboard menu above the counter, then at the man waiting to ring up his order. He hadn't remembered getting out of the car or walking into the restaurant.

"I'll have a Reuben and a coke," Macy said, then looked over at Theodore.

With everyone waiting, Theodore felt pressured. "I'll have the same," he blurted.

After finding a table, they waited until their number was called. Theodore got up to retrieve the food, returning moments later with two Cokes and two red baskets.

"I'm starving," Macy said, eyeing the pickle spears, the Rueben sandwiches, and potato salad. "I didn't eat lunch today, did you?" she asked.

"Yeah, some peanut butter crackers and a candy bar," Theodore answered, squeezing mustard on his sandwich.

"That's lunch?" Macy said. "Jeez, Theo."

Theodore picked up his Rueben. A lump of sauerkraut slipped out, falling into the basket.

"How long have you worked at DreamCo?" Theodore asked, stuffing the errant chopped cabbage back into his sandwich.

"A little over a year," she said. "I worked at an ad agency before that, Glennon/Gray Advertising." Macy slid her hair behind her ear.

"Sometimes I miss it," she said. "Being around all those creative people." She looked up, surprised by her own comment. "I don't mean that the people at DreamCo aren't creative. That's not what I'm talking about. It's just that at an ad agency you get to see things progress, unlike DreamCo, where everything is in secret codes that magically evolve into computer games. It's very creative, what you do, it's just that it's kind of a covert process."

He weighed her observation, having never viewed it that way. Code to him was a clear and precise language, nothing covert about it.

"That's what I love about doing pottery," she said, dabbing her mouth with a napkin. "I can watch a piece develop," Macy said, her eyes flashing joyously. "I love working with clay."

"Like on a wheel?" he asked, making a gesture with his hands as if he were forming a cylinder on a potter's wheel.

"Yeah," she said. "Have you done pottery?"

"No, but I've read about it."

"You should try it. It's wonderful. I even dig my own clay." Macy sipped at the straw. "Would you like to give it a try sometime?"

He nodded, his mouth full, then placed his sandwich back in the basket.

"Theodore!" a voice called from across the restaurant.

Theodore and Macy both turned to see a man with black wavy hair approaching. He was wearing pressed jeans, a white dress shirt, and a gray sports jacket. Macy looked over at Theodore.

"Theodore," Sid said, reaching out to shake Theodore's hand. "I hardly recognized you without the, uh… you know…" he said, glancing at Theodore's bald head, then smiled at Macy.

Theodore put down his fork.

"It's good to see you," Sid said, suddenly turning serious. "I'm really sorry about Sarah. Such a tragedy."

Theodore's expression went cold.

Sid continued. "It's just awful… and then that business in the newspaper today!" he said, shaking his head.

Theodore sat up, his face distorted. "What?"

"Hi, I'm Macy. Theo and I work together at DreamCo," she said extending a hand, as if purposely redirecting the conversation.

"I'm Sid Carter. Nice to meet you," he said taking her hand. "DreamCo, what's that?"

"We design video games. Theo is one of our chief designers," Macy told him. "He's working on a great new project." She looked at Theodore—who was still wearing a glum expression—then back at Sid. Sid was fixed on Macy.

"Really? Congratulations, Theodore!" Sid beamed. "I know you were always busy on that computer of yours." He grinned at Macy. "I'm not much good with technological stuff, more of a people person, you know?"

Macy smiled weakly, averting her eyes.

"I'm an insurance underwriter for TransMutual in San Francisco. People, corporations, numbers, tables, that sort of thing. Boring, boring stuff, but it gets me out of the city. I like to travel. No wife or family, so it works out pretty well," Sid told Macy, ignoring Theodore. "I just got in town today. A big venture with General American. Aw, but you don't want to hear about that." Sid laughed, giving Macy a grin that exposed his perfect teeth. "So what is it you do at DreamCo, Macy? You a computer genius too, like our Theodore here?"

"Sid! Go away!" Theodore blurted, surprising Sid as well as Macy.

Sid turned to face him. Theodore balled his fists under the table.

"I was just talking to the…" Sid started to say when Theodore shot up from his seat.

"Go!" he repeated, a few inches from Sid's face. "I don't want trouble. I just want you to go away and leave us alone!"

Heads in the restaurant started turning. Sid glared at him for a second, then reached in his jacket and pulled out a business card. He was about to hand it to Macy when

Theodore snatched it from him and ripped it down the middle. The manager walked out from behind the counter, but Sid turned to leave before he got there. In a few moments, the dull chatter of conversation returned to the restaurant and the manager stepped back behind the register. Macy reached across to touch Theodore's hand.

Theodore looked toward the door, then sat down, heat rolling up inside him, as if he were about to cry. He focused on the red basket, on the plastic weaving, the paper lining on the bottom, the sandwich, mustard dripping down the crust in a small mound near his potato salad. He heard murmuring in the deli, the cash register dinging, the drawer rushing open, change tinkling in the compartments. "Thank you. Here's your number, we'll call you when it's ready," the man behind the register told another patron. Then the door opened and a gust of cool air swept around Theodore's ankles. Chairs scuffed along the wooden floor, people talked about grocery shopping, the car accident on Clemmons Boulevard, the woman who was beaten and robbed, problems at school with a boy named Billy, until all the conversations whirled into one continuous rumble like oncoming traffic.

"Theo? Are you okay?"

He looked over, pausing a moment, then nodded.

He sipped his Coke and looked out the window into the dark, a light rain beginning to fall, glistening on the passing automobiles. Macy followed his gaze toward the window.

"Aren't you hungry?" she asked, glancing at his half-eaten sandwich.

He glanced at the remnants in the basket, then shook his head.

When Macy finished eating, they walked in silence out to the parking lot. They were almost to the car when Macy stopped and touched Theodore's arm. "Hey, you want a beer or something?"

"Not in there," he said. "I have some at my apartment?"

"That sounds good," she said, unlocking the doors to the Mustang.

On the drive he explained to Macy that Sid Carter had been one of Mrs. Bloom's gentleman friends, although casual, emphasizing the *casual* part. He also told Macy what a slime Sid was, hitting on Maria Lopez when Mrs. Bloom wasn't around. It almost felt deceptive, to Theodore, referring to Sarah as Mrs. Bloom when he was telling Macy about her, but it didn't feel right to call her Sarah in front of others, as if it was a secret shared only between him and Mrs. Bloom. For the rest of the drive to his apartment, he was mostly quiet, sunk into himself, answering questions when Macy asked, and speculating on Sid Carter: Why did he roam free, while Sarah had to die in the fire?

CHAPTER 17

M acy always liked this part of town, and knew Kent lived just a few blocks away in one of the new refurbished lofts. Even though the walls of Theodore's apartment seemed like they could use a fresh coat of paint, the space was cozy and uncluttered. To her it fit Theodore's personality perfectly, though she really didn't know him well.

"Glass or the bottle?" Theodore called from the kitchen.

"The bottle's fine," Macy called back, scanning the apartment from the couch, her hands on her knees. Theodore walked into the living room, handed Macy one of the cold beers, then sat opposite her on the cushioned chair, his face puzzled.

"What's wrong?" Macy asked.

"I was just thinking about Sid… I thought he died in the fire," Theodore said. "There was another body found at the house and it wasn't Maria and I just assumed that… well, that it was Sid. Maria and I were the only tenants. It was weird seeing him, you know, like a ghost or something."

Macy tugged at a corner of the label on the bottle, remembering the article in the morning newspaper, knowing now that Theodore hadn't seen it, wondering if she should tell him. But what good could it serve, she thought, to tell him that the other body found at Mrs. Bloom's house was Kendall Blannert?—a man who had grown up in foster homes, was in his late twenties, the same man who worked at the HARP office in LA, and who had access to files, fixated on elderly women that lived alone, preying on them, and who was believed to be the Glen Valley Killer. The details of the article rambled through her head. She wanted to tell him about Blannert so he wouldn't have to wonder. But then, eventually the same notion would seize Theodore that had seized her: What had happened to Mrs. Bloom that morning before the fire? Was she tortured, raped, then brutally murdered? Was she already dead when the fire started, or tied to her bed like all the other victims, being tormented by her attacker as the house burned around them? It was too ghastly to ponder. Macy tried to shake the image.

"So I don't know who it was…" Theodore said, raising the bottle to his lips, "…you know… in Mrs. Bloom's home? I've been wondering." He looked down at the scuffed coffee table, seemingly lost in possibilities.

"It doesn't matter, does it?" Macy said, reaching over to touch his hand. "That's over. What's the point in thinking about it?"

He shrugged.

"Theodore, can I ask you a question?" Macy said, wanting to change the subject. She had noticed his bed when she used the bathroom when they first arrived. The bed was angled in the middle of the room, away from all the walls, the legs sitting in bowls of water.

"What are the bowls of water for?" she asked.

She could see he was embarrassed and felt intrusive for asking.

"Is it like a religious thing or what?" she asked. "You don't have to tell me if you don't want to."

"No," he answered. "It's not a religious thing. My landlord has a bad roach problem. They crawl on me while I'm sleeping."

"Aghh," Macy grimaced. "That's disgusting."

"I figured if I moved the bed away from the walls and made sure the blankets didn't touch the floor, then the only way they could get into my bed was up the bed frame legs," he said, setting his bottle down. "So, I placed the legs in plastic bowls and filled them with water, figuring the little buggers would have to swim if they wanted to get to me. I don't think they can swim."

"Problem solved?" Macy asked, sitting back in the couch.

"Not exactly. I woke up Sunday morning with one crawling on my arm."

"Ughhh," she said, shivering. "I couldn't stand that."

"Yeah. I can't figure out where they're coming from. I've tried everything, including roach bombs. I guess I'm gonna have to call the landlord."

"You know, Theo, there are some nice places out where I'm living... and I don't think they'd cost you much more than this place."

Theodore pondered the idea. "Transportation wouldn't be a problem," she said, noticing he seemed to be anxious about something. "You could take the train in to work. You could even ride in with me...but I know you keep odd hours..."

Theodore stared at nothing in particular, some spot across the room as if trying to picture it. Macy wasn't sure if he was upset or hadn't heard her correctly.

"We could ride out there one day if you wanted to look?" she offered, brushing a few wisps of hair from her forehead.

Finally, as if awaking from a deep sleep, he said, "Yeah, thanks." He then asked her about the neighborhood, how long she'd lived there, all the usual conversation. She told him how quiet it was and that crime wasn't a real big problem, and she mostly felt safe. He went to the kitchen for two more beers. The subject slowly turned to work and home versions of computer games, then to Theodore's computer that burned in the fire, about what Redmond had said about the top floor collapsing. They sat for a moment listening to the street noise.

She placed her empty bottle on the coffee table and checked her watch. "I guess I better be going. Give you a hand with the bottles?"

"No, they're fine. The roaches will carry them off in the night."

"Ugh, God! Well, good luck," she said. "I had fun."

"Yeah. I'll see you tomorrow."

She pushed her hair behind her ear, then looked back at Theodore.

"Oh, I almost forgot," she said. "I'm heading up to the mountains this Saturday to dig clay. You want to come with?"

"Dig clay?"

"Pottery clay."

"Sure. What time?"

"In the morning, eight or so. Not too early. I'll pick you up, how's that?"

"Yeah, that sounds good."

"Okay then. Well, I'll see you tomorrow."

Her pumps clicked down the wooden stairs and out the front door. Walking across the street to her car, she wondered about Sid and how confused Theodore was upon seeing him, and felt horrible she had not mentioned anything about Kenneth Blannert, and what really happened to his friend, Mrs. Bloom.

CHAPTER 18

The phone on the nightstand continued to ring as Kent wrestled himself free from a disturbing dream. He pushed up on one arm and glanced at the dim red glow of the alarm clock—2:47—and couldn't figure out who would be calling at this hour. Fumbling to lift the receiver from the cradle, Kent turned it right way around, untangling his wrist from the cord, then pushed it against his ear.

"Hello?"

For a moment there was only silence.

"Hello?" he said again, about to hang up.

"Do you like working at DreamCo, Kent?"

Groggy and half asleep, Kent struggled to recognize the voice, thinking maybe it was some kind of prank. "Who is this?" he finally said, squinting across the dark bedroom.

"Because if you do like working at DreamCo, you better get your shit together, Tanaki!"

"Mr. Cantwell?" Kent rubbed his eyes, trying to wake up. "What's wrong?"

"That vagrant from Bakersfield is what's wrong! The fucking chipmunk! Theodore!"

"I don't understand… what happened?" Kent said, sitting up on the edge of the bed. He reached over and switched on the nightstand lamp.

"You don't know? What kind of a ship are you running, Tanaki! That fucking lunatic was riding in the elevators all night, up and down, up and down, like a fucking mental patient. When I confronted him, he told me you said it was okay, that whatever he needed to do to *get his creative juices flowing* was just fine with you, even if it meant burning up my goddamn elevators! Do you know how much those cost to fix? Do you? Would you like me to take the repair charges out of your pay? Or maybe I'll just make the elevators off limits to everyone but me, and the rest of you can break your asses taking the stairs!"

Kent shook his head in disbelief. He knew something was going on with Theodore and the elevators and was frustrated trying to figure it out. Theodore was strange, of that there was no doubt, but so was Cantwell, who seemed equally enamored with the lifts. The other disturbing aspect was Cantwell never referred to Kent by his last name; Cantwell had achieved a new level of outrage Kent was unfamiliar with.

"Are you still there, Tanaki?"

"Yes sir, absolutely. I'm here."

"Well?"

"Well what?"

"Well what? What the fuck are you going to do about it? Jesus, Tanaki, don't make me regret giving you control over the entire creative department. You have to reign these nutballs in. We're not running a nursery school for geeky losers, here! Tell me what the fuck you're going to do…"

Kent took a deep breath, trying to make sense of Cantwell's wrath. He'd always been a bit peculiar, and harbored an extraordinary brand of passion that bordered on fury, the part of Cantwell's personality Kent had never been quite able to warm to.

"I'll have a talk with him tomorrow. It won't happen again. I promise," Kent said, grimacing, instantly sorry he promised.

Kent waited for Cantwell's next salvo, the receiver pressed to his ear, nervously hoping that the solution he just offered would be enough to quell the storm. The silence coming from the phone seemed to stretch out indefinitely, an uncomfortable void both timeless and irritating. When the refrigerator clunked on and started humming and buzzing, Kent thought he might need a new one soon, then took his attention back to the call. He waited a moment longer, the time now 3:12, then said, "Mr. Cantwell? Are you still there?"

"Fire him!"

"What?"

"Fire that ridiculous derelict!"

"But Mr. Cantwell… I think I can talk with him and—"

"I know that little bastard leaked *StarField* to *Modern Gaming!* He has to go!"

"I confronted him about that," Kent said. "He told me he didn't. He said he had nothing to do with it… and I—"

"You believed him! Jesus, Tanaki, were you born yesterday? We are the laughing stock of the video game industry. *StarField* was going to put us on the map… make us leaders instead of losers…"

For all Cantwell's verbose bravado and long-winded philosophy, Kent knew he was conservative at heart. Cantwell would much rather stow away on someone else's success than chance something unproven. He lacked any real vision. Though rowdy and garrulous, Cantwell was not adventurous when it came to forging the new frontier in video games.

"I need a head on a platter, Kent. Do you hear me?"

"Yes sir, head on a platter... I'll fire Theodore first thing..."

Another long silence. Kent hated waiting for Cantwell to formulate his thoughts. Most of all, he hated to have to fire Theodore. Kent really liked OBO, and Theodore, and truly believed Theo's game might be the fresh idea DreamCo had been looking for.

"We'll discuss that when you get in..."

"Sir?"

"The firing of young Theodore. We'll discuss that when you get in. Now get some sleep. I don't want to see you dragging around the office all day!"

Kent waited until he heard the click on the other end of the line. He placed the receiver into the cradle, a little unnerved. Not only by the call, but what he thought he'd heard as Cantwell was hanging up the phone.

"Was he laughing?" Kent said to himself.

CHAPTER 19

The morning was humid and warm. Macy parked her Mustang, locked the door and was halfway to the entrance of DreamCo when she spotted Kent sitting in his BMW.

"Kent," Macy said, tapping on the window.

Kent turned toward her, pulled his elbow back, then hit the switch for the window. She was greeted to a cold blast of air conditioning and a loud riff of Led Zeppelin. She didn't recognize the song. Kent turned down the stereo.

"Come sit a minute," he said.

She walked around and got in. "Isn't this dangerous, sitting here with the engine running and the windows closed?" she said, placing her briefcase in her lap and shutting the door. "Carbon monoxide or something?"

"Not in a Beemer," Kent said flatly, then adjusted the air-conditioning control to make it cooler.

They sat without talking for several minutes before Macy spoke.

"So, what's up? I don't think I've ever seen you like this."

He looked over at her, his features like clay, his eyes unable to hold her gaze.

"Cantwell called me at three this morning," Kent said. "Screaming at me about Theo." He shook his head, looking out the window for an answer.

"What?" Macy said, dumbfounded.

"Yeah. Three in the morning," Kent said. "Seems that Cantwell caught him playing on the elevator last night. I just don't get it, I mean—"

"Last night?" Macy interrupted. "I was with Theo last night."

Kent looked over, narrowed his eyes, surprised. It seemed to take Macy a second to decipher his meaning.

"Not *with* him! Not like that. I mean we grabbed a sandwich after work, then went to his apartment for a couple of beers. I left him around nine-thirty."

Kent turned back toward the windshield. "Well, I don't know anything about that. All I know is Cantwell called at 3 a.m. to tell me that Theo was fucking around on the elevator, excuse my Japanese, and that I should…" Kent stopped to consider his statement. "Frank told me to fire him."

Macy said nothing, her eyes drifting back down to her briefcase.

"I don't want to fire Theo. I like him. I like his game. I like what he brings to DreamCo, but ever since he got here things have been bonkers. Cantwell is driving me nuts, calling me to his office practically every day, chewing on my ass about one thing or another, mostly about Theo. I don't know what's with those two."

Macy touched Kent's hand on the seat and smiled. "Are you going to fire him?"

He glanced down briefly, then back out the windshield. "Cantwell and I are supposed to discuss it today." Kent shook his head. "Did you see what *Modern Gaming* wrote about

StarField?" said Kent. "I mean we barely have the game in production and the entire industry knows what we're doing. We're a joke."

"I don't think it's that bad," she said. "But there is one thing that troubles me."

"What?"

"You're starting to sound like Cantwell, and that *is* scary!"

"Christ, I hope not." Kent smiled. "I just don't know what to do," he said, suddenly sullen again. "Cantwell thinks Theo ratted out *StarField!*"

"What do you think?" she asked.

"I don't know…."

Just then, Kent saw Theodore walking across the parking lot toward the entrance.

"Look at him," Kent said.

Theodore was swaying back and forth under the authority of his limp. He stopped for a moment to look at the lettering above the doors, his black beret falling to the pavement when he tilted his head back. He bent over, brushed off the beret, placed it back on his head, then went into the building.

"He's so smart… and so pitiful," Kent said, shaking his head, staring at the spot where Theodore had been standing.

"Hey, he's been through a lot," Macy said, touching Kent's arm. "The fire, losing his friend, Mrs. Bloom. And to top it off, I think he feels responsible for the fire. It's sad."

Kent looked over at Macy, wearing a look as if he'd detected something in her voice that signaled more than compassion. "Macy, what's going on here? I thought you and…"

"Yeah, yeah, nothing's changed," she said. "It's just that Theodore could use a friend or two."

Kent was smirking, his eyes tight on hers.

"What?" she said, shrugging her hands out. "There is nothing going on between us. I mean it!"

"Hey, it's none of my business," Kent said. "But he is strange, Macy. As much as I like Theo, he is very strange."

"You're strange too, Kent," Macy smirked. "Maybe you haven't noticed."

Kent watched out the window as more employees entered the building.

"You ready to go in?" Macy asked.

Kent nodded, shutting off the engine.

As they strolled toward DreamCo, Macy asked him if he'd read the article about the Glen Valley Killer in yesterday's paper.

He nodded. "Weird, huh?" Kent said. "Does Theo know?"

Macy shook her head. "No, and I'm not going to tell him. What's the point? I think he has enough to think about without that crap.

CHAPTER 20

Theodore hadn't slept at all the night before and couldn't concentrate. Sitting at his computer, he recalled the previous evening, returning to DreamCo after Macy left his apartment. He had hoped to gather data on the elevator, find clues, but all he found was Cantwell's snarling face.

"What the fuck are you doing?" Cantwell had screamed when the elevator doors opened. Even now, Theodore felt embarrassed, remembering how he'd just stood there, holding his note pad, staring at Cantwell.

"I don't pay you to burn up electricity and wear out my elevator, using it like some fucking carnival ride," Cantwell had shouted, his dark silhouette ghosted against the dimly lit hallway, then stepped forward, into the elevator, under the harsh light of the overhead fixture.

Theodore eased backward, the rear wall of the elevator blocking his retreat.

Cantwell bent close to his face.

"What is your problem?" he whispered, his stale cigar breath causing Theodore to blink. "You don't get it yet, do you," Cantwell said, his eyes like flickering, dying flames. "You remind me of my father, Monroe. You remember him, don't you?" Cantwell's sinewy hands opened and closed as if they were breathing. "I told you about him the first day you were here. Monroe, my old man. Just like you, he didn't know he was a loser, either!"

Theodore pictured Monroe in his three-piece suit, dapper, like Frank, but with kinder eyes. He remembered how Monroe had sat down next to him at the indoor pool, had listened to his story about the stairwell, and all the doors with "6's" on them, and how scared he had been. Monroe was attentive and hadn't made him feel like a fool. Monroe told him about his own son, Frankie, and the strange thing that had happened to him on the elevator. Then Monroe gave the Trumballs a free dinner at the hotel restaurant.

"Monroe wasn't a loser," Theodore had said to Cantwell.

Cantwell said nothing, straightened up, narrowing his eyes to slits. His features hardened under the bleak light, his chin protruding like the prow of a ship.

Theodore felt himself slump unintentionally, averting his eyes to the brightly swirling carpet at his feet. In a few moments, Cantwell's shadow separated from his, and without raising his head, he listened as Cantwell walked away and down the hall.

"Can I come in a minute?" Kent asked, poking his head into Theodore's office.

Theodore bristled, shaken from the memory of the previous evening.

"We seem to be having a lot of these heart-to-heart talks lately," Kent said, but his light demeanor evanesced quickly. Kent hesitated a moment, as if searching for a way to get into this conversation, finally deciding it best to just dive in.

"Cantwell called me at three this morning, Theo, complaining that you were riding up and down on the elevator and... you know the rest. He wasn't happy." Kent finished talking and stared at him.

Theodore contemplated his desktop.

"Are things all right? Do you need some time off?" Kent asked.

Embarrassed, Theodore found it difficult to push any words past the lump in his throat. He wrung his hands under the desk where Kent couldn't see, and waited for an explanation to surface, glancing at Kent, then back at the desktop.

"We have to do something, Theo. Cantwell's pissed!" Kent pleaded.

Sensing Kent's exasperation, Theodore began to feel alienated, upset that they now seemed on opposite sides. "I'm sorry, Kent. I don't want to cause you...."

Kent waved his hand as he stood. "Forget it, Theo. It's okay. Everything's cool. Just don't... you know... just watch the elevator, okay?" Kent said, pushing the chair back against the wall. "Let's go over OBO later with production, okay?"

Theodore nodded as Kent left.

CHAPTER 21

The remainder of the week dragged by as summer imbedded itself in the city in the form of a heat wave. Even the nights were hot. Sitting before his computer screen, he tried to concentrate on OBO, but Sid kept surfacing like a stubborn stain, hauling Sarah up with him. Flames broke out behind Theodore's eyes. He heard Sarah's screams, saw her beating the flames with her robe, fire scorching the walls brown, paint peeling, boards curling black. Realizing the fire was out of control, maybe she tried to escape her fiery bedroom, but a twisted pyre of two-by-fours and gypsum board spoiled her exit. Maybe the flames crawled along the walls fueled by the stale air rushing into the burning hallway. Maybe she fled to the window, screamed for help, the ceiling beginning to sag above her unnoticed, weakened from intense heat. Maybe the fire forced her to the center of the room, pinned her there, spreading through the carpet, licking at the seam of her nightgown, biting into the silk, devouring it with ravenous speed.

Theodore jumped up from his computer, ran to the window, wedging himself in behind the Levolor blinds. The window seemed stuck, or locked. He jerked up on the handle, the thin blinds crinkling tinny against his back. "Open, dammit!" he shouted. The window flew open. A blast of warm night air swept across his face, thick in contrast to the thin, cool air conditioning in the office. He gulped it in, then slowly sucked it to the bottom of his lungs, calm easing through him like warm blood. On the street below, car horns blared, people shopped and walked and waited at bus stops, a small dog barked, someone yelled for a cab, brakes squealed, a distant siren whined— fortifying sounds to Theodore's ravaged mind.

For the last few nights he had left DreamCo when everyone else did, but returned late in the evening to write code and spend time in the elevator. It was too hot to sleep anyway; his apartment had only one window air conditioner and it seemed free of Freon. He would stay until one or two in the morning working with his numbers, then return to his apartment after the cool night air had settled over the city. But he was getting nowhere with the elevator—no clues had emerged and no patterns that he could discern. There had to be some way to control the process of shifting between realities, predict the moments that physicist Hugh Everett III referred to as "choice points" or what good was it?

After locking his office, he headed for the elevator and in minutes was scribbling formulas in his note pad, pressing elevator buttons, waiting, hoping to find the mirror elevator, like before, but nothing happened. Exasperated after a couple hours of riding up and down, he decided to call it quits.

When he stepped off the elevator into the deserted lobby, he heard someone clear his throat.

"Working late, Edward?" a voice said.

Theodore peered toward the dark corner of the lobby past the large plants that stood between him and the lounge chairs, cocked his head slightly and tried to focus, wondering why the voice had referred to him as Edward.

"I've been watching you, Edward," the voice said again.

Theodore heard him inhale, saw a glowing nub of orange light illuminating a vague puff of smoke. The hot light evanesced back into darkness as the odor of cigar wafted slowly toward him.

"Mr. Cantwell?" Theodore said.

"Edward, Edward, you are a mysterious lad. I don't know one other person who uses an alias, and I know a lot of people." Smoke swirled faintly behind the plants with the grace of an apparition.

"I really don't care why you go by an alias, but I am interested in why you spilled *Starfield* to *Modern Gaming*. They don't pay that well."

"I didn't, Mr. Cantwww—"

"Oh, I don't really care, not now. I'm more interested in what it is you do on my elevator every night, Edward."

Washed in light beneath a solitary ceiling fixture, Theodore stood dumbfounded, shuffling his feet.

"I'm sorry, Mr. Cantwell," Theodore blurted. "It won't happen again."

"My dear boy... you've got me all wrong." The cigar glowed brightly, like it was about to explode, then went pale. "I don't mind you riding up and down on my elevator... hell, I do it all the time... clears my head, you know? Does it clear yours?"

Something creaked lightly, coins and keys shifting, tinkling. Theodore pictured Cantwell readjusting in the chair, crossing or maybe uncrossing his legs, maybe sitting back, getting more comfortable to listen to an explanation. The change settled, the cigar burned, the smoke swirled faintly orange and for a moment Theodore thought he could see Cantwell's angular nose protruding from the shadows of a face.

"No… you're searching for something, aren't you? Yes, of course, that's it. You're searching for something miraculous. Am I right? You can tell me, Edward."

Theodore began to fidget, suddenly uncomfortable with the direction of Cantwell's interrogation.

"Kent told me that you were in St. Louis years ago with your family," Cantwell continued. "Some sort of vacation or something. Said you stayed at The Baldwin Hotel. Isn't that curious, Edward? I guess we have something in common. You probably met my old man, Monroe, maybe became good friends. I guess that's why you thought he wasn't a loser. Well, Edward, just like Monroe, I want to be your friend, too."

The change in Cantwell's pocket shifted again, tinkling against something metallic, maybe a lighter.

The bright light above Theodore made it difficult to see, keeping his pupils dilated. He heard a tinny rustling, a click, then the hushed hum of escaping butane as the flame from a lighter shot up in the area where the cigar had burned brightly. The flame floating in air reminded him of a picture he'd seen of Jesus with a dollop of fire hovering above his head.

"Did Monroe do a good job? —fresh towels, little soaps, shampoo and all that? —clean sheets?"

Theodore nodded, choosing not to speak, afraid his voice might crack. He was surprised by how much Cantwell knew.

"Good! Monroe was always good at those things—fresh toiletries, clean sheets, and the like. What happened, Edward? I'm curious. You know, The Baldwin Hotel was a strange place… strange energy, if you know what I mean. I could feel it. You probably could too, couldn't you? Maybe that's what scared you?"

Theodore realized that Kent had told him everything.

"Nothing to be ashamed of, Edward. It would scare a grown man. It scared me!"

Theodore felt his eyes narrow on the dark space behind the plants, his questions about Cantwell answered, about what Monroe had told him that day at the hotel sixteen years ago, about his son, Frankie, being trapped in the elevator, about Cantwell's so-called morning meditations. Cantwell was searching for the same thing. Then Theodore recalled what Kent had told him about Cantwell's sudden wealth, gambling on sports, on the stock market, but there's no gamble involved when you know the outcomes.

"When The Baldwin Hotel burned down, I damn near didn't make it out alive, the elevator machinery crashing down in a ball of fire, exploding into the lobby. What a site, Edward. A few burns. Nevertheless, I wasn't about to give up... like my old man. He couldn't handle it and let himself go insane. I hope you're not a quitter, Edward. I hope you don't go insane."

Theodore swallowed hard, thinking about taking a step forward, but it seemed too risky. Better to keep some distance between himself and Cantwell.

"Me... I went to the elevator company and met a cute little thing who was more than happy to research every building that had the same model elevators installed as The Baldwin. Oh, she was so beautiful, and so helpful. You'd be amazed how many there were. A bunch in Chicago and Kansas City, but I was done with the Midwest. Too damn cold. And some on the east coast, but I never liked it there. Then she handed me a slip of paper with a whole list on the west coast, but one in particular caught my eye, a wonderful little nine-story building in LA. Same model elevators. Even the metal stairwells were manufactured by the same outfit as the ones in The Baldwin. All the building needed was a new entrance! Imagine my good fortune. I just happened to have one."

Theodore wasn't sure what to make of the story. He was about to ask a question when Cantwell said, "Time." Smoke bellowed up from between the plants. "Time, Edward. Our minds have been conditioned to believe in Time, in tomorrows, and we trick ourselves into thinking we had all those yesterdays, but it's just an illusion, Edward. In reality, there is only today. It's always today, always this moment, and nothing else."

Theodore coughed when the smoke reached him. He cleared his throat and for a moment thought he could see Cantwell beyond the plants. He waited for the burning orange button of his cigar, hear the spare change jangling in Cantwell's pocket...

"Theo, you all right, boy?" a voice spoke from behind him.

Theodore spun quickly, his heart pounding. "Adam!" he said, surprised to see him standing there. He hadn't heard him approach.

Adam stood next to his rolling bucket, holding the handle, staring at Theodore with a peculiar expression of bewilderment.

"I was just talking with..." Theodore said, peering past the manicured vegetation, the area oddly devoid of anything but darkness.

"Who you talking with?" Adam asked, leaning sideways to see around him.

Theodore regarded the space where Cantwell had been. "Nobody," Theodore said, then hurried toward the revolving doors.

CHAPTER 22

Sleep came roughly to Theodore, vivid dreams riding the backs of other dreams, fragments of images jammed into one another forming disturbing indiscernible dramas. Driving his newspaper van down a deserted one-way street, he came to a dead end. A huge bulldozer, with numerous bright spotlights, broke through the barrier, roaring toward him, spewing smoke. Throwing the van into reverse, Theodore twisted in his seat, pressed the gas pedal, but the van barely moved. With the accelerator flat against the floor, the vehicle barely crawled backward, the bulldozer closing fast, the roar deafening. Glass exploded into a billowing firework when the steel bucket of the bulldozer crashed through the windshield, smashing the front end. Trying to escape from the van, Theodore struggled with the door handle, the stench of burning oil and diesel fuel filling the cab. Moving backward now, the van being pushed down the street under the power of the huge earth mover, Theodore figured he'd be crushed like a tin can. The bright light burned red through his closed lids, the thunderous roar ripped at his eardrums, a loud thump, then silence. He thought he was dead. He opened his eyes and the machine was gone. Getting out of the van, he stepped to the pavement, looked up the street, then down—nothing.

"Bring me one of your beautiful ruby gazanias, Theodore," a woman's voice said. Lying behind the vehicle was a body covered with stacks of blank newspapers. Falling to his knees, Theodore shuffled through them, but the faster he did, the more newspapers there seemed to be. The voice called again, "Bring me one of your beautiful ruby gazanias, Theodore." In his haste, he tossed newspapers haphazardly, exhuming the body beneath the rubble. There was movement under the stack, then the fragrance of Sarah's perfume. "Sarah, hang on!" he screamed, slinging newspapers, finally exposing the face— the bloated blue visage of Porky, his teeth rotted, his breath fetid and sour.

Theodore sprung up in bed, sweating. He felt something crawling on his cheek, and groped for the intruder, feeling the hard shell of a thick roach. "Ah! Fuck!" he screamed, slapping it away. The insect cracked against the wall. "Fuck," he said again, throwing back the sheet, his body soaked with perspiration.

Checking the time—6:35 a.m.—he decided sleep was no longer an option. He showered, dressed, then bolted down the stairs of his apartment building, heading for the coffee shop. When he hit the sidewalk, a wall of warm sticky air seized him, a westerly breeze mixed with the smell of salt and ocean and exhaust fumes. The sun, a reddish disk cloaked in a violet scarf of smog, seemed unable to free itself from the horizon. He hurried down the sidewalk, listing from side to side under the infirmity of his dwarfed leg.

After getting coffee, he sat quietly at a table near the front window, expunging the last residue of his nightmares. Someone had left yesterday's newspaper on the chair next to him, and unlike his dream image, this one was filled with print and headlines.

Kendall Blannert, the Glen Valley Killer, Dead!

Theodore read down a few lines to discover that the police, after successfully obtaining dental impressions from the corpse, traced his residence to an apartment on the outskirts of Glen Valley. The article said he worked at the HARP office in LA. When the police searched his apartment, they found Polaroid pictures of his victims, the pictures taken during their torture and after their deaths.

Disgusted, Theodore threw the newspaper back on the chair before he reached the part of the article explaining how Blannert's body had been discovered at the burned-out residence of Mrs. Sarah Ann Bloom. The article went on to postulate, based on the close proximity of the dead bodies, that Blannert may have been in the act of assaulting her when the fiery ceiling collapsed on them.

Theodore looked out the coffee shop window and saw an old man, rumpled and dirty, staggering along the sidewalk. He had only one shoe, the other foot protected by a worn sock, his face ruddy and red like a sorrowful sunset. The man peered through the window at Theodore with flat, dim eyes that seemed to be floating in blood. Theodore looked away, down at the steam rising from his coffee cup, then searched the small café for a place to bury his thoughts, finally opting for the sports page on the chair next to him.

CHAPTER 23

"What's going on?" Theodore asked Otis when he arrived at DreamCo and noticed the yellow tape blocking off the elevator.

"Hey, my man!" Otis said, folding the newspaper down onto itself. "How are you today?"

"Good, Otis. What's with the elevator?"

Otis began to laugh a little, shaking his head as he scanned the lobby, then started speaking just above a whisper.

"Mr. Cantwell was caught in the elevator this morning when I come in, pounding on the doors, swearing like a marine!" Otis said, pausing to chuckle, then rocked his head slowly from side to side. "I yelled to him that I would get him out but he just kept swearing. I don't even know if he heard me. I had to get a crowbar from my trunk to pry open the doors. He came out of there looking like a newborn baby, all red and wet and fuming!" Otis covered his mouth. "I know I shouldn't laugh, but..."

"What are they doing to it?" Theodore asked.

"Oh, something up in the motor house," Otis said, leaning to the side and pointing toward some nebulous spot above them. "We got the other elevator, though." Otis averted his eyes across the lobby smiling. "It seems to work just fine... well, most of the time anyway. Both them elevators is older than roaches!" he said, laughing again.

"Older than what?" Theodore asked, not certain he'd heard correctly.

"Roaches!" Otis said, hosting a more serious expression. "Did you know roaches are one of the oldest creatures on the planet? They survive everything. It's no wonder they so damn pesky, they feel like they own the place!" His somber expression gave way to another fit of laughter.

Theodore knew about the tenacity of roaches. But maybe it wasn't tenacity after all, just some freaky cosmic joke that this most hated and despised creature would ultimately have the last laugh. The lowly only needed staying power to succeed, he thought.

"Theo," Macy said, touching his arm.

He swiveled toward her.

"Hi, Macy," Otis said before Theodore could speak. "Did you hear what happened to Mr. Cantwell?"

As Otis told the story again, Theodore watched Macy, letting his eyes follow the trail of fine naked hairs down the side of her cheek that ended at the soft edge of her jaw. His concentration was broken when she laughed.

"Did you hear that, Theo?" she asked, still musing with Otis.

"Yeah, Otis just told me," he answered, forcing a smile, suddenly remembering the peculiar conversation with Cantwell the evening before. Had Cantwell tried to find one of Everett's "choice points" to jump realities after Theodore left? How did Cantwell know about them? And more disturbing, had he found one?

"Hey, are we still on for tomorrow?" Macy asked Theodore, her smile enthusiastic.

"What's tomorrow?" he asked, not sure what day it was.

"The mountains? Digging clay? Do I need to call you in the morning so you'll remember?" she asked.

"No, I'll be ready. What time?"

"Around 8:30," she said. "And if I don't get to work soon, I may still be here until then." She touched Otis's hand, smiled, then touched Theodore's shoulder. Her hair edged out from behind her ear and her right hand instinctively swept it back in place.

"That is one fine lady," Otis said, watching her disappear into the working elevator.

CHAPTER 24

———

The sky, a milky gray void beyond the drab landscape, hung timeless above the highway, while the distant peaks of the San Gabriel Mountains appeared diaphanous and vague, veiled in clouds. Misty rain congealed into watery tendrils at the edges of the windshield, escaping the whoosh and thump of the wipers methodically clearing wide swaths of glass. Theodore, mesmerized by the swipe of the blades, lost in the hum of the tires on pavement, was unaware of Macy sitting next to him, except when the fragrance of her perfume interrupted his wandering, drawing him back inside the Mustang.

Balancing the McDonald's coffee cup in his lap with his left hand, he noticed that it still felt warm, comforting, contrasted with the cool wet glass of the passenger side window.

"Do you know what group this is?" Macy asked, noticing the song playing on the radio.

"No, who?" Theodore asked.

"Fleetwood Mac. *Mystery to Me* album," Macy said, reaching over to turn up the volume. "It's called *Hypnotized*. I love this song."

He hadn't noticed the song, his attention on the wet pavement disappearing past the hood of the Mustang. Sarah's record collection came to mind, the thin cardboard sandwiches of album jackets pressed against each other, the colorful artwork, the photographs and typography, the details floating like billboards inside his head. Theodore never really listened to music all that much, but Sarah's collection enchanted him, the lustrous black vinyl discs. How could so much sound live in such infinitesimal grooves, entire worlds of horns and pianos and violins and drums, sopranos and tenors and baritones, all the beats and notes and compositions etched into vinyl? It was mind boggling.

"You still here?" Macy said, flipping on her turn signal, even though there wasn't a car anywhere in sight.

"Yeah, sorry," Theodore said, regarding her briefly before raising his cup to his lips. The coffee had grown tepid, tasting bitter on his tongue. He lowered the cup back to his lap.

The static on the radio had all but drowned out the music when Macy twisted the knob to find a new station. He noticed her sour expression, as if she were pondering some problem without a solution.

"You really like music, don't you," Theodore said.

Macy shrugged, her attention on the road ahead. "Doesn't everyone?"

Theodore wasn't sure. "Have you ever heard of Billie Holiday?"

"Of course, though I don't listen to her music," Macy said. "I'm more into rock."

"Sarah, my landlord, she had a Billie Holiday album." The song started playing in his head, the one Sarah had rushed from the bedroom to turn off. He couldn't quite understand the impact of music, as if that gene was absent from his biology.

Macy gave Theodore a sideways glance, then checked her speed before settling her eyes back on the glistening asphalt ahead.

"I'm sorry about the other night, that outburst with Sid at the restaurant," Theodore said into the hum of the car on the wet pavement. "He's not a very nice man."

Macy smiled over at him. "You don't have to apologize…" The rain had stopped and Macy turned off the wipers.

Theodore waited a moment before he apologized again. "I'm not much company today. Sorry. I'm preoccupied, I guess." But he was always preoccupied with something; a philosophical quandary, a mathematical improbability. Even so, with Sarah there seemed to be no disconnect, no awkward stillness, no buried thoughts. They shared so many aspects of life, the garden, the flowers, the new greenhouse, her baking, her joy of being… Then there was Sid. How could he still be alive? Who was the mysterious other body the firefighters found?

"So, tell me about digging clay," Theodore blurted out, attempting to get back in the present, form a connection to Macy.

"Better than that," Macy said, slowing to turn onto a gravel road. "Why don't I just show you!"

A bright strip of blue breached above the trees in the otherwise seamless white sky. Theodore was surprised; the ride seemed to take no time at all. Sage-scrub and big-cone firs lined the rugged road, the ground overgrown with yellow-flowering shortpod mustard. The gravel path soon turned to dirt and mud with deep pockets and gullies. They bounced along slowly, Macy guiding the Mustang carefully through the ruts, maneuvering it several hundred yards down the gutted road. They came to a small clearing of grass on the right and pulled over slowly, coming to a stop near a rusted barbed-wire fence. Light drizzle sprinkled the windshield.

"Do you ever get stuck up here?" Theodore asked, turning to look out the side window at the gravel, a few areas beginning to soften to mud.

"We'll be fine, really. I do this all the time," she assured him, then jumped out of the car and walked around to the trunk.

"Ooh, it is getting muddy," she said, kicking her sneaker against the tire and knocking a clump of wet dirt loose. Theodore was joining her at the back of the car when she popped the trunk and started handing him pails and tools. She grabbed some rags and threw them in with the spades, then pulled another sack from the trunk. "Lunch," she announced, without looking up at him. "There, let's see," she said, biting on her thumbnail, her eyes roving over the articles in his arms, apparently checking them off the list in her head. "I think that's all we need. Oh, wait… here, rubber gloves. I don't use them anymore but you might want to. I also have a couple of Cokes in that small cooler in the back seat. Would you get that?"

Theodore walked back to the passenger side door, pulled the seat forward and reached for the cooler, dropping the buckets in the mud.

"Everything okay?" she said, her voice muffled as she dug deeper into the entrails of her trunk.

"Yes," Theodore answered, bending over to pick up the stuff he'd dropped.

"Oh, Theo, I only have one pair of boots," she said, disappointed. "I forgot about them. I always come up here alone."

"I don't need any," he answered, gratified that he was allowed into her solitary world. He walked to the back of the car juggling the equipment.

Macy laughed. "Here, let me take some of that…"

After they divvied up the load between them, Macy slammed the trunk lid with her elbow, then swiveled her hip against the driver's side door to shut it.

"This way," she said, her arms full, pointing with her forehead, and started trudging down a path along the road that eventually led into the brush. Theodore followed.

As they fought through the understory, Theodore watched Macy push limbs aside, bending under branches, the seat of her worn jeans ostensibly stained from previous clay hunting trips. A few times the sweatshirt she had tied around her neck caught, pulling her back, causing her to stumble. Theodore would hear her laugh. Once in a while she would glance back over her shoulder to check on him, smile, continually plodding forward. Theodore couldn't take his eyes off her; she was radiant.

"Almost there!" she announced without turning around.

In a few moments he heard the rush and gurgle of the stream, along with twigs snapping under Macy's feet. She pushed through a dense opening and into a clearing, holding the branches back for him. After stepping through the space, he stood on the bank of a stream several yards wide and crystal clear.

"Wow! This is incredible," he said, staring at the water purling above head-sized dark stones.

"It is, isn't it?" Macy said. "I'm sorry it was so rough. I got lost back there. It's been a while since I've been here. We just need to follow the stream down a ways to the spot." She looked over at Theodore and motioned with her head. They walked another five minutes until they came to a clearing.

"Right here," she said, dropping her load to the ground. "I love it up here." She stepped to the edge of the stream and removed the sweatshirt from her shoulders, laid it on the ground next to her, then bent down, cupped her hands and dipped them into an eddy, pulling clear water up to her face. "Ahh. That feels so good."

He couldn't stop staring, watching water drip from her chin, her hair falling down along the side of her face, stringy wet at the ends. He wanted to bend down next to her, kiss her. Just then, she stood up, smiled, and turned back toward the pile of tools strewn across the grass.

"Ready to work?" she asked, turning a bucket over to sit on. She untied her sneakers, placed them on the ground next to her, then slipped her boots on. She led Theodore to the edge of the stream, showed him the eroded bank and how to separate the clumps of bluish gray clay from the dark earth. He worked along the undercut while she dug from beneath the streambed, the water barely a foot deep.

For a long while they worked in silence. Thoughts that had been pleasantly absent during the short hike, returned; Cantwell and the night before. If Cantwell made the "shift" in the elevator, how would Theodore know? Did it matter? He couldn't figure Cantwell's game.

"Macy," Theodore said, dropping a small chunk of clay into his bucket. "If you could change the past, would you?"

She looked up. "Change the past? How do you mean? Like, are there things I would do differently if I could do them over?"

"Kind of, I guess. What I mean is, if you really could change them, would you?"

Macy laughed a little, brushed some hair from her forehead with the back of her hand, leaving a smudge of dirt just above her right eyebrow. "You mean like travel back in time, in a *time machine,* or something?"

"No, not a time machine," Theodore said rather brusquely, impatient with the idea of *time travel;* he had little regard for the mechanistic notion. Kent had assumed the same thing, that Theodore, when talking about alternate realities, had been referring to *time travel.* A split second later, tormented by a troublesome dread, Theodore realized that his conversation with Kent about time travel had only transpired in Theodore's head. He took a deep breath to center himself, assailed by the disquieting notion that most of his reality unfolded behind his eyes, not in the physical world. Yet he was almost certain that whatever happened in the elevator at DreamCo, or in the stairwell sixteen years ago at The Baldwin Hotel was not due to the engineering of the stairwell, or the engineering of the elevator, but could maybe be attributed to power spots or energy vortexes housed in them—much like the ones he had searched for in Sedona years earlier with Woody. Theodore didn't believe that machines could produce such magnificent possibilities, but that the human mind and physics could. After all, parallel universes were scientific theory, while time travel was merely science fiction.

Nearly composed, Theodore went on, "I guess for a moment, just imagine that you could shift to an alternate past, would you do it."

Macy looked puzzled, as if she needed a tangible operation for performing such a feat, some kind of workable metaphor. "Like going to a hardware store to pick out a paint swatch from thousands of possibilities?"

"Yes! Yes, that is exactly what I'm talking about," Theodore said, ebullient over Macy's analogy, and at the same time perplexed he hadn't thought of it himself.

Macy hesitated, her eyes narrowed on Theodore. "Is this about regret?"

"Maybe. I don't know. Does it matter?" Theodore said. "I mean, would you change outcomes if you could?"

Macy looked back down at the water, dug her spade deep into the streambed, bringing up a scoop of drippy mud and rocks. Staring at the mucky gunk on her spade, she picked lightly through it, dropping some bits of clay into her bucket, then lifted her eyes toward Theodore.

"No, I don't think I would," she said, "but it would be a hard decision. I remember an article I read not too long ago about that very thing. The article was written by these two researchers who examined the phenomenon of regret."

She swished her hand in the water to rinse it.

"The article talked about people creating alternate worlds in their head. Like, if a person had an unfortunate experience, he would start imagining a different reality where the event never happened, playing it over in his mind, 'if only I had done that one little thing differently….'"

Theodore considered the clay in his bucket, the water rushing by.

"I think that's part of the addiction with video games," Macy said, staring over at him. "Getting to do it over! As many times as you have quarters for!" Macy stepped lightly on the slippery rocks, moving toward the bank. "The whole idea of being able to redo your life when things go wrong is a little frightening to me." She said, padding from the stream to set her bucket on the grass. "I mean, sure, in video games… who cares. But in life?"

"Why?" Theodore asked, placing his bucket on the ground near hers. "Why is the idea of being able to change events so frightening to you?"

"I don't know," Macy said. "Maybe because I feel like… this may sound silly, but… well, I guess I believe in a grand plan for everyone and the events that happen in our lives."

"Fate?"

Macy shook her head lightly. "No, not fate. That makes it sound like you're just a mindless cog without choices. I don't believe that either. I believe we have choices and they make a difference." Macy paused a second. "I think that our decisions impact others and that our choices somehow determine our reality."

"Well, then, why wouldn't changing the past… or choosing a different outcome… why wouldn't that be the same as what you're talking about?" Theodore asked.

Macy pulled an old blanket from a cloth bag and spread it on the ground.

"I told you, I'm old-fashioned," she said, shyly. "But if I were able to select the past I wanted, it would always be from my limited perspective of life. I couldn't know how my choices affected others... you know? Too much responsibility."

"But what if you knew what had happened, and it was horrible, affecting people you loved?" Theodore said, with a hint of pleading in his voice. "Wouldn't you want to change it then?"

Macy looked down at the blanket, at her boots and started to pull them off. "When I was nine, my brother was eleven and we were playing in the tree house our dad had built in the huge sycamore in our backyard. We pretended to be super heroes. I was Wonder Woman, he was Superman. The *creep alarm* had just gone off. The creep alarm was an old wind-up alarm clock that my Mom gave us. We would set it to go off after a few minutes and when it did it was time to fight evil. This time it was Godzilla crushing Glen Valley. Kenny was in front of me and we were running toward the ladder of our tree house to fight Godzilla, when he tripped on his cape and fell from the tree house. It was only about six feet, but I guess he hit wrong and snapped his neck. He was dead before I could get down the ladder."

Macy reached in the paper sack pulling out two sandwiches and a large bag of potato chips. "I hope you like tuna?"

Theodore nodded and took the sandwich.

"Anyway, when Kenny got killed I had so much regret. I felt like I could've prevented his death, that I should've done something, like grabbed him or maybe I should have been first to the ladder, I really don't know. I even made myself believe that I had grabbed Kenny at the last second and that he was okay. My father forever regretted building the tree house, and a week later, after the funeral, he hooked a rope to his pickup and pulled it down. My mother was devastated by my brother's death, angry with my father forever building the thing, hating herself for letting us play in it. We all constructed alternate realities where Kenny didn't die, and I don't know that I've ever completely let go of mine. But no one was to blame. There was nothing that anyone could've or should've done differently. It just happened. Sometimes crappy things happen."

"But what if you could switch pasts and have your brother back?"

"Why are you asking all these questions?" Macy said, her eyes dampening. "I miss him terribly, but... no, I wouldn't switch pasts... I don't know. I can't even consider it because it's not possible and... it's just stupid to think about." Macy put her sandwich down on the blanket and stared at the stream.

"I'm sorry," he said, tuna from his sandwich falling unnoticed onto his trousers.

"No, it's okay," she said, forcing a smile. "I thought I had dealt with that. I guess you never can, not entirely." She looked at Theodore, then pointed at his trousers. "You're losing your tuna."

He wiped the tuna salad off his pants with a napkin.

"You seem obsessed with the idea of being able to change the past," she said, grabbing some chips from the bag.

"I don't think I'm obsessed," he said, sounding defensive even to himself. "It's just something I think about, that's all."

She said nothing, continuing to eat her lunch. "Do you want a Coke?"

He nodded, thinking about her reaction to his questions, to her idea of a greater plan. He guessed she was referring to God, or something like God. It had been so long since he had considered God. Maybe because if there was a God, then He would certainly condemn him for what he had done to Porky. But why was he given the opportunity to switch pasts, to invoke a different outcome, if not for the sole purpose of changing things? And if that were true, wouldn't the ability to alter the events have had to come from God, or the Master Planner, or whatever this powerful force was? And wouldn't this force have to be benevolent? Or was this force nothing but a trickster, a cosmic prankster not much different from Cantwell, or himself, for that matter, setting up traps to fall into, planning pranks for no other reason than a colossal empyrean laugh. Was that also part of the grand plan?

Macy finished her sandwich and stretched out on the blanket.

"Feel like digging more clay?" she asked.

"Sure," he answered. "How much do you need?"

"If we fill three buckets, that should be more than enough for right now. Besides, we won't be able to carry much more than that. We still have a long walk back."

The sun broke through the clouds behind a stand of tall pines, painting long shadows across the blanket. Macy and Theodore rested a bit longer before they resumed digging. After filling all three buckets with clay, they rinsed the tools in the stream, packed up the supplies and hiked back to the Mustang, this time on a more defined trail. By the time they reached the car it was almost six in the evening.

"It'll probably be dark by the time we get back," she said, placing wet rags over the clay in the buckets to keep it moist. She stuffed blankets in next to the containers to keep them from turning over, then laid the tools inside. Sitting on the edge of the trunk, Macy poked at the mud on her boots with a stick.

"How long have you been doing pottery?" Theodore asked, cleaning his shoes.

"About eight years," she said. "I started doing it in college, kind of playing around with it and really liked it, but didn't go crazy with it until a few years ago when my fiancé bought me a kiln."

Macy started talking about throwing on the wheel, making pinch pots, and hand building, but Theodore didn't hear much of it, his mind spinning with the notion of her fiancé.

"Jeez, listen to me go on about firing clay," she said, laughing and shaking her head. "I'm sure you could care less." She looked over. He was staring at the ground.

"Do you need to wipe your hands?" she asked, holding the rag out to him. He hadn't noticed.

"Theo?" she asked again. "Do you need the rag to wipe your hands?"

Theodore shook his head, looked down at the ground, then looked up. "I didn't know you had a fiancé," he said, trying not to sound alarmed.

Macy seemed embarrassed. "Yeah," she said, averting her eyes toward the ground. "Kent's the only one who knows at DreamCo. My fiancé is in medical school at Rush in Chicago. He has another year before he starts his residency." Macy threw the rag on top of the clay and shut the trunk. "He got kind of a late start because he was studying to be a marine biologist, but then decided to become a surgeon. It feels like he's been in school for a decade." Macy pondered her statement. "It has been a decade!" It seemed to Theodore that she was no longer speaking to him.

"You ready to go?" she asked.

He plodded through the mud to the passenger side and got in. Macy slid behind the wheel and started the car. "I guess you think it's strange that I've kept my fiancé a secret, huh?"

Theodore shrugged, suddenly saddened by her disclosure, as if a door had blown shut inside him.

"It's been such a long engagement that sometimes I wonder if we'll ever get married," Macy said, checking her face in the mirror out of habit, not noticing Theodore's dour expression.

"It feels easier not to say anything in case it never happens. That way I won't have to deal with everyone else's disappointment on top of my own."

Macy backed the car up slowly, the Mustang swaying gently from side to side as the tires rolled through the ruts. She turned it hard to get it back on the dirt road and pointed it down the mountain.

CHAPTER 25

Theodore arrived at DreamCo early Monday morning before anyone else. The elevator had been fixed over the weekend so he stepped in, and pressed the button, pondering the trip to the mountains with Macy, and her fiancé, what she had told him about regret and alternate worlds. Was everything that had happened an illusion? —the stairwell in The Baldwin Hotel? —Porky? —the beating Woody had taken? —his first day at DreamCo? He pulled a quick inventory of what he knew to be real, and what wasn't. It was futile. How could he possibly know? Everything seemed real, then not real—funhouse mirrors and slanted floors, trapdoors and curtains, mirages shimmering above hot sand, sleight of hand. Even the past seemed real, but where was it? It wasn't here in the elevator, it wasn't in the lobby or his apartment, or in the bloodshot eyes of the ragged man seated next to him on the bus that brought him across town—so where was it? Just stashed in his head, a charlatan reality? Was Cantwell right: there is only today?

The jagging thought propelled him from the elevator and down the hall to his office. He slammed the door and flopped down in his chair, poking the button to boot his computer. As he waited for the screen to propagate with code, he deliberated on Cantwell. If Cantwell knew something about all this business then wasn't that proof that it was real? —that it had happened, the elevator, the "jump," everything?

As the morning progressed, Theodore became aware of the slow wakening of DreamCo, the subtle bustling outside his office, commotion on the street below, the rumble of the elevator straining upward through the hollow shaft.

The phone rang.

"Hello. Theo speaking."

"Theo, it's Woody."

"Woody! Hey, hi!"

"How about lunch today? I'm in LA this morning looking at some new lab equipment and I should be done in about two hours. Can you get free?"

"Sure, yeah. You gonna pick me up?"

"What's the address?"

Theodore gave him directions. Woody arrived just after one in the afternoon. After a brief tour of DreamCo, Theodore couldn't wait to show Woody his office. He was so proud. He only wished he could feel the same about his horrible apartment.

"Wow," Woody said, surveying the sleek interior, the aluminum desk, the huge windows, the view from the seventh floor. "This beats Ballas Photo Lab. You hit the big time, Theo."

Theodore felt like he had.

"Edward," a voice bellowed from the doorway. "Oh, we have company today, I see." Cantwell entered. "I'm Frank Cantwell, president of DreamCo." Cantwell walked directly to Woody and thrust his big hand forward. "And you are?"

"I'm Woody, Theodore's friend. Nice to meet you."

"Hmmm," Cantwell said, still palming Woody's hand. "Woody... Theodore... Linus... your parents and Theodore's must have watched a lot of cartoons!"

Theodore's face flushed. Woody chuckled. "Yeah... probably. Your offices are amazing. I was just telling Theo—"

"Theo! Yes, our Mr. Trumball certainly has a variety of monikers," Cantwell said, briefly shifting his attention to Theodore before turning back to Woody. "I prefer Edward. How do you keep all your friend's names straight? Teddy... Theodore... Theo... Edward?"

Woody looked over at Theodore, seemingly confused by the question.

"We're just heading out for lunch," Theodore said, ready to escape Cantwell.

"Sounds good. Maybe I could join you?" Cantwell said, his gaze radiating a peculiar light. Something collapsed inside Theodore. He couldn't speak. Woody looked at Theodore then back to Cantwell.

"Oh, darn," Cantwell said, feigning disappointment. "I forgot an appointment I have. Well, maybe another time then. It was sure nice meeting you, Mr. Woody." Cantwell turned to Theodore. "Have a nice lunch, *Edward!*"

Cantwell was almost to the door when he spun back toward them. "I can't wait to see those new modifications you made on BOBO! ... Kent told me all about them. We'll have a meeting later, just the three of us... well, I guess the four of us if you count BOBO!"

When Cantwell left the office, Woody turned toward Theodore. "BOBO? What's that?" Woody said.

"My game, *OBO,*" Theodore said, nearly in tears over his humiliation.

The drive to the restaurant seemed to ameliorate some of Theodore's embarrassment; Woody talking about his kids, his job, married life. Woody didn't ask much about Cantwell, probably detecting that Theodore didn't want to talk about him, even though Theodore's combatant boss still commandeered his thoughts as they pulled into the restaurant parking lot.

The host showed them to a table. Food arrived a few minutes before Theodore felt the need to sidestep small talk and pose a difficult question to his best friend. "I've been wondering something for a long time," Theodore said to Woody.

Woody looked up from his plate, chewing a bite of food. "What?"

"Did you believe me when I told you about that stuff that happened in St. Louis... you know, when we were kids?"

Woody looked confused.

"The Baldwin Hotel," said Theodore, trying to stir Woody's memory.

Woody brightened, then swallowed the mouthful of food. "To be honest, Theo, I *didn't* believe you... not at first anyhow," he said, raising his iced tea. "I remember you calling me when you got home, going on about the Arch, and the stairwell, I thought you'd lost your fucking mind! But then you told me something that changed all that. I've never doubted you since."

Theodore shrugged, unsure what he was referring to.

"I came over one afternoon and you were sitting on your bed like a zombie and all of a sudden you looked over and said, 'Woody, the day you win the spelling bee, don't go home through Tathum Cemetery. Promise me!' I remember feeling a little scared." Woody returned his drink to the table after a short swig.

"You told me that Porky and the Boneheads were going to be waiting for me and give me the thrashing of my life if I went home from school that way," Woody said. "You remember?"

Theodore regarded him silently, nodding.

"You were sick the day of the spelling bee," Woody recalled. "You made me promise, *'cross my heart and cut a fart'*, that I wouldn't go through Tathum Cemetery." Woody crossed himself and farted at the table, just the way they did as kids, then grinned.

Theodore chuckled at the childhood gesture, but his smile faded as he pictured what had happened to Woody in the more gruesome version of their lives, the day Woody *had* gone through Tathum Cemetery. Woody's mother, Edith, had called that evening. Theodore could still see Madeline's face twisted with anguish, listening to Edith on the phone. Occasionally he overheard the muffled high-pitched cries of Edith through the receiver. When Madeline hung up, she breezed past Theodore as if he were invisible, disappeared into the bedroom, and shut the door. He heard sorrowful weeping as she related the story to his father.

His father was the one who had to tell Theodore what had happened that afternoon. How a gang of boys had jumped Woody in the cemetery and beat him until he was unconscious. They knocked out teeth, broke his nose and several ribs, and left him blind in one eye. It was almost four months before Woody came out of the coma. Theodore became anxious over the memory and quickly reminded himself that none of that was in this reality.

"What's wrong?" Woody asked, scanning the pained expression on Theodore's face.

"Nothing," he said, forcing a smile, glad that beating would never be part of Woody's consciousness.

"I don't know how you knew about the spelling bee," Woody said "But when I won it, I figured I better not chance going home through Tathum, so I called my dad."

Theodore quietly picked at his food, recalling the cemetery and Porky.

"I still can't believe what happened to Porky... falling in that grave like he did," Woody said. "Then having the unfortunate luck of being impaled on a pick ax. Jesus!" Woody shook his head obviously recounting the story that had circulated in school the following day. Theodore pictured it too, but from a different perspective. It wasn't unfortunate luck that brought Porky to his premature demise. Theodore had found the pick ax by one of the other gravesites and carried it to the one he'd prepared for Porky.

"After that, I would've walked over hot coals if you told me my feet were made of asbestos!" Woody said, stabbing another chunk of steak.

Theodore said nothing, pushing his plate away.

After they finished dessert, Woody checked his watch. "I need to get back to Bakersfield. Shelley made dinner reservations for tonight."

"Oh... I almost forgot. Happy Anniversary," Theodore said.

Woody shut his eyes, letting his head fall forward. "Damn!" he shouted loud enough to turn a few heads in the restaurant. "I completely forgot! I can't walk in without a present. What am I... is there a Berrie's Bath Shop around here? Oh, hell, how would you know! Never mind, I've gotta get going," Woody said, jumping up from the table and dropping his napkin on the seat.

"Actually, Woody, I get all my toiletries at Berrie's!" Theodore joked.

"Do they really keep your skin silky smooth like the ads say?" Woody asked, in a serious tone.

"Yeah, like *butta!*"

They both laughed.

"There's a Berrie's in the Meadow View Mall in Glen Valley," Theodore told him. "It's not exactly on your way home, but you could swing through there...."

"You're a god!" Woody said. "Shel loves that shit!"

Theodore paid the check and they drove back to DreamCo.

"Tell Shelley hi for me!" Theodore shouted as Woody pulled away from the curb.

CHAPTER 26

Theodore pushed away from his monitor, glanced at the clock: 5:43. A brilliant evening light was spreading outside his windows. He thought maybe he'd leave, then come back later to work on the list of code malfunctions Kent had dropped off shortly after he'd returned from lunch with Woody. Maybe see if Macy wanted to have an early dinner together. He was just getting up from his desk when Kent knocked and entered.

"Hey, Theo, sorry I didn't get to meet your friend today," Kent said, coming over to Theodore's desk. "Mr. Woody, right?"

"No, just Woody. That's his first name." Theodore hadn't thought about Cantwell all afternoon and was miffed Cantwell had lied to Kent about Woody's name.

"Okay, well, we're having a meeting right now if that works for you," Kent said. "Were you leaving?"

Theodore wanted to say yes, mostly just to avoid seeing Cantwell, but also to check with Macy about dinner. "No... I'm good. Cantwell's office?"

"The viewing room," Kent said. "About ten minutes or so?"

Theodore nodded, then tidied up his desk as Kent was leaving. He picked up his phone to call Macy's extension, but then placed the receiver back in the cradle, figuring he probably wouldn't have the energy to share time with her after the conference with Cantwell.

Padding down the hallway toward the elevator, Theodore was struck by how quiet it was. He stood at the elevator doors for a moment, feeling an unnatural current thrumming beneath his skin, then pressed the call button. The elevator trundled inside the long, empty shaft, rumbling up toward him, the noise growing louder the closer it came. The lighted numbers above the elevator flashed the floors. It arrived with an almost hydraulic halt, a slow, deliberate liquid decompression. A moment's pause before the gears engaged to slide the doors open. Theodore had been staring at the floor before he looked up.

"Good evening, Theo," Cantwell said. "Glad you could attend our little shindig."

Heat rose in Theodore's chest. "Hello," Theodore said, stepping in and glancing at the lit button for the ninth floor. The doors slid shut. The elevator moved with a jerk, then smoothed its ascent, picking up speed as it rose, the whirring buzz playing along the taut skin of Theodore's eardrums.

"Does that sound right to you, Theo?" Cantwell said into the vacant space.

"What?"

"The elevator. Does it sound right to you? Otis thinks I should replace these old things. What do you think?"

Theodore only shrugged, unsure where Cantwell was headed with this conversation.

"I'd hate to get rid of them now… we're so close. At least it feels that way to me. How about you, Theo. Do you feel we're close?"

Theodore couldn't bear the riddles. What did that even mean: *Do you feel we're close?* Theodore hadn't felt the elevator stop but was relieved when the doors shot open. He bolted from the elevator and headed for the viewing room, feeling Cantwell's eyes on his neck, hearing Cantwell's footfalls a stride behind.

Kent had the game queued up on the main computer screen when they entered. Cantwell took his seat at the center of the table, Theodore finding refuge at the far end. Kent was the first to speak. "So, I think we're on the right track, but some of our testers are saying that Daisy is erratic, that she doesn't always reveal the wormholes when they hit certain scores. We're not sure what's happening with that." Kent looked over at Theodore. "Any thoughts?"

Theodore had to think a moment. Benchmark scores were predetermined but were associated with the actual time to reach those goals. The further a player fell behind on time, the less chance a wormhole would be revealed, no matter what their score.

After clearing his throat, Theodore began to speak when Cantwell interrupted. "I think I know what the problem is," Cantwell said, sitting forward with his hands clasped on the table, a knot of thick fingers entwined like ropes.

"What's that, Mr. Cantwell?" Kent asked.

"Well, our little Daisy here is so much like Theo, I think she is just stubborn about granting access to these magical passageways…"

"I don't understand," Kent said.

"I think our little Daisy hates keeping score as much as Theo does," Cantwell said. "That's why our little blossom is acting like such a—"

"I don't think that's it," Kent said, interrupting the president, shifting his attention to Theodore. "I think the algorithm might be off, maybe, or... Could that be it, Theo?"

The tightness in Theodore's chest felt like a steel trap. He tried to take a deep breath without letting Cantwell see his discomfort.

"Well, Theo? Is our little Daisy having a bad algorithm day?" Cantwell said.

Theodore closed his eyes, trying to calm his thudding heart. Before Theodore could answer, Cantwell's secretary buzzed in on the phone.

Cantwell pressed the button. "Yes, what is it?"

"Sir, Mr. Trumball has an important call on line seven."

"Thank you," Cantwell said, pushing the phone toward Theodore. "For you."

Theodore stared at the flashing light, the clammy warmth of perspiration filling his shirt. He looked at Cantwell, then at Kent. He wanted to take it privately, but it seemed that wasn't an option.

Cantwell handed him the receiver. Theodore pressed the lighted button and said, "Hello?" Cantwell got up from the table and lit a cigar.

"Teddy, it's Linus."

"Hey, Linus. This isn't a good time... I'm in a kind of important meeting and—"

"There's been an accident, Teddy..."

"What? Who, Mom?"

"No... Woody. Car accident. He, uh..."

"Is he all right, Linus?"

There was a long pause. Theodore glanced toward Kent, then back at the table, at his own knuckles, his eyes drifting down to his fingernails. "Linus?"

THEODORE

I don't know how it worked. At first I thought it had something to do with harmonics in the elevator, or maybe the sequencing of numbers, or some kind of magnetic array in the shaft, but after much contemplation, I concluded that it had nothing to do with the physical properties of the machinery, or the revolving doors, or the building itself, but instead, maybe had to do with energy vortexes and intent.

In 1969, just before Woody left for the Air Force, I talked him into driving to Sedona in search of energy vortexes. I had heard about them from a gardener named José who was originally from San Miguel D'Allende and had lived for a while in Arizona. He told me that the vortexes contained strange powers and that the people who visited them experienced anything from miraculous healings to UFO sightings. We searched a long time and never found them, but we did come across a Native American who invited us to a peyote ceremony when we told him what we were searching for.

We drank peyote tea while a young dark-haired man played a water drum. Woody vomited when he first drank it and I wished I had. The rest of the night we spent in front of the fire, listening to the drum, nursing bizarre vistas and hallucinogenic creatures and trolls, until we both fell asleep.

The next morning, feeling surprisingly refreshed, we set off for Mesa Verde in search of the Anasazi "cliff palace" ruins. The Anasazi, "the ancient ones," built amazing dwellings that contained intricate wall markings indicating a vast knowledge of the stars and cosmos. But around the 1200s, after living in that area for over 700 years, the Anasazi vanished suddenly from their homes and no one has ever been able to figure out where they went or why they left.

My intention was to find out if energy vortexes could have accounted for their strange departure. We found the astonishing ruins but little else to support my theory.

CHAPTER 27

―――――――

Rain plinked against the bedroom window. Theodore, still dressed, his bedroom dark, was lying on his back, staring at the ceiling, at the frosted glass light fixture above him, and thinking about Woody, about Shelley, their kids.

Disillusioned, and falling quickly into despair, he rolled over on his side, pulled himself into a ball. Fighting back the tears, he tried to think about OBO, about code sequences, about anything else, but unsolicited images leaped before his eyes like deer leaping in front of a speeding car—images of the woman at the intersection driving through the red light, smashing into the side of Woody's Datsun, killing him instantly. He gave in to the tears, sobbing lightly, pulling the sheets haphazardly up around his shoulders and knees, leaving his back exposed to the dark.

The phone rang over twenty times before Theodore pulled himself from bed and shuffled to the living room to answer it.

"Yes," he said, picking up the receiver, staring at the floor.

"Teddy, it's Linus. You okay?"

Theodore studied the black scuff marks on the floor, as if someone had tried to move a heavy object across it, like a refrigerator, maybe, or a washing machine, or a couch.

"Teddy? Are you there?" Linus shouted from the other end of the phone.

"What?" Theodore said.

"Goddammit, Teddy!" Linus screamed, then softened. "I'm sorry. I didn't mean to yell, but damn… sometimes it's hard to get through to you!"

Theodore listened now, remembering why Linus was calling.

"Teddy," Linus said. "Shelley's in a bad way. You need to call her. She needs to hear your voice."

Theodore envisioned the woman driver seeing Woody's Datsun starting through the intersection, glimpsing the red stop light as she passed under it, pressing the brake as hard as she could but knowing it was too late, the awful crash. Macy was right. Theodore could feel an alternate world forming in his mind, one where he hadn't wished Woody a Happy Anniversary, where Woody didn't go to the Glen Valley Mall, and where he arrived home without a gift for Shelley, but at least arrived safely.

"Teddy? Say something so I know you're there, will you?"

"I'm here, Linus," he said, flatly. "I'm listening." But he wasn't. He was thinking about lunch with Woody, about the car accident, about the brilliant physicist, Hugh Everett III, his concept of "choice points," making "jumps," realigning his world, finding a different outcome.

"They're laying Woody out on Friday," Linus said. "Do you want me to come get you, bring you back to Bakersfield for the funeral?"

Theodore said nothing, seeing the red light, listening to the crash.

"Do you want me to come get you?" Linus asked again, raising his voice.

"No, Linus! I don't want to talk about this anymore." Theodore hung up the phone.

He went back to his bed, sealed himself in the rumpled sheets, contemplated choice points, alternative worlds, regret, grief. Something crawled on his cheek. He reached up and felt the hard shell of his arch nemesis. "Dammit, where are you little bastards coming from?" He squeezed the insect between his fingers, heard a crunch, then flung its body against the wall. Kneeling up in bed, he scanned the darkness for the source of the pests. Another hit his head.

"Dammit," he yelled, slapping at the bug, then seeing it scamper across his sheets, a dark shape running erratically, seemingly blind. Jumping up, he ran to the doorway and flipped on the light. "Where are you little fuckers coming from!"

His eyes darted around the room, searching for the source of the scourge when another one hit the sheets running. He glanced up at the light fixture. A roach was crawling across the mountain and deer etched into the glass light cover.

Climbing onto the mattress, he reached up and unscrewed the knob holding the glass cover in place. Two more roaches fell inside before he could get it undone. After removing it, he could see another roach squeezing through the gap between the white metal housing of the fixture and the ceiling. He swatted the insect from the opening, then ran to the kitchen for a screwdriver. In minutes the light fixture was hanging from the ceiling by its wires. Several roaches rushed through the new breach, falling to the bed like skydivers from an airplane.

Theodore stomped at the frisky dark shapes as they rushed to the edges of the bed and disappeared under the mattress. "Shit! Shit!" he screamed as more of them fell on him and the bed. He kicked at the fleeing vermin, howling, reminiscent of a war dance, until he suddenly stopped and turned his attention back toward the ceiling. He glared at the opening, began to pick and prod until finally he began pounding at the ceiling with his fists. Large chunks of plaster fell onto his head, onto the floor. All at once the hole broke open and a black hoard of roaches, hundreds of them, poured from the gaping rupture, covering his bed, crawling over his feet, racing across the floor. "Fuck!" he cried, then heard someone pounding at his door.

"Hey, asshole, keep it down in there!" an angry voice screamed through the wooden door. "I'm trying to chill over here!"

Theodore bolted toward the door, threw it open and found himself face-to-face with the scowling young musician from across the hall. The young man, with his dark unkempt hair exploding from his scalp, glared at Theodore. Filling the doorway, the man stood resolute, wearing nothing but boxers and undershirt, unruly hair protruding from his armpits and covering his chest.

"We're trying to watch a movie. It sounds like fucking World War III in there. Keep it down!" the young man screamed and turned back toward the open door across the hall. A woman's laughter issued from the apartment and the blue glow from a television set filled the opening, silhouetting the young man's large frame. Theodore recalled the nights he'd endured the sorrowful wailing of a poorly played saxophone.

"Fuck you," Theodore shouted. The musician spun around and padded back toward Theodore, his eyes fixed, his cheeks glossy and tight. But before the musician could register his dissatisfaction with the parting comment, Theodore caught him hard on the jaw with a right hook, dropping him in the hallway. The musician groaned, tried to get up, but Theodore caught him again, this time with a foot to the stomach and it was over. He grabbed the musician by the feet and spun him a quarter turn until he no longer blocked Theodore's doorway, then slammed the door.

Moments later, he heard the door across the hall slam. As he walked back into the bedroom, he saw that the roaches now covered everything like a splattering of brown paint. Except these paint specks moved with such frenetic urgency it seemed the room itself was alive.

He grabbed his beret off the dresser, carefully checking for bugs before he put it on, then rushed into the hall, slamming the door behind him. He glanced over his shoulder at the musician's door, half expecting a second bout with the young man, almost welcoming another chance to release his rage. In the stillness of the bleak hallway, a surprising shadow of remorse drifted over Theodore, picturing the man lying on the floor, grimacing in pain when he had kicked him. Turning back toward his own door, he locked it, and wondered why he was securing his apartment—there was nothing to steal except roaches, he thought—then hobbled down the stairs, pushed through the front entrance of the building, and stepped onto the wet sidewalk.

Cars rushed by in the cool evening, spraying water, disrupting the colorful reflections in the black puddles. He hailed a cab, popped open the door and jumped in, detecting the stale odor of cigarette smoke as he slammed the door.

"The nearest Catholic Church," Theodore shouted, throwing a glance back at his building, nervously rubbing the knees of his trousers, thinking the portly musician might come charging through the door at any second.

"Churches are closed," the driver said, checking his watch, turning toward the back seat.

"I don't care. Take me to one that's closed then."

The driver flipped the flag on the meter, slipped the shifter into drive, and sped away down the wet street.

Some forlorn orchestral composition played on the radio as traffic lights switched to green, then red, a brief interlude of yellow in between. Bright store windows flashed by like a passing train, the smell of grime and cigarette smoke rising from the stained vinyl upholstery. Automobiles and delivery trucks shot through intersections, headlights splashing along the pavement, passing and honking, trailing a wet red glow behind them. Vehicles turned abruptly on perpendicular streets and the chaotic pattern of traffic made Theodore wonder why there weren't more accidents. Woody. Dead. It was impossible. They'd had lunch only that afternoon, laughing, sharing stories, how Woody's eyes became bright ornaments upon entering Theodore's steel and enameled high-tech office. His children, his luminous wife, Shelley, her features now certainly wrecked with grief, her eyes bloated and crimson with tears.

When the taxi pulled to the curb, the driver turned in the seat. "Will this do?"

Theodore swiveled his head to find the structure, an impressive stone cathedral with a large rose window above the narthex, pointed arches and flying buttresses and a tall transept spire that pointed toward the heavens like a compass needle, as if directing the faithful toward the answers they sought. The church seemed out of place, out of time, its antiquity garishly updated by a few unimaginative buildings with little architectural merit, maybe to house Sunday school children, or lawn mowers and weed trimmers and wheelbarrows and rakes.

Theodore pushed a twenty into the cabby's palm as he jumped from the vehicle, then went up the walkway leading to the massive oak and metal doors. A single spotlight illuminated the façade, while another one shone brightly on the masonry marker situated at the edge of the manicured lawn and engraved with the words, Saint Catherine's.

A sticky hush engulfed him as he traversed the stone steps—no cars or people anywhere, just the solemn rush of rain on the standing puddles and concrete surfaces. Water dripped from the front edge of his beret as he grabbed the brass handles on the front doors and pulled. The dead bolt rattled, but the doors were fixed. He walked along a stone path that led to the side of the church to find another entrance and spied the rectory, a free-standing edifice near the back of the parking lot, connected to the church by a covered walkway of modern construction. A light burned on the second floor of the building.

Rain sizzled along the chintzy corrugated roof covering the pathway. Theodore checked the side door of the church—locked. Standing beneath the canopy, temporarily out of the deluge, he glanced toward the rear of the church at a stand of pin oaks that blocked the view from the street. Running stiffly, careful not to slip on the wet grass, he came to a basement window that was partially hidden from the rectory and the street. With the rain slashing at the grounds and buildings, Theodore was certain no one would hear him kick the window in.

After picking the remaining shards of glass from the frame, he squeezed through the opening and felt himself standing on a hard, cold floor in total darkness. Motionless for several minutes, his eyes adjusted on a sliver of light along the floor some ten feet away. He shuffled cautiously toward it, figuring it was at the base of a door, but his foot caught on something and he stumbled forward, bumping a table. He caught himself just as something shattered to the floor. "Damn," he whispered to himself, standing stock-still, listening to hear if anyone stirred above him. Nothing. He moved nearer, reached out, felt the rough wood of the door, letting his fingertips trace down the grain until they found the cold, metallic surface of the knob. Twisting it gently, he waited until the latch clicked, then eased the door open.

He found a stairwell that led from the basement into the sacristy, and finally, the altar. It felt strange to be back in church. The familiar fragrance of incense filled the space as if it had been absorbed into the walls, the cabinets, and the wooden pews. To the left of the altar stood a metal rack stair-stepped with tiers of votive candles flickering in deep-red glass vessels, bringing to mind the many times he had lit one as a young boy after confession.

Across the church was a statue of Jesus, standing three feet high and recessed into a steeple-shaped alcove along the wall. Jesus had his head bowed slightly, shoulders slumped forward, but just barely (he had never noticed that Jesus seemed to slouch a bit), with the first two fingers of his right hand frozen in an eternal gesture of blessing. He seemed remarkably peaceful in contrast to Theodore's pounding heart.

After a quick survey of the empty church, he walked toward the statue, his wet shoes squeaking on the marble floor, echoing in the hallowed space. When he reached Jesus, he stared a long time at Him, at His knowing soft eyes, His unhurried brow, the characteristic beard, mustache, and long flowing hair that framed His glowing face. Instinctively, Theodore bowed his head and crossed himself, something he hadn't done in years, then pulled the heavy statue forward from its space until he could grasp it in a bear hug. When he had it secure, he lifted it from the alcove and carried it across the church, setting it on a pew just outside the confessional. He tugged at the door to the smallish space until the flimsy lock gave way. Turning back toward Jesus—the statue standing in the pew like a child during Sunday services—he picked Him up and carried Him inside the confessional booth, placing Him on the seat that the priest would normally occupy. He adjusted Jesus so that He faced the wooden lattice dividing the priest from the penitents, then stepped out and closed the door.

Theodore sat down in a pew, pulled at the kneeler, then knelt on the padded red leather. Bowing his head, he tried to order the jumble inside his skull by whispering a Hail Mary, surprising himself by the total recollection of the prayer. When he finished, he stood up, left the pew and walked to the deep-red curtain of the confessional, pushing through it after a moment's pause. Inside, he felt the same nervous anxiety he had always experienced as a boy, the dark cramped space, the scent of oak, but something was missing—the smell of Father Edward's Old Spice.

Theodore knelt down in front of the oak screen and saw that Jesus was ready, His unblinking eyes fixed on him, His hand forever ready to bless and forgive.

"Bless me father… I mean, Jesus, for I have sinned. It's been… I don't know… a really, really long time since my last confession," he said, suddenly embarrassed, not because he was talking to a statue, but because he hadn't been to confession in over sixteen years.

"Look, I'm not going to bore you with the minor stuff," he said to the indefatigable statue just beyond the screen, "because I have some serious issues to discuss." He looked up, as he always had when he was a boy hoping to catch Father Edward reading or sleeping, but only saw the painted eyes of Jesus staring back. Theodore nodded his head as if agreeing with himself on some salient point he had made or was about to make.

"Okay, then… let's see," he said, unsure where to start, feeling he should've prepared himself better in the pew. "Well, I guess I need to talk about Porky… you know… what I did." He found it hard to verbalize the tragedy in its rawest description, even to the statue. "I killed him!" he finally blurted out. "I killed him and I'm sorry I did, but… There was no other way! It was him or Woody! I had to…."

He stopped abruptly when Woody's car accident skidded into his head. At once, his attempt to save Woody all those years ago seemed futile, Woody was dead anyway, but now it was worse, now there were kids and a wife left behind.

As if besieged by some inexplicable and troubling revelation, Theodore began to pummel the statue with questions. "Is that it? You took Woody's life to show me that You had the power? What about his family, his kids? What about them? What are they supposed to do now?

"And Sarah, why her? Why did you take her from me?" An image surfaced in the dark cavern behind Theodore's eyes, Porky lying in the grave, a pick ax protruding through his chest like a cathedral spire, the red life oozing into the mud. He began to tremble when Porky reached up, shaking his head, wearing an expression of sadness, compassion. Porky looked like Jesus on the cross, anguished, but absent of malice.

"That's it, then? Punishment for killing Porky? Is that why you're taking everyone from me? My dad? Almost my mom? Sarah? Now Woody! Jesus! How can I pay my debt? When am I free? How can I make things right? How?" Theodore screamed. "Say something, goddammit!" He slammed the oak latticework with his palm. Jesus stared back, unfazed and loving, administering His eternal blessing. Theodore banged the wall above the small window, over and over until his arm fell weak. He slumped on the kneeler, his head falling toward the grid.

After resting it there a few moments, he got up, wiped his eyes, and glared at the statue. Jesus remained vigilant, peaceful, understanding.

"You don't get it, do you? How could you? —you're plaster!"

Theodore sniffled, squinted at the statue, then wiped his sleeve across his nose.

The rain had mostly stopped when he climbed out the basement window of the church. He hurried along the drenched street. After going several blocks, he decided to hail a taxi. The driver dropped him on the street in front of DreamCo.

Standing at the revolving doors, he dug in his pocket for his keys, looked up at the words inscribed above them—The Baldwin Hotel—and suddenly felt stranded in a freakish dream. Inside the dimly lit lobby, just beyond the glass, Theodore glimpsed a crowd of people, milling about, waiting, as if embedded in liquid amber. They all turned to look at him. He stared back, trying to recognize their faces, then placed the key in the lock and twisted it. Placing his hand on the upper edge of the revolving door, he pushed it until a wedged-shape opening left just enough room for him to squeeze through. With palm on the metal handle, he guided the door around until it spilled him into the lobby.

Once inside, he knew exactly who they were. There was his father, Frank Trumball, and a cousin that died of pneumonia, and Monroe in his three-piece suit standing next to a stranger he couldn't identify. Then Randall Bloom stepped forward, (he recognized him from Sarah's photo) then Macy's brother, Kenny, (unsure how he knew this young boy) and Charlotte from high school, (he didn't even know she was dead!). And Jesus was there, still a statue, but with a radiant golden gloriole circling His head, the intricate filigreed kind from Renaissance paintings. Then a woman stepped forward with two men. Sarah, with Porky on one side of her, Woody on the other, and all at once Theodore knew he was dead. He'd read how people died and walked into a bright light and were greeted by deceased relatives. But there was no bright light, just the dim lobby of DreamCo, the huge model of Saturn suspended above him. Dr. Melvin stepped forward from the crowd and touched his shoulder.

"What are you doing?"

"Am I dead?"

"Theodore, I want you to stop and think."

Theodore looked down at the floor, the puddle of water forming around his shoes. "I have thought it out," he said. "I must get my life back."

"No, you have to forget all this nonsense, Theodore. This is another crazy delusion of yours. You have to learn to live within reality, live with life as it is."

"Live within reality? Whose reality—yours? You and your shock box!"

"Theodore, give this up now. Look at yourself. The madness is starting again and you won't be able to control it."

Theodore looked over at Sarah, then Woody. His father was gone and so was Porky.

"Theodore, don't try to alter the past. Think about the lives you will be affecting, the people that will be hurt. It won't change what you did to Porky. Nothing will change that."

"Who will it affect? Who will it hurt?" he asked.

"What about the Glen Valley Killer, Theodore? He will be free again if you do this."

Theodore recalled the newspaper article and realized that Dr. Melvin was right. The Glen Valley Killer would no longer be dead in the new reality. "I'll take care of that."

"It's not that simple, Theodore. Don't do it."

A bright light shown on Theodore's face, blinding him temporarily.

"What are you doing?" the officer repeated from the squad car, the spotlight trained on him.

Theodore turned to face the voice, suddenly realizing he was standing outside DreamCo in the rain, his beret dripping, his trousers and shirt soaked. He wrestled his attention past the plate glass window, past his own reflection, and into the dark lobby. It was vacant and dim and lifeless, like the interior of an excised human organ. "I work here," Theodore finally said, feeling groggy, holding up his key. "I forgot something."

"It's awfully late," the officer said. "You have some ID?"

Theodore fumbled with the wallet in the back pocket of his trousers, then handed the license to the officer. The policeman held the little photo ID under his flashlight for a moment, then handed it back.

"Okay," the officer said, pulling away slowly.

As the cruiser departed, Theodore was just about to push through the revolving doors when he stopped cold, seized by a powerful and disturbing sense of déjà vu. Have I done this before, he asked himself? He looked around, first at the departing police car, the spotlight shining along the building, the taillights burning bright red in the puddles, then at the entrance to DreamCo. Something was off. The nerves in his legs sizzled with a low dismal current, as if he were being charged with tiny flashlight batteries. He adjusted his beret, then unlocked the revolving doors and pushed through the merry-go-round entrance.

Once inside, he hurried across the marble floor, his wet sneakers squeaking and leaving puddles, until he was standing in front of Otis's desk.

As he shuffled through the pile of newspapers, he noticed his hand trembling and wished he had a cigarette (the first time he'd thought about smoking in a long while). After a few moments, he found the article about Kendall Blannert, then searched the desk for a pen or marker. Pulling his shirt tail from his trousers, he lifted it to expose the pale skin of his belly, carefully printing the name and address on his white skin, a few inches above his navel. To the left, next to Blannert's name and address, Theodore printed the current date, his own name, then *Woody* and *Shelley,* and their two children. To someone else looking at Theodore's stomach, the name and address would be printed upside down, and angled slightly. He spent a few moments committing Blannert's name to memory just in case something went wrong. It was difficult to focus on an anonymous name in a newspaper, but he had to if his plan was going to work—call the police and tell them who the Glen Valley Killer was, maybe give them the address, even though it may seem a bit suspicious. After tucking his shirttail in, unaware that the back still bloused out clumsily over his belt loops, he went to the elevator. A morbid foreboding rose up in his gut when he found himself giving the lobby of DreamCo one last curious look, a final farewell of sorts, then pressed the call button.

THEODORE

In front of the coffin, looking down at my dad, I thought he looked younger, but too stationary, like someone pretending to be asleep, holding his breath, and any moment he would blink, then laugh, and we'd all go to a grand party. Of course, my mom would be upset that my dad had invented such a cruel prank.

My mother walked up behind me, took my arm, and gently led me from the casket, but I refused to go. I made quite a scene, announcing that we had to wait for dad, had to wait until the prank was complete. "No, Theodore, come now, please," she had said to me, crying.

"Don't you get it, mom," I told her. "Dad's playing a trick on us. He is!"

CHAPTER 28

―――――――――

"Mr. Cantwell!" Theodore said, surprised to see him standing in the elevator when the doors opened.

"I *knew* tonight was the night, young Edward," Cantwell said, standing erect as a soldier, arms folded behind his graphite gray suit, his blue eyes blazing like neon. "The *rain*, boy! How often does it rain in LA this time of year? *Never!* That's how I knew!"

Doesn't he ever go home? Theodore thought, shocked by the unexpected intrusion. And what did Cantwell mean?—*I knew tonight was the night.*

Cantwell seemed to expand as the doors slid shut, consuming more than his share of real estate in the small elevator. And with his features ghastly lit from the cold fluorescent tubes, his large hands clasped together in mock prayer, he had the appearance of a glowering ringmaster in some furtive, sadistic carnival. Theodore shuffled backward until his heels wedged up against the metal wall panel, the powerful stir of déjà vu filling his stomach, his chest, his head, as if it were consuming him from the bottom up.

"You know, Edward, I thought for sure you would recognize me the day of the interview," Cantwell said, grinning. He turned his head toward Theodore, then followed with his body, slowly twisting, like a serpent, until he had him blocked in the corner. "But you didn't... that threw me for a while, made me think I had imagined everything."

Cantwell closed his eyes as if in meditation, his face softening, smiling angelic. Suddenly his eyes popped open like spontaneous blazes, glaring down on Theodore. "Ah, but then there was that game of yours... OBO, right? Yes, when you demonstrated *that* 'dog' I knew I hadn't imagined anything. My memory was perfect as usual," Cantwell said. Then, with a gloating pause, his eyes growing wide, his mouth stretched into a sinuous grin, he pronounced, "That's when I knew you were in *my* reality, Edward!"

His reality? Confused by Cantwell's riddle, Theodore commanded his mind to sort out the possibilities. Cantwell droned on about something, but Theodore, frantically searching for clues, was no longer listening, caught up in his own disturbing web of questions. How could it be that he would not remember Cantwell, but Cantwell would remember him? Did he, Theodore, exist in this reality only from Cantwell's perspective? He knew that he existed in others' lives only from their perception, accounting for the fact that everyone he knew saw him differently. Certainly, Linus had a different perception of him than Woody, or his mother, Madeline, or Macy. But where was Theodore's own consciousness? Didn't his consciousness exist only in his own reality? —isn't that the source of his experience? Many of the greatest minds in science today postulated, but more than that, suggested empirical proof of the existence of parallel universes, but how had they accounted for what was happening to him?

If one electron could be in two different locations at the exact same moment, wouldn't they share the same consciousness? — or were they separate, two independent entities with one source? If so, which one recorded the event? Theodore became anxious over the apparent illusion of his existence and who controlled it. Then it hit him. All those years ago, just as Theodore had had complete knowledge of the events of the *shift* at The Baldwin Hotel, the alternate realities, his parents, and his brother Linus, as well as Woody himself, had had no knowledge that anything odd had happened; a seamless, uninterrupted experience of time. Only Theodore had been privy to the shift. Now it seemed to be Cantwell who was in charge of choosing another reality—and Theodore was now caught in Cantwell's world. *How could this have happened?*

"Yes, we've done this all before," Cantwell said. "That morning you left I knew you had found it, that you could control it—I needed to know how. I couldn't think about anything else as I rode back up on the elevator that morning, about how you had manipulated time in this damned thing, just how it had happened unwittingly to me years ago in St. Louis. Anyway, a week or so later, as you lay in the hospital in that blasted coma, good fortune, being a fickle and pernicious mistress, shined upon me and the elevator opened into itself. I knew I had made the *jump;* I had shifted between realities?" Cantwell turned to face Theodore with a knowing grin. "But it's not about time travel, is it? Or parallel universes?"

Cantwell didn't wait for Theodore to respond. "I just didn't know how I did it. But I decided to learn from you, the master, the Messiah, when you returned to DreamCo, just as I knew you would." Cantwell smiled, then scratched at the gritty stubble on his chin.

"That fucking game of yours, Edward. I hated that game and had to suffer through the demo twice, all those stupid…." Cantwell trailed off, his scowl softening when he apparently realized he had sidetracked himself with the recollection. "God, am I glad the charade is over. I felt like goddamn Ronald Reagan trying to remember my lines," Cantwell said, frowning toward Theodore, then added, "...Reagan when he was still an actor, of course, not a goddamn governor!" He stared straight ahead, darkly, as if pausing to consider Reagan.

"But it was worth it," he said with renewed joy, "...all the waiting, all the acting, remembering my lines so perfectly, careful not to alter a thing..." Cantwell nodded to Theodore like an accomplice, waggling his finger in the air. "Just so we could get back to this moment... or should I say, this new, more prosperous moment!" Cantwell chuckled. "Oh, and that little incident with the storeroom your first day, well... I couldn't resist that little prank. It was an improvisation that I figured wouldn't alter the outcome of things very much, and"—Cantwell paused to laugh, as if remembering how sweet the prank was—"if you hadn't been the butt of it I think you, a bright boy like yourself, would have appreciated it as well!"

Cantwell paused a moment, in contemplation of some new notion, said, though not directly to Theodore, but into the ether of the elevator, "Synchronicity, young Edward! That's what we have here. Certainly you've read Carl Jung. If you haven't you need to. We have moved into a higher realm of experience, one of the upper tiers of human potential."

Theodore was struck by the comment, a million tumblers in his brain locking into position at once, suddenly recalling what Macy had said at the stream when they'd been digging clay, talking about the addiction with video games. "Getting to do it over!" she'd said. "As many times as you have quarters for!" Of course Theodore had considered that notion when thinking about video games, the addictive quality of getting do-overs, but until Cantwell's statement, Theodore had never posited that maybe that's what happened to him at The Baldwin Hotel, not some kind of time travel, or even parallel realities, but something much more bizarre, a sort of cosmic do-over that had nothing to do with science or physics or Everett's so called "choice points," but something far more insidious, or miraculous, something inexplicable and disturbing. Especially so when he considered Cantwell and DreamCo. Cantwell was from St. Louis, but happened to move to California, and happened to open up a video gaming company that Theodore—who just happened to design video games—just happened to get an interview with at DreamCo, which happened to be close to where he lived, where Theodore just happened to meet Frank Cantwell who was the son of Monroe, the man who operated The Baldwin Hotel in St. Louis! Coincidence? More like preposterous! Too much chance and happenstance for any rational mind. Until you viewed it through Jung's lens. Synchronicity, Jung called it, part of a higher order of events beyond all odds, something beyond scientific reductionism, beyond logic and reason, a noncausal principle—like a force or energy permeating the universe—where the external world becomes aligned with the experiences of the individual, mirroring, or echoing, the personal thoughts and desires of the individual, possibly resulting in some kind of cosmic do-over, as in Theodore's case. Yet there was a similar supposition in physics, where it was theorized that the observer of the experiment influenced the outcome of the experiment.

Theodore was in the throes of his new thesis when Cantwell, his demeanor suddenly gentler, more contemplative, leaned uncharacteristically close to Theodore, and said, almost in a whisper, his eyes glistening with intoxication, "Imagine it, Theo, the physical, external world of matter bending to our personal will and desire. It's the grist of the gods, the power of Odin."

Cantwell's genuineness unnerved Theodore. Never had he called him Theo, or spoken to him with such respect—for the first time absent of malice—almost as an equal. "It has to be,"

Cantwell continued, easing back, his eyes focused now on some distant, preternatural space. "Think about it. How could it be that I develop video games, and you design them? Sure, if our paths had never crossed before, there would be nothing to mull over, nothing worth mentioning. But no, dear Edward, this is so much more, destiny and fate and yes, synchronicity, and I can't wait to get started."

Cantwell, rasping his meaty palms together like a praying mantis, was fixed on some delightful notion, seemingly unaware of Theodore. "I am more prepared now than ever before," Cantwell spoke, convincing some invisible audience. "I have memorized every stock that has gone up or down, every baseball score, every horse and dog race around the country and, you'll love this, Edward... every winning lottery number in every state that hosts a lottery. It's fucking brilliant! And it's all up here." Cantwell poked the tip of his thick forefinger against his temple. Just then, he glowered down at Theodore.

The gentler, kinder Cantwell was gone, the previous devious one back at the helm.

"That is what I will take with us," he said, then added, "...and I don't mind sharing some of it with you, either, my boy. Our private little enterprise, you might say."

Confused over Cantwell's ramblings about comas and pranks and baseball scores, Theodore was still puzzled. Theodore had never been in a coma, had never been in a hospital since the shock treatments. A coma! He would certainly recall that, wouldn't he? He stared at Cantwell who now looked like a ravenous beast in danger of slobbering down the front of his six-hundred-dollar suit.

"Oh, and I'm sorry for what I said about your game, Edward," Cantwell said, apologetically, supplying a sad smile as proof of his remorse. "But the good thing is, it doesn't matter anymore, none of it! We will have more money than you could ever dream of!" His eyes glazed for a moment.

"It's not about games anymore, Edward," Cantwell said, his eyes blazing, spittle spritzing from his mouth, "...*This,*"— he stated emphatically, thrusting his fat forefinger skyward— "*This*... my boy... is the *real thing!*"

Cantwell stared at some crystal-clear picture in his mind with a visage of imbecilic intensity. Just then, Theodore saw Cantwell as someone possessing a maniacal, obsessed, almost useless sort of intelligence, as Cantwell blathered on about wealth and power and control. But then a disquieting revelation hit him—that he was no different from Cantwell, no less maniacal, no less obsessed, no less consumed with power and control, except that he, Theodore, disguised it as good intention. But maybe my intelligence is actually more destructive than Cantwell's, Theodore thought; after all, Cantwell didn't seem capable of murder; the rigorous inventory took him by surprise.

"Oh, and that fucking Kent. He was on to us," Cantwell said. "He knew something was up and would've loved nothing more than to get his hands on a big wad of cash and start his own company, leave me twisting in the breeze! I had to drive a wedge between you and him, that's why I leaked *StarField* to *Modern Gaming* and made him think it was you. It was perfect. These last few days he was so worn out from me chewing on his ass he could hardly walk. Well, fuck DreamCo, fuck Kent, and fuck the arcade video biz! This is what it's all about!"

Just then, Cantwell's face flashed like a traffic signal toward Theodore. "Let's get started," he said, his tongue darting out between wet lips.

The elevator sprang to life as Theodore pushed buttons in an arbitrary sequence not only for Cantwell's hawkish eye, but also to free his own mind of deadening thoughts. Unable to contain himself, Cantwell began firing questions about the pattern Theodore was using. Feigning authenticity, and to further boggle Cantwell, he consulted his spiral note pad scrawled with mathematical computations.

"You won't fool me with notepads this time, my boy," Cantwell said, pulling a cigar from inside his jacket and slipping it between his teeth.

Theodore ignored him, trying to focus his thoughts on one thing, all the while pushing buttons without an inkling of logic. The doors opened on dimly lit halls, then closed again. Nothing was working and to make matters worse, Cantwell had lit his cigar.

"Get it to work!" Cantwell cried, shooting Theodore looks as hard as bullets. "This is the night!" Cantwell started his grandiose arm gestures. "It has to work. Everything's set. It must work! It's time! It's destined to be, written in the stars! Make it work…"

"Shut up!" Theodore shouted in frustration, his hands pulled into tight knots. "Here," he said, disgusted. He tossed the note pad toward Cantwell. It landed at his feet. Cantwell glared once again at Theodore, then gave the harmless pad a kick toward the doors.

"I can't concentrate if you're talking!" Theodore said.

But Cantwell wasn't listening, puffing his cigar, flicking ashes on the new carpet.

Theodore, slipping deeper into his own thoughts, pictured himself in Sarah's house, in the hall the night of the Angels game, flipping on the light, laughing, her smiling eyes aimed at him. He sensed her warm hands on his skin, her lips against his, the taste of her breath on his tongue; he saw the newspaper sitting in front of her door, the vase, the dandelion, the smell of the fresh-cut flower, the morning light bleeding into the narrow space, the steps leading to his upstairs apartment, the hot plate, the tangle of extension cords and the rug he'd placed over them. He saw smoke rising from the rug, a flame shooting up, the fibers of the rug dissolving in fire, turning black, spreading until the flames broke against the couch like a wave, engulfing it quickly, the fabric dry and hungry. The floor sagged under rolling flames, consumed quickly beneath Theodore's feet, heat rising around him, sweat prickling his skin, melting, burning. He heard muffled screams, or talking, felt the house moving up off its foundation, picking up speed, moving sideways, then abruptly up, then down, then swirling madly until he thought he would be sick.

"Are you okay?" Cantwell said, blowing smoke in his direction.

Theodore coughed and felt the weight of Cantwell's enormous hand on his shoulder. He had to do more than picture Sarah, more than resurrect past memories, or give into useless imaginings. He had to focus his thoughts, give them substance. Just then, he formed the words silently with his lips and spoke them into his smeared reflection in the elevator doors. "I want a reality where Sarah and Woody are still alive, even if—" (here his mind bucked and reared up like a spooked horse, but he had to commit, give his thoughts gravity, otherwise the guilt over Porky's death, the ECT and the torture over the past twenty-nine years was all for nothing) "...even if it means my death."

"What's that, boy?" Cantwell said, leaning in closer.

Swiveling his head slightly toward Cantwell, Theodore became aware of the shaking. A moment later the elevator doors opened and they both turned to see the interior of an identical elevator before them. Theodore moved quickly into the mirrored space, Cantwell hastily following. The elevator began to move again, but this time jerky, sporadic, jumping up in spurts, then falling fast until they couldn't tell which way they were moving. The lights flickered as they picked up speed, jerking from side to side, then up, then down. Theodore braced himself in the corner, while Cantwell, eyes wide and demonic, spread his legs farther apart to brace against the gyrations.

Without warning the elevator came to an abrupt stop, tossing Cantwell off balance, making him giggle before he straightened himself once again to regain his position in the center of the machine. He glanced over at Theodore for a brief second before the tiny space was thrown into utter blackness.

"Shit! Are you there, Edward?" Cantwell asked, reaching out to find him.

"Of course I'm here!"

A loud groan echoed above them in the elevator shaft. The elevator dropped in a jerk, followed by a loud crash. Something ricocheted off the interior of the elevator shaft, something old and metal and important, and landed on top of the roof above them, out of sight, but unmistakably there.

"What the hell was that?" Cantwell whispered in the darkness. The elevator dropped again, but faster this time until they could both feel the pressure in their knees. Theodore hunkered deeper into the corner, sliding his back down the wall until he was seated on the floor, pulling himself into a tight ball. Unable to see in the absolute gloom, Theodore found it unnerving to hear Cantwell whooping and howling like a kid on a roller coaster. The elevator jerked sideways a couple times, throwing Cantwell toward Theodore, then tossed him away again, into the darkness.

Explosions thundered above them. The elevator seemed to be free falling as if it had been dropped from a plane. Theodore covered his head, preparing for an impact that would certainly crush them. And it came, a deafening collision that shot up through the floor, a shock up through his tailbone, his neck, and into the crown of his head. He heard a loud thud and commotion when Cantwell crashed to the floor. For a moment Theodore couldn't move, dizzy, disoriented in the dark. They had stopped but the door hadn't opened. The thunderous clatter rumbled above them. Objects started falling onto the top of the elevator with loud clunks and clanks, ringing in

Theodore's ears. One object whistled down the shaft toward them like an approaching siren, bursting through the ceiling in a cascade of wood splinters and steel, slamming into Theodore's knee. He howled in pain, his knee throbbing and quickly wet with blood.

He heard Cantwell groan, then felt Cantwell's hand on his foot.

"You alive?" Cantwell moaned, tugging at Theodore's shoe.

"Yeah," he said, pushing to his feet. "We have to get out of here!" The grumbling above them began to crackle, the noise echoing down through the shaft.

Theodore felt his way toward the doors, working his fingertips into the narrow crease between them. Barely pulling at the slit, the doors popped open. Daylight flooded in. Cantwell was balanced on all fours.

"You did it, boy! You did it!" Cantwell screeched, staring at the floor, pounding his fist on the linoleum. "You did it. This is the old linoleum. I had it replaced with that God-awful carpet the day you came for your interview. That way I'd know."

Theodore was already out of the elevator. Followed by Cantwell. With both of them clear, the elevator doors went shut. Theodore listened for a moment to Cantwell's exhilaration before turning back toward the entrance to DreamCo.

"You did it!" he yelled again, but Theodore kept walking.

A loud crash startled Theodore as he reached the revolving doors. He spun back toward the sudden noise to see a sheet of thick blue smoke seeping from the crack between the closed elevator doors. Cantwell, brushing debris off his suit, also turned to find the source of the din. Facing the elevator, they both looked up, their eyes fixed on a deafening clatter inside the shaft, like a freight train hurtling downward toward the lobby. All at once, the elevator doors blew out, the metal sliding doors spinning and tumbling, screeching across the lobby floor. The motor platform had collapsed from above and smashed the elevator compartment, bringing with it the motor and elevator cables, belching flames and smoke. One of the greasy cables, writhing from the fiery opening, slashed at Cantwell who was trapped under one of the doors.

For a moment, with Cantwell caught, surrounded by flames, Theodore thought to flee, let Cantwell perish in the fire.

Cantwell, groggy but still conscious, looked up, reaching out to him, almost as if he knew Theodore was about to leave. But Cantwell's hand suddenly became Porky's. Cantwell's eyes filled with the same desperation, wearing the same expression of someone intoxicated by epiphany, purged of hate, free of torment, ready to make amends and forgive the world its trespasses. The image confused Theodore, scared him, forcing him back toward the entrance of DreamCo, away from the helpless figure. With his hands on the revolving door, Theodore heard another loud racket behind him, could feel the heat of the flames coming closer. Spinning around, he saw Cantwell face down on the floor, unmoving. More debris had fallen from the shaft and tumbled into the heap covering Cantwell. Theodore ran back and grabbed Cantwell's limp outstretched arm, tugging at his massive, unconscious body until it eased forward along the floor, out from under the burning wreckage. He quickly ripped off Cantwell's shirt and slapped at his burning trousers. Flames rushed up the wall above the elevator and had already spread to Otis's desk. The papers and furniture were shrouded in fire.

When Theodore got to the entrance, he folded Cantwell's heavy body into one wedge of the revolving door, then pushed hard to move him through. Once outside, he grabbed Cantwell's arm, dragging him to the curb. As he released

Cantwell to the pavement, he looked up and saw Otis walking across the parking lot.

Not wanting to explain why he was there and what had happened, Theodore took off running toward his white newspaper van at the back of the parking lot. Otis yelled at him to stop. Theodore kept running, popped open the door, then grabbed the keys from under the mat, and started the engine. It fired instantly. By now, Otis was running toward him, waving his arms for him to halt.

"Cantwell's hurt," Theodore shouted from the van window as he sped past. "Call the fire department!"

Otis glanced toward the building. The revolving doors were filled with smoke.

In the rearview mirror, Theodore watched as Otis's face registered the calamity. Otis paced a second, glared at the departing van, then pulled a pen from his pocket and wrote something on his palm. Theodore glanced at his side mirror to see Otis rush to the entrance and hoist Cantwell onto his shoulders, carrying him across the lot like a wounded soldier in an old John Wayne war movie.

CHAPTER 29

———————

I t was only after he exhaled that Theodore realized he'd been holding his breath when he turned the van onto Rosemont. He fully expected to see the street glistering with fire engines, police cars, news vehicles and onlookers; there was nothing. The neighborhood was quiet except for Miller's beagle that seemed unable, as always, to stop barking. He brought the van to a stop in front of Sarah's house. Then, as if instructed by a voice in his head, he reached behind the driver's seat and pulled a newspaper from the floor.

GLEN VALLEY WOMAN FOUND BRUTALLY SLAIN.

GLEN VALLEY KILLER BLAMED. STILL NO SUSPECTS!

Another woman was found raped and killed in her home on Monday!

13 women in last 5 months.

He remembered the headline, but checked the date to be sure. Cantwell was right. Things had changed. Running across the lawn, Theodore was struck by the notion of Cantwell, recalling his eyes in the elevator, the look of someone possessed with money and power, then recalled the same eyes trapped under the burning debris, the eyes of the mourner, the penitent, the reborn! But Theodore knew it wouldn't last; he knew that as soon as Cantwell was healthy, if he lived, he would forever pursue Theodore for the secret. But there was no secret, at least not one Theodore could figure out.

The thought made him almost wish he'd let Cantwell burn in the flames along with DreamCo, and that would be the end of it. But what disturbed him even more was that killing was suddenly becoming easier, at least the thought of it, a solution to insoluble problems. He hurried across the lawn, moving faster as if he could outdistance the lumbering, deadening notion of murder.

When he reached the back porch, he threw open the screen door and went quickly through the hall, up the stairs to the door of his apartment. He fumbled with the keys, then pushed inside after unlocking the door. Rushing to the hot plate, he saw that the burner was on. He switched it off and went to the throw rug, feeling the burning hot lump of extension cords nestled beneath the fabric. He tossed the rug aside, unplugged all the appliances, then unplugged the extension cords from the wall. Still not satisfied, he rushed downstairs to wake Sarah and get her out of the house.

Pounding on her door, Theodore saw someone in the margin of his vision walking up the back-porch steps, approaching the screen door. Theodore pounded harder, yelling for Sarah as the stranger positioned himself at the back entrance. Theodore yelled her name, glancing over, wondering what the stranger wanted. Bright morning light silhouetted the man, his wide-brimmed hat seeming odd for June. Theodore turned toward him, called Sarah again, and was about to confront the stranger when Sarah's door burst open. Startled, Theodore spun around to find a husky man standing in Sarah's doorway holding a Polaroid instant camera. He was about to question the unfamiliar visitor, when the one at the screen door wearing the hat said, "Are you Theodore Trumball?"

Confused by the confluence of these two strangers, Theodore tried to respond to the hat man at the screen when a brilliant flash of light blinded him, causing him to throw his hands up over his eyes to rub away the red spots inside his head. In the confusion, he heard the faint whir of a tiny mechanized device; the Polaroid camera spitting out a square, flat image already in the process of developing. Finally able to see, his eyes were drawn to the shiny, vague photograph bouncing on the floor at his feet, then felt the sudden shock of a sharp object thrust into his gut. The pain shot up into his chest, ripping though his torso as he fell backward against the wall. Slumping to the floor, he saw the man at the back door rush into the hallway. Theodore feared another attack, but was unable to move. The hat man rushed past him, chasing the Polaroid camera man into Sarah's apartment, followed by a gunshot.

Police descended upon the premises in seconds, charging into the hallway, one of them stopping to squat down next to Theodore.

"Call for an ambulance," the officer yelled out to someone.

Theodore winced when the policeman put pressure on his stomach, a curious numbing chill spreading through his body. Theodore watched a deep red stain eating through his shirt, unable to believe that the blood leaking to the floor was his. The officer picked up the Polaroid picture lying at Theodore's feet, studied it a second, glancing briefly at Theodore, then stuck it in his pocket.

"You're gonna be okay, kid," the man told him.

Moments later, Theodore heard a siren draw nearer, then a commotion in Sarah's apartment, followed by shouting.

"Someone untie her. Call for another bus," a man's voice yelled. "You, over there, grab that blanket and cover her."

There was a shout, then a scuffle, followed by muffled conversation. Ambulance attendants rushed into Sarah's hallway, the gurney rattling and clanging. Theodore felt hands all over him, lifting him, his body cold, sagging in the middle under its own weight.

"Wait," Theodore mumbled, as they slid him onto the gurney. Another medic cut away the bloody shirt and applied pressure to the wound. "Is she okay? Sarah! What's going on here?"

No one answered as they rushed him from the house, down the steps and into the yard. He heard murmuring as the ambulance staff rolled him across the lawn. "Isn't that the young man that lives there?" a voice said. "I heard a gunshot," another one said. "Oh, I hope Mrs. Bloom's okay! I never did like that boy."

A siren approached and screeched to a halt on the pavement beyond his head. Leaves waved lazily in the limbs above while a bright sparkler of sun jumped in and out of the spaces between them. He felt a hand press on the wound, but the pain was gone. He could smell the dew still wet on the grass. The sun was warm once again on his face as they left the shadow of the large oak. Police car lights flashed blue and white off the branches of the massive canopy. Miller's beagle continued barking a few houses down, the dog's boisterous cry consumed by the ambulance siren as it carried him away.

CHAPTER 30

O n the fourth day of Theodore's hospital stay, Linus and Madeline arrived to find him sitting up, eating breakfast, and looking much spryer. Sunlight streamed through the opened curtains, highlighting the gazanias on Theodore's nightstand—the only color in the pale room.

"Who sent the flowers?" Madeline asked, bending to smell them, then lifted the card dangling from one of the stems, read it, flipped it over, letting it fall from her hand, sniffing the flowers once again. Linus threw himself into a chair tucked into the corner under the television.

"You look like you've joined the living again," Linus said, leaning forward to inspect Theodore's breakfast. "But *that* stuff could send you back to the valley of darkness."

Theodore smiled and continued eating, lifting the plate of orange gelatin cubes as an offering to Linus. Linus leaned back, declining with an outstretched palm. Madeline looked for a place to sit, then strolled over to the chair next to the hospital bed and sat down.

"How are you feeling today, honey?" she asked, setting her purse on the floor next to her chair, leaning forward to examine the bland-looking breakfast, shifting her attention to the monitor that tracked Theodore's vital signs.

"Mom, you understand all that?" Linus asked sarcastically, winking at Theodore.

"Yes, Mr. Wisenheimer," she shot back. "That's his blood pressure…and, well, the other number I'm not sure."

"The *78,*" Linus said. "That's his IQ!"

Madeline frowned, without bothering to look over at Linus, then asked Theodore when the hospital planned on releasing him and who was taking care of his paper route in the interim.

"Nobody," Theodore said, suddenly remembering that everything that had happened at DreamCo now never happened, and that once again he was the owner of a paper route. "I don't really care."

A man in a suit knocked on the doorjamb, then entered the room, glancing briefly at the empty bed next to Theodore's. He introduced himself as Lieutenant Redmond and flashed an I.D. with a badge.

"Could I have a moment alone with Mr. Trumball, folks?" Redmond said, looking at Madeline, then glancing at Linus. Linus stood, whispered *Mr. Trumball* in Theodore's direction with a grin, then took Madeline's arm to escort her into the hall.

"Wait! Wait! I forgot my purse," she cried, tearing away from Linus's hand and hurrying back.

"Ma, I don't think the L.A.P.D. are going to rip you off!" Linus said, slouching impatiently.

"I need my purse, Mr. Smart Alec," she said grabbing the flowered bag, then smiled at Redmond, then swiveled toward the hospital bed. "We'll wait in the hall, sweetheart!" she told Theodore.

When they left the room, Theodore stared up at Redmond, at his curly red hair, short but thick, scattered across his head like cedar shavings, his slate blue eyes, and those long legs, rocking lightly, as if he had stilts under his baggy brown slacks. Theodore had recognized him as soon as he entered the room, but knew the recognition wouldn't be mutual.

"Theodore Trumball, right?" Redmond said, checking the note pad he'd pulled from his pocket. "We traced you to your residence in Glen Valley by your license number." Redmond consulted his note pad again. "Otis Williams gave it to us, said you were at DreamCo the morning of the fire."

Theodore nodded, then flinched, grimacing from a pain that sliced up through his gut into his chest. Redmond seemed to notice but offered nothing in the way of condolence.

Redmond asked more questions, gathering mostly routine information— address in Bakersfield, occupation, family— patiently building a bridge of questions to the real reason he had come to County General. "How did you know Kendall Blannert?" he asked.

"I didn't," Theodore said, pushing away the cart with the breakfast tray, his eyes fixed absently on the hospital band circling his left wrist.

"Were you working together?" Redmond asked, then tagged on another question without giving Theodore a chance to respond. "Did you have a disagreement, is that why he stabbed you?"

"I didn't even know who stabbed me until yesterday," Theodore said. "My brother told me that Blannert was the one who stabbed me and that he was suspected of being the Glen Valley Killer…"

"You had to know him!" Redmond said.

"I didn't know him…" Theodore answered, shifting his eyes toward Redmond without turning his head toward him.

Redmond's blue eyes narrowed to gashes, one side of his mouth twisting up. "You had his name and address written on your stomach, not three inches from where he stabbed you," he said, pointing at Theodore's abdomen. "The surgeon wrote it all down before he cleaned the wound." Redmond had grown impatient, blurting out the words, showing Theodore the scribbled surgical mask. "Care to explain that?"

Theodore thought a second, more for Redmond's benefit than for his own. He already knew what he would tell the police, what he had to tell them. "I'm psychic... sometimes... you know, clairvoyant..."

Redmond glowered at him, as if trying to burrow into Theodore's brain to find the truth. "Clairvoyant, huh?" Redmond stated flatly. "Why didn't you give the police the information when you had your, *psychic moment?*" Redmond shifted his weight from one foot to the other.

"I never had a chance," he said, hoping that Linus and Madeline couldn't hear what he was telling Redmond. "The name just came to me that morning driving home from DreamCo, probably when I saw the headline. It popped into my head and I wrote it on my stomach."

"You didn't have paper in a van full of newspapers?"

"What does it matter *where* I wrote the name?"

"Did his exact address also *pop* into your head?"

"Yes."

"Don't you find that just a little bizarre?"

"There's a lot of bizarre things in the world..."

"Really? You know, Mr. Trumball, every day I get up," Redmond began, letting his arms fall limp at his sides. "I shower, eat breakfast, go down to the station, put in my eight or nine, go home, fix dinner, take out the garbage, drink a beer and fall asleep in front of the tube, and I gotta tell you, in my fifty-three years on this planet I haven't come across any of these *bizarre things* you're referring to… only bizarre people feeding me bullshit!"

Theodore shrugged, and rolled his eyes.

"Why were you at DreamCo that morning?" Redmond asked.

"I had a job interview."

"Did you see how the fire started?"

"No."

"Did you start it?"

"No!"

Redmond checked his note pad. "Otis Williams said he saw you running from the building to your van. He waved for you to stop but you wouldn't. He also said you knew Frank Cantwell's name. How is that possible?"

"I had an interview with him. Of course I'm going to know his name," Theodore said, his voice crackling with frustration.

"Yes, I know you had an interview with Mr. Cantwell, but you had never met him. How could you possibly know that the man you pulled from the burning building was Cantwell? He could've been anyone! Are you telling me that the president of DreamCo was wearing a nametag?"

Theodore was stumped, staring back at the bracelet, twisting it around his wrist with his right hand. "I just knew it was Cantwell, that's all," he finally offered.

"Another *psychic moment?*" Redmond said, glaring at Theodore.

Theodore poked his tongue in the side of his cheek, then looked out the window.

"If you're so psychic, what's my next question?" Redmond said, his expression dull and unchanged.

Theodore let his eyes fall to the sheet covering his legs, his hand smoothing the wrinkles.

"Yeah, right," Redmond said, then checked his note pad again. "Why didn't you stick around when DreamCo caught

on fire, or call the fire department yourself? Otis Williams,"—
Redmond checked his notes again—"said you were in a pretty
big hurry!"

"I had a premonition that something was wrong at Mrs.
Bloom's house. I don't know. What am I supposed to say?"

"The truth would be a good place to start!" Redmond
snapped back.

"Look, am I under arrest for something?" Theodore said,
impatiently.

"Not yet," Redmond said.

Theodore turned away, fixing his gaze on a small golden
bird making a nest on the ledge of the building outside his
window.

"I'll be in touch, Mr. Trumball," Redmond said, stepping
toward the doorway, then stopping. "Oh, by the way, the fire
at DreamCo is being investigated. Might have been arson.
Have any psychic impulses or premonitions about that?"

Theodore, ignoring Redmond's comment, watched the
bird fly to the eave with a soda straw.

"See you soon," Redmond said and left.

He heard Redmond talking to Linus and Madeline in the
hall but couldn't tell what they were saying. It was only a
minute or so before someone entered the room. Theodore
looked over. "Woody!"

"How you doing today," Woody said, walking up to the
bed. "You look a helluva lot better than two days ago! Here,
Shelley told me to bring this to you. She's sorry she couldn't
come. You know… the kids." Woody handed Theodore a
small package wrapped in festive paper. "Linus and your mom
went to the cafeteria to get something to eat."

Theodore took the package and shook it. "Homemade
oatmeal cookies with M&Ms?"

Woody nodded, then pulled an envelope from his shirt
pocket. "Here," he said. "Just like you asked."

"You haven't told anyone, have you?" Theodore asked.

"Of course not."

Theodore sat up, grimacing in pain, and took the envelope from Woody's hand.

"Thanks," he said, ripping the flap off the envelope. "Was Shelley pissed?"

"Not really, but she couldn't understand why I had to go to New Hampshire on such short notice. I didn't either, but…"

"I promise I'll pay you for the ticket… and a big bonus to boot!" Theodore said, scrutinizing the lottery ticket, recalling the numbers Cantwell had handed him in the elevator.

There was a light knock on the jamb. They both looked over to see an attractive woman standing in the entrance. "Mr. Trumball? May I come in?" she asked.

Theodore recognized her at once.

She walked closer and handed him a folded note. "Hi, my name is Macy. This is from my boss, Mr. Cantwell, the man you saved from the fire."

He took the note, glanced briefly at it, then looked up at her.

"How are you?" she asked.

He thought he detected a glint of recognition in Macy's eyes. "Okay," he said. "You?"

She nodded. An awkward silence followed. "Well, I hope you're better soon," she said and turned away.

Theodore held up the note and was going to wish her luck on her engagement, but just watched her leave.

"Cute!" Woody said, when she was gone.

"Nice lady," Theodore said, unfolding the note.

"You know her?"

"Sort of."

Theodore read the note while Woody played with the remote, shifting quickly through the seven available channels.

"Everything all right?" Woody asked, glancing over at Theodore, detecting the sullen expression on his face.

"Yeah, just having a little pain," he told Woody, then tucked the note in the drawer of the food cart with the lottery ticket.

CHAPTER 31

Two workmen cleared debris from the front of DreamCo, then pulled a flatbed up close to the building. When the driver stopped, he jumped from the cab and walked over to Kent.

"What are we picking up?" the driver asked, jerking up on his trousers.

"Those," Kent said, pointing to the revolving doors protruding from a pile of rubble.

"Why?" the driver said, pointing. "They're trashed. Look at 'em. The glass is gone, they're covered in black…"

"I don't need a damage report," Kent said. "I need the doors moved to a warehouse on Camarillo Boulevard. Here's the address." Kent handed the driver a piece of paper. The driver inspected it, shaking his head, then looked up at the two workmen leaning against the cab smoking.

"Hey Billy, get the forklift off the truck," he yelled. "We're taking those doors." The workmen looked at the wreckage and grinned back as if he was joking.

"Move your asses, will ya," the driver said, walking toward the two men. They flicked their cigarette butts to the pavement, jumping up on the flatbed to unchain the forklift.

"I heard about the fire on the news the other night," the driver said. "They said it might have been arson."

Kent said nothing.

"*You* think it was arson? Insurance thing maybe?" the driver asked, wrestling again with his trousers.

Kent looked up at the driver and spread his arms as if to say, "How should I know?"—then walked away toward the burned-out remains of DreamCo.

After the men had the revolving doors secured on the flatbed, the driver walked over to Kent.

"That's it. All loaded," the driver said. "Did you work here, you know, before the fire?"

"Yeah," Kent answered brusquely. "You have the address?"

The driver patted the breast pocket of his shirt, then motioned for the workmen to get in the cab.

"Oh, who's paying for this," the driver asked.

"It's on the paper I gave you," Kent told him. "We do a lot of business with your company—did, anyway."

The driver pulled the sheet out to check it. "Oh yeah, Frank Cantwell."

"That's it," Kent said.

"Isn't he the guy got burned in the fire?"

"If that's all, I need to get going?" Kent said.

"Yeah, sure," the driver said, as he walked to the cab and pulled himself up. "Good luck," he yelled to Kent. He slammed the door, threw the rig in gear, then pulled from the parking lot, leaving a cumulous of black diesel smoke trailing out behind.

CHAPTER 32

———

Sarah was sitting next to Theodore's bed with her back to the doorway when Linus walked in. She let go of Theodore's hand and turned to face him.

"Hi, Linus," she said standing up. "It's nice to see you again. Is your mother with you?"

"No, she wanted to pick up a few things at the store. She'll be by later this afternoon," he said, pausing near the bed, then looked down at Theodore. "You look ready to go home!"

"I am," Theodore said. "Maybe tomorrow."

"Theo, I'm going to take off," Sarah said, stepping close to the bed. "I'll see you in the morning." She touched his foot through the sheet. "Tell your mother hello for me." Sarah regarded Linus, then turned back to Theodore once more before leaving the room.

Linus pulled up the chair Sarah had been sitting on. He glanced back toward the doorway to see if she was gone, then looked at Theodore. "She's a neat lady, Teddy, and I think she digs you. You need someone like her," he said.

"I told you before, we're just friends...." Theodore said, hoping Sarah was doing all right. They hadn't had much time to talk. Even so, Theodore could tell some of the spark had gone out of her. She was unable to talk about the attack, yet, but the horror of it was embedded in her features.

"Hey, little brother. Whatever you say, but love isn't in any great supply out there. If you find it—wherever you find it— you better grab it..."

Theodore looked down at the sheet covering his legs, then at the bandage bulging under his gown.

"I did what you asked," Linus finally said, breaking the silence.

Theodore looked over, his thoughts on Sarah, her recovery; would she ever be the dancer again, singing in her apartment, baking blintzes and pies, the crazy Astros' fan shouting from the bleachers?

"What did you say, Linus?" Theodore said, turning toward his brother.

"I did what you asked. I went to see Cantwell."

"How did he look?"

"Pretty fucked up. He has burns along the side of his face." Linus ran his fingers along his jaw and cheek to indicate the location of Cantwell's wounds. "And his left hand is nasty looking...."

"And?" Theodore said, pressing the controller to raise his bed.

Linus sat back and rubbed his palm over the whiskers on his chin. "I went to his room and told him that I was your brother and that you didn't understand the note he'd sent you, and that you didn't know who he was. Only that when you arrived for the interview you saw the smoke and rushed in and found him trapped in the fire."

"What did he say?"

"He said, 'Bullshit!' then screamed at me about how you two were in the elevator together and some other nonsense that I couldn't understand." Linus looked down at some grease under his fingernail, picking at it with the forefinger of his other hand.

"Is that true, Teddy, what he said?" Linus looked up at Theodore. "Were you there with him in the elevator when the building caught fire?"

"It doesn't matter, Linus. What happened next?"

"I repeated what I'd already told him, that you had no idea who he was, and that you hoped he was okay." Linus stared at Theodore, absently picking at the grease.

"Well, what did he say, Linus? Tell me everything!"

"He went off on another tirade, said you were a goddamn liar, and that he salvaged the doors and he would have them up and running soon. That's when the nurses ran in and tried to calm him, but he screamed, told them to leave him alone. He told me to close the door after they left."

"Did you?"

"Yeah. What the fuck! He wasn't about to hurt me; I don't think he can move his legs."

"Then what?"

"Then I sat and listened to the whole sordid story, and I gotta tell you, that fucking weirdo sounded a lot like you, little brother, no offense. He rambled on about… well, all manner of crazy shit! After a while I just looked at him, nodded my head, and listened to the Dating Game on TV."

"Is that it?" Theodore said.

"Then he asked about The Baldwin Hotel," Linus finally said, brushing a hand across his hair. "Told me the whole story about the stairwell and the Arch and all that shit! I couldn't understand how he knew all that stuff. I was a little shocked!"

"Could he tell you were surprised?" Theodore asked with new concern.

Linus shook his head, then said, "I don't think so... I was cool."

"What did you tell him?"

"I told him exactly what you told me to tell him. I said, 'My family has never been to St. Louis, or any Baldwin Hotel, ever!' He screamed at me, then called me a liar again. I stood up to leave, but he kept screaming, and started throwing plates from his tray. I got to the door and was almost trampled by nurses and doctors rushing into the room."

"Shit!" Theodore said. "Then what?"

"I think they shot him up with something, and told him he needed to calm down or he would ruin the skin grafts. He kept fighting, shouting at me, calling me a liar, calling you a liar. He kept referring to you as Edward. The fucker seemed real confused."

Linus paused a moment. "Did something weird happen again?" Linus finally asked.

Theodore looked over at him. "What do you mean?"

"I mean like what happened when we were kids, visiting Aunt Trudy in St. Louis. The Baldwin Hotel."

"You never believed that anything *weird* happened in St. Louis. Neither did Mom or Dad. Why do you think something weird happened now?"

Linus let his chin fall to his chest. He leaned away from Theodore, stared quietly before he spoke. "I didn't believe at first, but I remember in the hotel room when you explained to Mom and Dad what had happened. I thought you were fucking cracked. Later on, when they weren't around, you asked me if I remembered your twelfth birthday party, then you described it in detail, along with all the gifts you got. Of course, I couldn't remember any party because you were only eleven, so there couldn't have been any *twelfth* birthday party. I thought you were crazy. I didn't give it another thought until you turned twelve and Mom threw you the big party... the party that you had described in perfect detail months earlier, right down to each and every present. The only thing you were wrong about was Woody. You said he wasn't at the party because he was in a coma or some ridiculous shit, but he was there, remember? He gave you those cool Rock 'Em Sock 'Em Robots that we played with all afternoon until we finally broke 'em, and Dad tried to...." Linus stopped abruptly, as if noticing the hard expression on Theodore's face. "What?"

"Why didn't you say something!" Theodore said, jerking forward in the bed. "All this time you've known I was right! You could've told someone, you could've told Mom. You could've told Dad before he was killed and you said nothing! How could you do that! You saw what was happening to me...."

"I'm sorry, Teddy," Linus said. "I was scared, too! Yeah, I did, I saw what happened to you, the shock treatments, the whole fucking mess and I was scared. I was afraid they would send me to that fucking wacko, Melvin! I was scared shitless so I just forgot about it, chalked it up to my imagination, made myself believe that you had never described the birthday party, that I made the whole thing up in my head." Linus's eyes reddened. Madeline walked in.

"How are you today, sweetie?" she asked Theodore, walking past Linus to the bed. She glanced at the monitor, then bent over and kissed him on the forehead. "You have good color today. Are you going to the bathroom on your own?"

"Mom," Theodore said. "You worry too much!"

"I don't worry too much. I just wanted to...."

"What are you doing here?" Linus interrupted, getting up to let her have his chair. "I was going to pick you up from the motel later on."

"I took the bus," Madeline said. "I got tired of waiting for you. What's wrong with your eyes?"

"Nothing," Linus said, rubbing a finger across them. "Here, sit down. I was just getting ready to come get you."

She regarded him, then the seat, placing her purse in her lap, studying the monitor next to Theodore's bed. "Your pulse rate seems stronger today and your blood pressure's almost normal.

Linus and Theodore both rolled their eyes.

"Are you going home soon?" she asked.

"Tomorrow, maybe," he told her.

"Do you want us to take you home?" she asked.

"No, Sar… Mrs. Bloom is going to pick me up. But, thanks anyway."

"Mom," Linus said. "Remember The Baldwin Hotel in St. Louis, the place we used to stay when we visited Aunt Trudy?"

"The Baldwin Hotel?" she said, bewildered. "I don't remember a Baldwin Hotel. We stayed at my sister's house when we went to St. Louis."

"No, when it was too crowded to stay with her anymore, don't you remember, we stayed at The Baldwin Hotel?"

"Oh, yeah, after she had the twins," Madeline said, rocking her body back and forth in the chair, looking up to find the past in the ceiling tiles. "But I don't think it was called The Baldwin Hotel. I think it was The Muncie Hotel, or the Jefferson, something like that. Your father would've remembered, he remembered everything."

"Mom, it wasn't the Muncie or anything else, it was The Baldwin…." Linus insisted.

"It doesn't matter, Linus," Theodore said, cutting him off with a wave of his hand. He gave him a faint smile and shook his head lightly. "Let it go, okay? It's just not important anymore."

Madeline smiled, noticing the golden bird outside the window. "Oh, look! She's making a nest. It seems a little late to be making a nest."

"Mom, how's your garden doing?" Theodore asked.

"Oh, Teddy, it's such a mess," she said, making frantic gestures with her hands. "I would love for you to come home and work on it for me, but I'm almost too embarrassed to let you see it…"

"Why don't I drive out to Bakersfield in a few weeks," he told her. "See what I can do."

"That would be so wonderful, sweetie."

THEODORE

Cantwell was the ultimate prankster and I have to admit, he got the last one in on me. The lottery number he gave me on the elevator was bogus and ended up costing me a few hundred for the round-trip plane ticket to New Hampshire for Woody. I don't know what ever happened to Cantwell. Maybe he cashed in all his lottery tickets, and placed his bets on all his sports scores, but I didn't really care about any of that. Sarah was my only concern.

She was tough, tougher than I had imagined, but she wasn't made of steel, and although she rebounded with daring determination following Blannert's attack, the ensuing months and graphic memories slowly wore her down, until finally one day she blew apart.

She'd been taking pills to battle her insomnia, but sleeping that soundly made her afraid, and she'd often wake up in a cold panic. Many nights she went without drugs; those nights were usually sleepless. But on the nights she slept without pills, she complained of restless, explicit nightmares of being trapped in burning buildings and awful fires. She couldn't understand the dreams and as much as I wanted to offer an explanation, I refrained.

After a time, she quit eating and rarely moved from the couch except to go to the bathroom. One day, after a horrible fit, she collapsed.

Feeling incapable of caring for her properly anymore, I checked her into a private hospital.

Nolan Ryan took the Angels to the playoffs that fall just as Sarah had predicted. By then, Sarah was out of the hospital and we went to every game. The Angels lost to Baltimore three games to one. When the season ended, Nolan Ryan became a free agent and went to the Houston Astros, becoming the first baseball player ever in the major leagues to sign for a million dollars.

A few months later, Sarah and I moved to San Francisco. She bought a great three-story townhouse overlooking the bay. It had a small backyard and plenty of room for a garden. Sarah and I remained loyal Angel fans and I took a deeper interest in the game when she explained to me about batting averages, statistics, squeeze plays, and the importance of the sacrifice.

I watched the '80s usher in a new revolution in video arcade games—Pac Man, Defender, Donkey Kong, and I was envious for a while, not being a part of it, until I realized that it wasn't important anymore. Besides, I had become involved in a study at SRI International. The institute had been conducting extensive research on astral projection—out-of-body experiences, journeys into the space between time constructs. I never made the trip myself, but the OBE's we studied described it as a fantastic and frightening place nestled between life and death, where time was no longer the warder.

But here, in this corporeal construct, I realized that time, as an arbitrary construct of measurement, was a vigilant and sometimes analgesic sentinel. Every year that wedged itself between The Baldwin Hotel and today helped to dilute my perception of what had actually occurred, to the point that I doubted if any of it ever did. I began to wonder about the "shift" in St. Louis, the terrible beating Woody had taken at the hands of Porky—had any of it really happened?—or was it all the product of some powerful premonition, or worse yet, some convincing delusion?

When I realized that I may have killed Porky for no other reason than my own runaway imagination, that he had never harmed Woody, nor had ever intended to, I filled with a slow, ruinous despair. Frightened, I confessed to Sarah what I had done all those years ago. I'm not certain if she truly believed me, but the next morning she insisted we drive to Bakersfield and visit Porky's grave, a place I had never been able to go alone. We searched every cemetery in Bakersfield, but there was no record of a Raymond Tucker who had died in 1962, or '63. A week or so after returning home from our quest, I recalled that Raymond Tucker's family had been from Utah, and that after Porky's death, his mother, three years divorced, had moved back to be near her brothers and sisters. When I told Sarah, she suggested a road trip.

It didn't take long to find the cemetery in Salt Lake City, the etched name of Raymond Tucker, birth, his death, 1962. There it was, at least it seemed, proof I had not imagined the events of that tumultuous year. Shaking and crying, I rattled in Sarah's arms until we walked back to the car. We drove all night to San Francisco, her love for me seemingly undiminished by my horrible deed.

I still make a pilgrimage every year to Tathum Cemetery to lay flowers on the knoll where I had tricked Raymond Tucker to his death.

I turned fifty a few months ago and while Sarah, now seventy-two, enjoys a youthful, energetic health after her bouts with depression, she still struggles with sleep, at times sitting up reading through the night to avoid the nightmares. Most days we spend in the backyard, me working in the garden, her sunning her face, her eyes closed, delighting in the fragrance of honey-suckle and listening to the Angels on the radio.

ABOUT THE AUTHOR

Lonnie Busch is an award-winning author whose short fiction has appeared in *Southwest Review, The Minnesota Review, The Baltimore Review* and other magazines. Among his awards for fiction are the Clay Reynolds Novella Prize for his novella, *Turnback Creek,* finalist in the Tobias Wolff Award for Fiction, the Glimmer Train Very Short Fiction Award, and others. His first novel, *The Cabin On Souder Hill,* was released from Blackstone Publishing in September, 2020.

Busch is also a painter, animator and illustrator, and has created artwork for numerous corporations, ad agencies and institutions, including the "Greetings from America" stamps and "Wonders of America" for the USPS.

See Busch's other books, *The Cabin On Souder Hill,* and *Turnback Creek* at: https://lonniebusch.com